Fractured

Book one of the Rook Maison series

Brian Blackwood

UNQUIET TOMB PRESS

Dedicated to Michelle Morningstar,
who let me play in her universe and do it dirty.

Acknowledgements

It is no lie to say that my life had some changes during the writing of this novel. Some big, some small. Some monumentally huge. But, through it all, lifting me up and making sure I knew I had it in me to keep writing, I had my friends and family.

You see, I went from believing I'd never write another creative work again, to believing I would never write anything I'd want anyone to see, to believing I couldn't muster anything further than a short story, to finally believing I could write this novel. I didn't do this myself. I could only have done it thanks to some very special people.

Thank you, Michelle. When I met you, I knew I had to write with you. Your unapologetic style and captivating ideas caught me, and never let go. You did more than let me into your world; you helped me rebuild mine, and then together, we created a new one. And for that, I will be ever grateful.

Thanks also go to my mother Theresa, old friends James and Chris, and new ones Shanley, Michael, Tom, and Jefferson. Your support of my work, interest in my story, and sharing in my enthusiasm did more for me than you could ever know. Something so simple can mean so much when it happens at the right time, and you all were there to spur me on.

Thanks to those who passed. My father, Bob, who showed me the power of thought with a purpose. To my grandmother, Lorraine, who showed me the power of the written word.

And, lastly, thanks to you. You who are reading this. I might not know you, but through this novel, you now know a little of me. I created this work to share with you, so you could look into our universe and see us in it. So that you, too, know you can create. And maybe, just maybe, so that you might tell a story of your own. Who knows, maybe Rook, Azrael, Lucifer, and the rest will visit you, too.

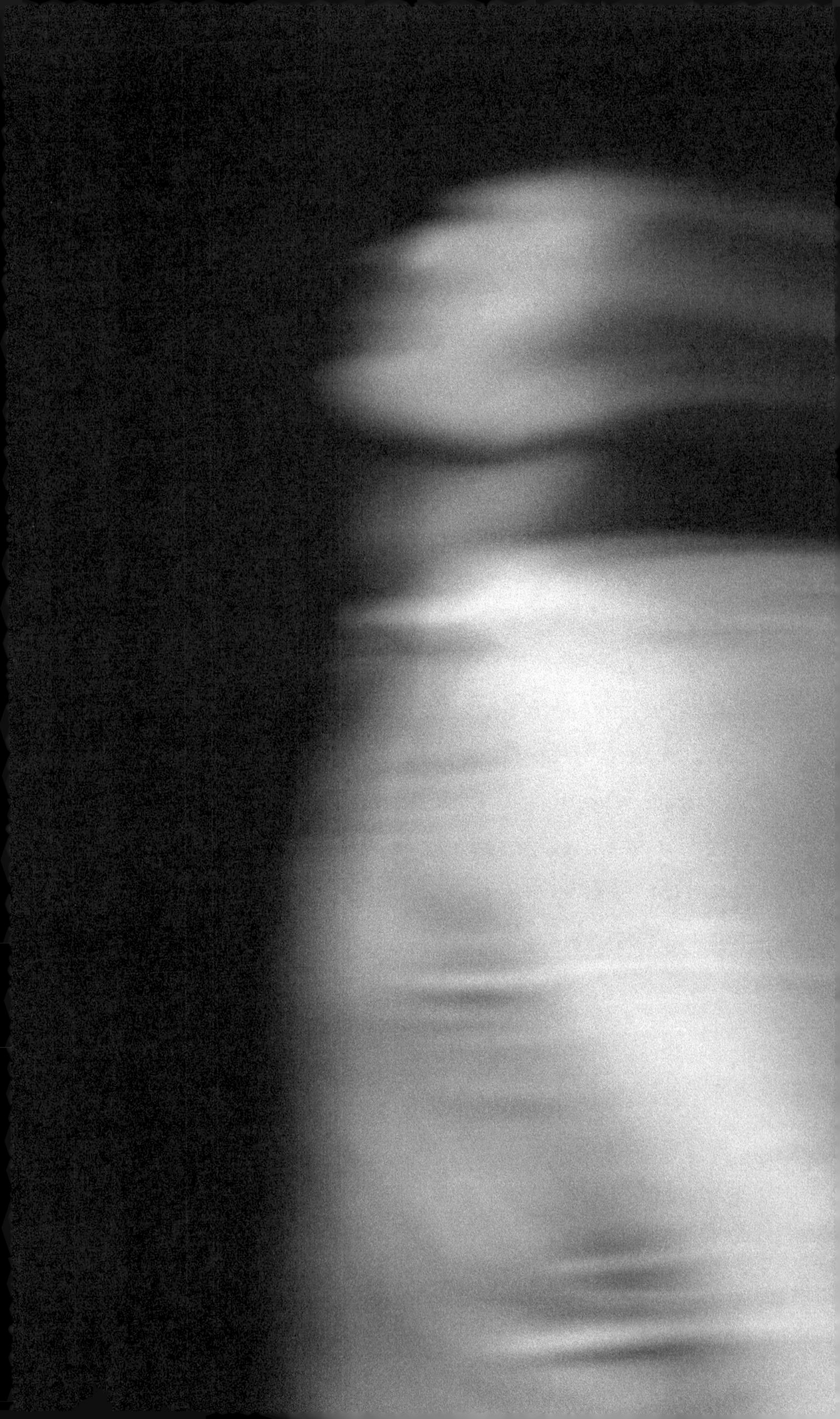

Chapter One

Rook screamed. His first breath was always a scream. It had to be. His soul would never neatly fit into another body again. None would ever be truly his again. The jagged edges of his spirit scraping into place, lighting every nerve on fire as if bared to the open air, would serve as a reminder that he was taking residence in a stolen shell. He was claiming someone else's body. Again.

With all his will, Rook gritted his teeth and forced strength into his new arms, straining against the pain. As he pushed his head up from the cool asphalt of the street, he flexed his fingers and dug into the dust and grime. Inch by inch, life returned to this body, his soul quickening the muscles each in turn as he focused on them. Thankfully, he was right about this body's heart. It thumped hard and powerfully. Yes, this body would suit him well.

Opening his eyes and sucking in the night air, Rook rolled back onto his knees. The pain was already subsiding, the alcohol in the body's system serving both as a painkiller and lubricant for the takeover. He looked about himself to remember his surroundings and get his bearings. There he was —the previous him— lying lifeless just a couple of feet away. His head —his previous head— bled slowly onto the pavement. Between them floated a wisp of feathery dark energy, quickly dissipating as Rook rose to his feet.

"So sorry, old chap," Rook said as he bent over to pull his coat off of his old body. Then, gesturing at himself, "Cheers for the upgrade. I'll take good care of this for you."

Rook chuckled to himself as he fitted his black Spector topcoat over his shoulders. He scoffed at the fashion choices this man had made, positing that he must have been in a mad dash to get laid tonight. Still, the clothes fit well, and the shoes had a classic British style. Something Rook could appreciate, despite them clashing with his favorite coat.

Turning away, Rook paused and thought a moment.

"Bloody cameras everywhere nowadays…" He looked at the body.

Shrugging, Rook pulled up the collar of his coat and walked away.

Rook fished the keys to his apartment door from the burgundy-lined pocket of his topcoat. His new fingers felt the bumps and grooves of each key as he searched for the least worn one. He had forgotten what most of these keys were for, but he kept them anyway. When he found the one he wanted, he lined it up to the deadbolt and pushed. A twang of pain ran through his fingers, and he dropped the keys to the floor.

"Bloody hell," he muttered. The bonding to the body wasn't finished yet; it still protested his presence. "Quiet down, ya bastard."

He leaned over and picked up the keys but straightened out to see the door already open. Standing in the doorway was a man of slight build with messy straw hair. His gray eyes stared at Rook with a sense of concern and urgency.

"Wh...," the man started.

"Broccoli. Radish. Pineapple. Whatever the bloody safe word is." Rook pushed past the man and entered the apartment.

"Rook?" The man took a step back and let the stranger pass.

"No, it's the Spanish Inquisition," Rook replied, dripping in sarcasm, as he tossed his keys into a dish beside the door and took off his coat.

The man sighed and closed the door.

"So, you did it again, huh? Couldn't help yourself?"

"Something like that."

"Well, at least I like the look of him. I can always be up for a twenty-something."

"Keep your goddamn hands off," Rook eyed him with a narrowing gaze. "It was a one-time thing, just me trying out new tricks. Now, let's get the hell on with it."

"You were my girlfriend, Rook."

"And it was bloody magical. But that bird's been cold in the ground for a year now."

Mark looked defeated. He hadn't really meant to engage with Rook, but it happened, and he paid for it by enduring Rook's cutting words.

Rook started to turn away but lingered on Mark's face. He could read the emotion in it, the sadness his words had just brought him, but he felt no pang of remorse or empathy.

"What the hell are you still doing here, Mark? You know exactly what I am and what I'm capable of. So why do you insist on sticking around?"

Mark looked up and met Rook's eyes.

"Because apartments in London are expensive, mate. Besides, I know your standards. This would never be on your menu," Mark gestured to himself.

Rook walked past Mark and patted him on the shoulder.

"You're too hard on yourself," Rook chuckled. Just think of yourself as a last resort if you insist on hanging about."

"Wow. Thanks."

"That's the state of it. You're living with a murderer. Your time is borrowed."

"And yet, this is the healthiest relationship I've ever been in…" Mark sighed and walked away. He headed for his bedroom and closed the door.

Rook smirked to himself.

"Remember, we're doing that old bookstore at seven," he yelled through Mark's door. "This bloke had a bundle of cash, so you can pick yourself something nice while we're there."

"Maybe something on tarot?" Mark's muffled voice came through the door.

"Don't give a toss about your fairy tales. Just make sure that angelology book is the bloody real deal."

Silence was all that followed. Rook paid it no mind and headed for his own room.

The golden light of the late-day sun spilled through the dingy windows of the antiquated bookstore. Three dusty old tomes, pulled from the shelves of the bookstore, sat upon a weathered wooden table before Rook. Their covers, painted in dark contrast to the fading light that spilled on them, faced him, each adorned with faded, flowing script. The first was titled *Eins Enoch* and possessed a subscript *Eine Deutsche Übersetzung*. The second was titled *The Paths of the Cross*. The third's title was too worn to read, but Rook could make out the words *formation* and *celestial*.

Across from Rook and the books stood a man of advanced age. He had struggled to lay each of the books out on the table, and now, having done that, he waited for Rook to make a selection.

"One Enoch?" Rook reached for the first book.

"Ah, yes. This is the German translation of the first book of Enoch. Very rare. Written three hundred years before any other translations were rediscovered in the eighteen-hundreds."

Rook opened the tome. The printing appeared old enough, and the pages were a thin parchment or vellum. It felt pleasing to Rook's fingers.

"You see, the monastic order of the Träumereien started this translation, and then it was hidden for years before being finished by the heretics of Lutheran and then being lost in the Wars of Reformation in-"

"Yeah, I noticed," Rook interjected. "This one's Middle German," he continued flipping through the book, stopping halfway. "But this part here is High German." He smirked. "These blokes weren't used to it yet. You can tell by how they keep switching between 'k' and 'ch.' Obvious as fuck."

The old man's eyes widened. "You can read Middle German?"

Rook scoffed. "Yeah. Came up on it."

The old man looked confused but then was horrified when Rook tossed down the book without a care for it.

"And who the hell hasn't read the Book of Enoch? This ain't gonna do us any good. Probably full of mistakes anyway."

The old man hastily snatched up the book and inspected it for damage. "Sir, I must ask that you really t-"

Rook pushed the second book away.

"That book, The Paths of the Cross? Total bullcrap. You better torch it before your whole rep goes up in flames, mate."

The old man looked aghast. "Sir, I assure you tha-"

"Burn it. Now this one..." Rook slid the last book toward himself and opened the cover.

A stained and blotched graphic, resembling something like a star chart or an interpretation of planetary bodies spread across the exposed pages. The artwork was hand-drawn by someone and meticulously detailed. It showed relationships between the various orbs presented on the page. This particular one highlighted an orb named Malakut, with the subtext underneath it in a script too faded to read.

The old man watched pensively as Rook motioned for Mark to come over.

"Oi, Mark! How about this one?"

Mark's head perked up from behind a display of tarot cards and several varieties of divination boards and path-finding cards. With a card pack in each hand, he came bounding over to purposely bump into Rook's shoulder and lean in dramatically to look at the book.

"Mmhmm. That's angelic script." Mark touched a knuckle of one of his full hands to the faded script and paused before nodding to Rook.

"Hmm..." Rook flipped through a few pages. The English was coming up rare.

"Enochian script," the old man corrected, "though it's been attributed to angelic writing. It's more believed that a proto-ca-"

"How much?" Rook interrupted.

"Not for sale." The old man looked at Rook with a severe expression.

"Really?" Rook was genuinely surprised.

"I'll not sell to a young upstart like you. You have no respect for the works here."

"Your glowing personality wins them over again, Rook." Mark chuckled, choosing between the card pack in his left hand or his right hand, deciding on the left, and looking up at Rook.

Rook's expression flattened.

"Tell me, mate, are you absolutely set on keeping this? I'll make it worth your while. Name your bloody price."

"No sale."

Rook and the old man fell into a silence regarding each other. Mark slid his chosen pack across the table.

"I'll take this one."

The old man stacked each of the three books on each other, making sure to place the one Rook wanted on the bottom. He then picked up the card pack and turned it over in his hand to read the price stickered to the back.

"Ten pounds."

"Rook?" Mark looked at Rook expectantly.

Digging into his back pocket, Rook produced this body's money clip. It was as sharp-edged and stylized as the shoes he wore. Pulling the stack of bills from the clip, Rook thumbed out a fifty-pound note and set it on the table, resuming his eye contact with the old man. They stared at each other as the transaction was made, but when the man held out the change, Rook turned on his heel and moved toward the exit.

"Thank you," Mark smiled as he took the change. He picked up his box and followed Rook.

Rook stepped outside and breathed in the cool air, looking out over the bustling activity across downtown London. Mark stepped up beside him.

"That script really on the level, kid?" Rook asked without looking at Mark.

"Absolutely. What are you going to do now?"

"Eh," Rook shrugged. "I reckon I have something to do after closing tonight."

Rook stepped off the curb and headed down the sidewalk.

Crosthwaite
BOOKS

Chapter Two

"You're sticking around here. If anyone comes sniffing, act like a lunatic or something."

Rook gestured vaguely in the direction of the alley that ran alongside the now-closed Crosthwaite Bookstore.

"I dunno, man. Is it worth it to break in? What if it's just a cookbook or something?"

Mark moved into place, looking uneasy as he shifted his weight from one foot to the other. The chill in the air caused him to puff out his jacket and shove his hands deeper into its pockets.

"And what if it's the bloody key to setting heaven on fire, eh? Or tells me how to control those angel wankers and make them do all sorts of debauchery and party tricks?"

Rook walked deeper into the alley and spied a drain spout, tugging on it to test its anchoring.

"Right. Point taken. Anything to take down the establishment."

"It ain't just about them, Mark," snarled Rook, giving Mark a hard look over his shoulder. "They ain't satisfied with just reigning over us. They abuse us. Manipulate us. Destroy us." He turned back to the grimy drain spout and gazed up at the window ledge above it. "I've been alive for five hundred years, and I can tell you one thing: dying while those bastards are still in power ain't worth a damn thing."

Rook hefted himself up and climbed the metal bracings to reach the window.

"Some of us don't have a choice, Rook," Mark muttered under his breath, turning his attention to the street.

Rook pressed his palm into the window's glass and shoved upward. To Rook's surprise, the window jostled in response. He pushed again and dislodged it from its jamb. Paint crackled from the frame as it slid up. With a wind-up practice swing, Rook flung himself into the open space and rolled through onto the upper floor of the bookstore.

Rook stood up, dusting himself off, and readjusted his Spector. Taking a quick glance around, he noted an abundance of boxes taking up most of the space on the floor, with several having been opened, their contents partially removed. They were clearly back-stock boxes, mostly full, containing the garish knickknacks no self-respecting consumer should ever purchase, Rook thought.

Making his way toward the stairwell, Rook descended into the store proper. With the lights off, the cluttered shelves and over-burdened tables looked like a sinister flea market, though the bookshelves lining the walls and the paperback islands proved easily navigable. Rook made his way to the table where he had last seen the books. Nothing remained from his previous conversation with the bookshop owner. Leaning over to inspect the back corners and the space behind the table, Rook saw nothing more to clue him in on the book's location.

Rook vaulted the table and looked at the back shelves from his new vantage point.

"If you were an incredibly precious book," he muttered as he looked in either direction, "stashed by some old codger, where would you be?"

Rook's eyes passed over the cash register, which sat perched on a cabinet with a large, central storage space with a narrow drawer below it. He paused, his eyebrows raising, as he realized he stood a chance to make a profit for his time here. He quickly looked around for anything to break the register open when he noticed no lock seemed to secure the cabinet. Rook tugged on the knob, and the cabinet door popped open.

A tiny, red light blinked lazily from the depths of the darkness inside, fused to the inner side wall, just inside the edge. Each blink illuminated the interior, and after a few, Rook noticed a stack of three tomes resting on the bottom of the cubby.

"Oh." Rook's eyebrows raised again.

He looked over the tome's covers as he removed them,

dropping the two he had rejected earlier to the floor. He tucked *formation* under his arm.

"And yet...," he smiled to himself as he returned to rummaging through the cabinet. Pulling open the drawer, he spied a long, metal letter opener that sat upon a stack of what he could only presume were bills and the like. Taking the blade, he brought it up to the register's drawer and slid the edge under the lock. With a quick shove, the simple latch popped, and with a ding, the till became exposed.

Rook sighed. "And yet, barely worth it."

He reached in and grabbed the handful of singles and fivers, shoving them into one of the three asymmetrical pockets of his topcoat.

"Rook!"

Mark's voice broke Rook's concentration, penetrating the pane of glass of a bottom-floor window that faced the alley.

"Rook!"

Rook cleared the table again and bounded to the window. He felt for the latch across the top of the pane, unhooked it, and slid the window up.

"Oi, what?"

"You hear that?" Mark pointed upward and down the main street.

Rook looked and held his breath to listen. Sirens. Police sirens.

"The bloody Yard, innit?" Rook's gaze flicked to Mark. "How long you been hearing it?"

"About since I heard you thud somewhere downstairs. They're getting closer."

"Shit, I must've set something off. Here," Rook lifted the book and thrust it through the window, "take this and get the hell back to the apartment."

Mark took the book and looked it over, confused.

"What are you going to do?"

"We need every damn second we can get with that before it's swiped. Can't have it looking like a bloody heist."

Rook pulled himself back from the window and started looking around the shop again.

"What are you going to do, Rook?" Mark asked again, stretching the syllables out as he posed the question.

"What did I say about 'The Paths of the Cross?'"

Rook saw what he was looking for. Nestled among the scented candles, incense sticks, and rolls of bound sage were a series of book-quote-themed match tins.

"Hilarious." Rook smiled to himself.

Mark followed his gaze, "Rook, no! Just get out of there!"

"Fuck off already! Don't be anywhere around here when they get here." Rook sped off toward the matches.

"Shit!" Mark looked both ways down the alley and then back at the window. He huffed, turned, and sprinted down the sidewalk along the main street before ducking into another alleyway.

Rook grabbed the match tin and tossed it up in the air to snatch it out of free fall as he walked back to the books he had left on the floor. He picked up "The Paths of the Cross," opened it to a random page, and set it on the table. He slid the tin open and took out a match.

"Strike-anywheres."

He then dumped the rest of the matches over the book, table, and floor. Sliding the match across the wooden surface of the table, it lit ablaze. He paused, only briefly, to take in the smell of sulfur and then tossed the match onto the book.

Dry and brittle, the tome caught on fire easily. As the embers raced out toward the edges, they met the strewn-about matches. Pops and hissing gave way to an inferno as the fire ate through the abundant fuel.

"Martin Luther, eat your Protestant heart out."

Rook took the book by its binding and flung it at the paperback island in the center of the shop. As it flew, pages cast ash along the floor with a chunk of the book-that-was clumping on the ground and catching the matches there.

Rook ran across the floor back to the matches and grabbed another tin. He repeated his vandalous effort twice more, tossing a fireball at the hardcovers along the wooden shelves and another at the sage rolls.

The sirens blared through the growing noise of the fire, and Rook could see the blue pulsing lights through the storefront glass. He eyed the window he left open, and thought to help increase the airflow by opening another, before taking up station just inside the main doors to await his guests.

Within a moment, the police were at the door. They shouted at each other, something about heading this way and that, to see about containing the fire. Rook wondered for a moment if they were even going to try the door and decided to help them out. It was getting a bit too warm, after all. He reached out and unlocked the storefront door. It was at this moment that the officer standing on the other side noticed Rook for the first time.

The officer reached for the door and flung it wide open. His wide eyes took in Rook in his dark overcoat and slim-tailored slacks and processed what he was seeing. It took a moment before he realized that Rook wasn't acting as though he was in danger, and the smirk on Rook's face sealed the suspicions that immediately formed in his mind.

"Halt!"

He brandished his nightstick and lunged at Rook, who raised his hands and shrugged.

"I wasn't planning on heading out, bobby. But it was getting a mite toasty."

The officer crossed the distance and used his nightstick to lock one of Rook's arms, sliding up behind him to force him out onto the street. Rook didn't resist but did complain as he stumbled forward and out of the blazing bookstore.

"Oi, mate, I'm not fighting you. You got me. Pat on the back, have a tea."

The officer forced Rook to the ground as another joined to assist him. After zip-tying his wrists together, they lifted him, each under an arm, and brought him to their vehicle, sliding him in the back seat. The car rumbled to life as a couple of the officers jumped in and pulled away from the bookstore, leaving the rest to deal with the blaze.

Rook leaned his head against the window and watched the fire burn.

Rook thumped into the metal chair inside the interrogation room. It was altogether too flat, too unforgiving for a living thing to rest in for too long. Cold, too, as he no longer had his Spector on to protect him from the metal backing. Perhaps that was the point, Rook thought, as the officer cut the second zip-tie to bind Rook's wrists that night. Reflexively, he rubbed where the plastic had been and waited for the officer to sit in the decidedly more comfortable chair across the table.

"Alright, Mr...Morten? Mind explaining what you were doing at the Crosthwaite bookstore in the middle of the night?"

The athletic, muscular officer sat across from Rook. His

freshly removed, standard-issue patrol cap was placed on the table in front of him, revealing his matted hair, carelessly groomed a dozen or so hours earlier.

"Morten?" Rook raised his eyebrows. "I thought it was 'Marten.'"

The officer looked confused and checked the papers he had in front of him on the table. He had said the name right, and so he narrowed his eyes at Rook and restated the question.

"What were you doing at the bookstore, Mr. Morten?"

"Trying not to breathe in that bloody smoke, honestly." Rook shrugged.

The officer sighed and slid the papers to the side before clasping his hands together.

"I don't see any reason to make this difficult for either of us," the officer stated. "Though your record is clean, except for a scuffle outside the fabric nightclub, we apprehended you inside the building while it was burning."

Rook nodded.

"And we found smoke permeating deep into your coat, suggesting you were there when the fire started."

"I'd like that back, by the way."

"But that's after we caught you plainly on the surveillance cameras setting the fire."

"Bloody cameras," Rook muttered to himself, looking to the side. He wondered where they were and if he was seen taking the book. He slid his eyes back to the officer and continued waiting.

"So, I'll ask you one more time, Mr. Morten," the officer leaned over his clasped hands. "What were you doing in the bookstore?"

Rook pondered a moment and then cocked his head.

"Need a good read, mate. Nothing better than settling in on a quiet evening next to a roaring fire. Don't you think?"

The officer frowned.

"Fine, fine," Rook sighed, "but it'll be easier to show you. Get some lackey to grab my coat and drag it in here. I'm sure you wankers didn't suss out what I had stashed in it."

"How about you just tell me, Mr. Morten?" the officer responded with a cool tone.

Rook smirked.

"There's no way you'll find it, mate. You'll probably trash it trying to." Rook leaned back in the chair. "Besides, what can I do with a sodding coat? I'll sit right here the whole time and guide you."

The officer looked incredulous, continuing to stare at Rook for a moment as he worked through the possibilities of what could be hidden in the garment that their X-ray and metal detectors didn't pick up. Still, he saw little harm in bringing the coat into the room.

"Officer Raynes!"

The door cracked open, and a young officer leaned in,

glancing at Rook and then at his commanding officer.

"Sir?"

"Bring me Mr. Morten's coat. Check it for any suspicious contents or substances before you do, though."

"Right away," and with that, the door was once again closed.

The officer's eyes met Rook's again. They left it silent for a moment longer before Rook decided to speak.

"You a religious man, officer?"

The officer narrowed his eyes again. "I'd appreciate not trying to delve into my personal life, Mr. Morten. I don't see how it's relevant."

"Don't give me that bloody nonsense," Rook smirked. "Even the worst of the lot will pray to some god or another. So, tell me, which one do you bow down to?"

The officer leaned back and let out a breath slowly, measuring the sense of the question. He crossed his arms and decided to answer.

"Christian."

"Ah, Christian," Rook's eyebrows raised in mock interest. "What denomination?"

"Anglican."

"Oh, one of the luckiest bastards to survive the Reformation," Rook nodded.

The officer continued to study Rook through a pointed gaze.

"So, your church a bunch of pompous pricks or more of a loosey-goosey kind of deal?" Rook gestured with a flip of his hand.

"I don't see what any of this has to do-"

"Tell me," Rook leaned in on the table, smirking in the harsh light, "when was the last time you confessed?"

The door to the interrogation room opened, and the young officer came in with Rook's coat in a thin plastic bag. Rook smiled as it was handed over to the senior officer.

"We found nothing out of the ordinary on it, sir," Officer Raynes said. "The only metal was a bottle opener hanging from the inside pocket zipper."

The older officer took the bag and opened it, the room filling with the smell of smoke. He whipped it once to lengthen it and then held it up in one hand, just far enough away from Rook as though to taunt him with it.

"Thank you, that is all," he said to his junior. Officer Raynes nodded and left the room, closing the door again.

"There it fucking is," Rook grinned, "a bloody masterpiece, innit?"

"Alright, tell me what we need to know about this coat, Mr. Morten," the officer said, looking to Rook and noting his smile with a growing sense of concern.

Rook's eyes locked onto the officer's.

"Oi, copper. You gonna answer me, or are you too busy counting your Hail Marys?" Rook sneered. "Been to confession lately?"

The officer lowered the coat to his lap and swallowed. The hair on his arms and the back of his neck rose. His stomach knotted. Everything about his body was telling him to leave right now. But, he had a duty, and so he screwed a measure of steel into his face and stared back at Rook.

"What does it matter to you?"

"One should never meet their maker with a heart full of regrets."

On full alert, the officer dropped the coat and pushed his chair back, watching Rook intently. The hair on the officer's body began to itch, their roots excited by something in the air around him. The air in the room quickly cooled, and the light began to dim. Looking around the room, the fluorescent lights seemed to struggle to emit their glow and began to scream in a barely audible whine. The officer looked back to Rook to see the man leaning back in his chair, the smile of a madman on his face, as the growing darkness surrounded him. Bits of the darkness glinted in the light as it swirled around Rook, appearing like a haze of gossamer caught in a whirlwind. Through it, the officer could see Rook's body going limp and sliding down in the chair, but above it rose a condensation of black mist that knitted together into a form like a living shadow. A shadow made of broken glass.

The officer shot up to his feet and backed away, knocking into the table and toppling his chair. He looked around the room in a desperate attempt to find something that could protect him but found nothing in this barren place.

Rook rose over the officer, his broken and fractured soul whipping into a frenzy of spinning glass. He paused, savoring the moment, his essence pulsing with anticipation. He waited for the inevitable pull of the underworld to tug on him, challenging it to take him before he would take this man's body, relishing how it was taking longer and longer for the familiar calling to attempt to claim him.

"Holy mother of G-" the officer gasped.

Rook dove forward, slamming himself into the officer's body. Being of nothing but soul, the man's flesh gave no resistance to Rook. Instead, Rook connected with something much more solid and resilient, deep within the officer's body. Rook latched on and tore, ripping the soul from the officer's body, disconnecting the solid thing, and snapping it off like a shard of ice. Discarding it, Rook descended into the body, bearing down on the brittle remnants of the previous owner's soul and anchoring to it. He watched as the officer's soul was flung away; the damage Rook caused it snaking fractures up the essence like the slow, shattering of a pane of glass. *Let's see how fast I can get it*, Rook thought as he forced his soul into the extremities of the body and arrested the necessary control. The pain began to well up in the body, and it mingled with Rook's own consciousness until it was no longer the body's pain but his own. He felt the rush enter his new lungs, giving fire to his new muscles and jump-starting his new heart.

He screamed. Rook's first breath in a new body was always a scream. It had to be. And Rook opened his eyes to find himself leaning back against the corner of the interrogation room. He looked at his new hands and legs, and then over at his old body, still limp in the chair, and finally at the black soul that hovered in between them. He smiled as he saw the soul, form wavering, the shards of it clinging to each other magnetically, as it became aware of itself again. He watched as the eye-less voids in the vaguely humanoid form began to smolder like embers as the spirit's inborn anger and resentment shaped and transformed it. As it lost its purpose as a soul, it gained a new one as a wraith, and it set its hatred on its old body. But, as it began to drift forward and form claw-like appendages, it suddenly jerked downward.

"Don't fret, mate," growled Rook with a smirk, "I reckon the place is top-notch."

Like a sudden shift in gravity, the wraith fell into the floor and receded from view. Brushing himself off, Rook walked over, picked up his Spector, and slid it on.

"Aw, bloody hell," Rook scowled as the burgundy lining of the coat cut into his larger frame, the fit too tight to be comfortable. Still, Rook would not be without it and got it on despite how it fit. He flipped the collar up and walked toward the door. He took a breath, gave himself a good once-over glance, and then opened the door. He walked down the hall with a long gait, keeping his eyes forward, ignoring the confused and questioning looks the other officers gave him.

"What was that scream?"

Rook walked through the front doors of the precinct and out into the street.

Chapter Three

A stream of black energy pierced through the white haze that blanketed the entirety of an unmeasurable expanse. The energy moved with a steady flow, heating up and brightening from black into cardinal blue as it gained speed and descended. It bent, twisted, and looped on its path as it was drawn deeper into a mass of like-colored molten energy. This blue gave way to bright white when the energy, combined with countless other superheated streams, became a massive ribbon that flowed through a superstructure made of pure light. Around the structure in sprawling masses were countless other streams, from a myriad of angles, that all fell into it, churning the glass-like matter endlessly.

A man stood before this complex structure, a spec of darkness set against this massive, roiling machine of light. An expression of concern tinged his otherwise immaculate mocha features, turning the angular ridges of his brows, set atop his pointed nose, into a scrunched and creased contortion. His amber eyes watched as one of the flows of black energy seemed to be sprinkled with bits of something broken, glistening against the backdrop of ambient light. As it traveled down its path and joined the rest of the mass, the fractured energy diffused but refused to brighten to its expected hue, instead suffusing itself upon the structure and darkening the energy that encountered it.

The man's concern turned into determination as he steeled himself and took in a deep breath. His skin lightened, white light from within forcing itself through his form. Quickly, the light outshone his loose blouse and over-tight dark pants. He transformed, all semblance of humanity washed away, as he assumed a presence of pure full-spectrum light. He reached out his hands and willed his energy forth, issuing a torrent of iridescence at the darkened section of the structure. As his light impacted the dark, it ate away at the edges and seeped into the cracks. The rainbow hues solidified within the cracks, filling the cavities, but did little else to erase the dark.

The light receded from the man, and he returned to his base form again. He breathed hard, the effort having winded him. He looked upon his work with a tempered measure. *It will have to do,* he thought. He caught another glinting stream from the corner of his eye and turned his head to look at it. And then another. And another. Gravity replaced his expression, and he rushed from the structure into the mists beyond.

Navigating the impossible space of haze and semi-solid

corridors seemed natural to him, running and making turns as needed, lifting into the air, and flying as required. The structure was clouded from view nearly instantly as he made his way, moving at an unknowable speed until he breached into a realm of green and earthy colors. A narrow path of grass was before him, flanked on either side by still waters that led into a forest clearing. In the center of the clearing was a thatch hut of modest size, smoke rising from an opening in the roof. The man ran down the path to the hut, pushing open the reed-enforced door before entering.

On the other side, he was surrounded by the dampness of a dark, dank cave, the breadth of which was massive. Set far in the distance was a structure made of stone, a temple, lit by candles lining its facade. Carved into the stone were symbols of cycles: the rising and setting of the sun and moon, the turning of the seasons, and the birth, growth, and death of a tree. Over the entrance, the bulb of an orchid plant was carved.

The man crossed this distance in an instant, moving through the entrance and into the temple. He stumbled forward into a small stone room illuminated by a light coming through the hole in the center of the floor. Across the room stood an old woman dressed in woven cloth of earthen hues, leaning on a staff of twisted wood. When the man entered the chamber, her eyes, filled with the birthing and dying of stars, moved from the light and onto him. As the man collapsed to his hands and knees before her, she lifted her staff and came around the hole in the floor, stopping at his side.

"Adrian," the crone spoke, her voice rasp and harsh, "you pushed yourself too hard, didn't you?"

"Gaia," Adrian strained to catch his breath, "something's wrong with the Agglomeration. Too many fractures are coming in. I can't heal them all."

Gaia knelt next to Adrian and offered her hand to him, a slender hand dimpled with the flushed flesh of a child. The little girl closed her eyes. With a hum of energy, she infused the man with a violet light that traced through his body and disappeared within him. Adrian opened his eyes and strained to stand, nodding his thanks to the small girl.

"I know," the child said, "I've been watching it from here."

When Adrian reached his feet, Gaia turned away and looked into the light, her long red curls framing her now adult face as she peered downward. Adrian joined her and dropped his gaze into the light.

"You didn't train me to handle this, Gaia," Adrian started, "it's using me up too fast. Every time I seal a crack, more come rushing in."

Gaia looked at Adrian, the galaxies in her eyes shifting as she thought.

"You were never meant to heal...this," she gestured at the light, "these aren't just fractures; they're shattered. Things in tatters. I know of nothing that can do this to a soul save a divine decree of destruction from Raziel."

"What do we do? If I keep this up, I'll burn out, and you won't have any Noden left to help you."

Gaia's silver-lined, faded curls continued to frame her face, the lines of time etched into her skin and made even deeper by the glare of the light.

"I can't help you. I'm afraid the only one who can is the one who built the Agglomeration, and Min has been missing for some time." She reached out into the light and pulled in a stream of glinting, black energy, inspecting it as it flowed through her hand. "No, we're going to need to figure out what's causing this. Stop it before it spreads too far for you to heal."

Adrian nodded. "Great! How?"

Gaia sighed, the sound like a shrill wind as it escaped the small girl's body.

"I'll go to Malakut. Those that kill and reap must know what is causing these poor, fractured souls."

"Malakut?"

Gaia closed her eyes, envisioning a long stone hall with a ceiling too tall to see and a floor submerged in murky water. It was lined with sandstone columns etched in angelic script. The entirety was lit by a setting sun, frozen in place outside. She reached out a hand and touched Adrian on the forehead, the vision of the realm flooding his mind's eye.

"Duat. Purgatory. Where souls were judged before we did away with such things. Now the home to the Cataclysms. With this image, should you need to go there, you will arrive in the central hall."

"Cataclysms? Like Azrael."

Gaia, appearing fully grown again, nodded.

"Yes. Where the Four Horsemen reside."

Gaia turned to the side and stepped forward, fading from view before her foot hit the ground. Adrian stood, looking at where she had been a moment before. The light in the room darkened, and he turned to look through Gaia's portal into the Agglomeration to see a large, scintillating mass trace through a channel of energy.

Gaia stepped out into the great hall of Malakut. To either side of her, hallways spread outward, mists concealing the expanses after some distance. Before her rose a stone-cut stair that broke the water lazily flowing at her feet and climbed upward toward the frozen sun. She walked forward on the water, never breaking its surface, until she set foot upon the ancient stonework steps. And then she began to climb.

The stairs crested and expanded out flat before her into a grand room. The sun's light poured through openings cut into the stone walls on either side of her, illuminating the hall and room beyond as if it were large enough to take up the entire sky. Just before her stood an altar, larger than she, with an immense set of measuring scales sitting atop. Dust-covered books and a giant feather lay strewn about near the scales, their disuse apparent.

Gaia walked around the altar and proceeded further into the room. On the other side of the altar were two water channels carved into the floor that led parallel to the far end. There, they terminated, spilling their unending waters into nothingness. Standing near one of the channels, resting his side against the wall, stood a man whose form towered over Gaia in any of her stages. At eight feet tall, dressed in a black cassock, the figure put into perspective the massive halls and room, as even he was little more than a spec set against it.

"Samael," Gaia spoke as she neared the man. In response, the man turned toward her, revealing his light skin, fiery red hair that ringed his otherwise bald head, and long, red beard. He held a book in one hand, closing it as he turned toward the voice.

"Gaia," Samael said, his voice tinged with sorrow, mirroring the scent of old graves, crumbling stones, and petrichor that accompanied him. "What brings you to Malakut?"

"There's a problem at the Agglomeration." Gaia's young voice belied her serious tone. "Fractured souls are arriving at an increased rate. The Noden can't heal it all, and it won't be long before too many humans will be born Fractured."

Samael pushed off the wall and turned toward Gaia fully.

"Fractured begets Fractured," Samael agreed, "but why come here? We're not in the habit of shattering souls."

"No, but you are the Harbinger of Misery, reaper of suicides. And you were once the Angel of Death. Do you not know of a way to track down what's causing this?" Gaia asked, her voice remaining tense as her body became mature. "Between you and your successor and the other Cataclysms, you can find out how these unnatural deaths are occurring and put a stop to it."

Samael thought for a moment.

"There hasn't been a Fractured among the Sorrowed I've shepherded lately. But maybe there's been one among the usual and murdered. I'll summon Azrael."

Gaia nodded.

"But," Samael continued, "it may be a moment before Azrael can respond. Would you be able to hold the next few Fractured aside so we can examine them?"

"The mechanism to direct souls no longer exists," said the old crone as she gestured at the two canals behind her, "and nowhere but the Agglomeration for a soul to go. Adrian will hold one or two in stasis for you at the Agglomeration, but that will last only as long as his essence holds."

"That'll have to do, thank you."

"Be quick in your investigation, Harbinger. I've only

just trained this gray soul into a Noden, and he is already nearly spent with the burden of healing the fractures in the Agglomeration alone. There is no prospect of another worthy of this path and no other option to keep the slow shattering of life's engine at bay. If you don't stop the Fractured and save Adrian, there will not be another to replace him in time."

"Understood. Let him know we'll arrive as soon as we can."

Gaia nodded again; heart heavy in her chest. She turned and walked away, taking only a few steps before disappearing.

Samael stood silently, weighing his book in his hand to help him think. As he pondered, the smell of freshly turned earth wafted through the space, and Samael turned to see another man before him. Matching him in height, the other wore a double-breasted black suit, a long overcoat, and a dark woven shawl covering his short black hair and revealing his gaunt, nearly skeletal face. No eyes sat in this companion's sockets; only darkness peered back.

"Azrael," Samael smiled wistfully, "thank you for coming."

"Of course, old friend." Azrael's thin, bony fingers grasped and pulled down the shawl onto his shoulders. "Your summons felt urgent. I came as soon as I could."

"We have a situation. Gaia came here to inform me of it herself."

Azrael raised a brow.

"Come, let's go to the Agglomeration. I'll explain there."

Azrael nodded and faded from view. Samael tossed his book in the air and willed it to cross the empty space and set itself upon the altar. Then he, too, faded from view.

When the pair reformed, they were illuminated by the light of the Agglomeration. They looked upon it and saw the streaks of darkness and jagged edges scoring the roiling mass that caused Gaia's concern. Their faces fell as they looked over the damage and then looked at each other.

"Azrael!" A voice rang out. Azrael and Samael turned to see Adrian floating toward them. They saw the spirit enhanced by his Noden training, possessing far more corporealness, vigor, and color than a ghost normally would. Azrael couldn't help but smile.

"Adrian," Azrael nodded, "how are you faring?"

"Uh," Adrain said, clearly flustered, "I mean, the job's great, but it's a lot, you know? A year ago, I was trying to find some rich sugar daddy to rock my world, and now I'm trying to keep the thing together that's literally our entire world." Adrian wiped his brow with a sheepish smile. "Drucilla would kill me if I told her I was doing this, let alone that it was killing me." His face dropped. "Y-you haven't told her, right?"

Azrael shook his head and clasped a hand on Adrian's shoulder.

"That is up to you in your time. I am glad you have

done well here, and that is what we will focus on for now." Azrael turned and gestured to Samael, "This is Samael, my predecessor and fellow Cataclysm."

Samael offered a slight smile.

"Samael, sure, nice to meet you, but we'll have to do meeting the new DILF thing later. I don't think we exactly have the time."

Samael laughed at the comment, but Azrael raised a brow, not catching the meaning of the new word.

Adrian motioned for them to follow and flew across the expanse toward a pocket of iridescent energy. The pair turned, and each unfurled a set of black angelic wings before taking to the air and following. When they got closer to the energy, they could see it enveloping two black humanoid forms, anchoring them in place. They stopped before the specimens, hovering near Adrian, who checked his containment cell for any weakening.

"Gaia said you needed to see a couple of them, so I caught these guys just before they were rejoined. My snare is good for now, but..."

"Thank you," Azrael said as he pushed through the shell of energy and came before the dark figures. Samael followed and, once on the other side, hovered close to the souls, looking over their edges.

"Wraiths," Azrael noted, "intact. So, these are not from novice necromancy."

Samael leaned closer, reaching out a finger to feel along the lower extremity of a wraith.

"And they weren't born Fractured, either," Samael added. "Look. Here. You see this sharp edge?"

Azrael and Adrian both looked to where Samael was touching. Azrael crossed his arms and straightened back out, but Adrian squinted, not quite seeing what they saw.

"Right here is where the Anima connects to the Animus. And there's no Animus here. These were fractured when this was broken off."

"Wait, I know this," Adrian said. "The Anima is the part of the soul that is 'us,' our personality and memories. And the Animus is the part that tethers us to our physical bodies, the anchor."

"Right," Samael said, "and when you die, the entire soul, Anima and Animus, returns to the Agglomeration."

"And these guys are missing their anchors?"

"Yes," Samael said as he stopped hunching over and turning to Azrael.

"How does that happen," Adrian asked.

"They were forced out of their bodies," Azrael said.

"What?" Adrian asked, looking back and forth between Azrael and Samael.

"The only way an Anima and Animus can be separated from one another is by forcefully ejecting the soul from its body," Samael explained, "and the only way to do that is with a very poor use of necromancy on a living body, or…"

"Or possession," Azrael finished Samael's thought.

Samael met Azrael's gaze and nodded.

"Most likely."

Azrael turned toward Adrian.

"You don't need to hold these any longer; we've seen all we need from them. I'm afraid if you release them back to the Agglomeration, the damage will be too much for you to handle, but I don't wish for you to hold them here and unduly tax yourself further."

"Yeah, I don't really have a better choice. I can't do both. While I have them here, I can't spend any energy healing at all. I've got to chance it," Adrian said, a grim expression crossing his face.

"If I may be so bold as to offer a workaround," Samael said.

"Please!"

"Unravel them," Azrael said.

Adrian's mouth fell agape. Before leaning in, he looked around to see if anyone else could see or hear them.

"That's against the celestial laws," Adrian said. "If I get caught doing that, I could lose my place here. Or worse, get tossed in! I've heard the stories!"

"Desperate times, my friend," Samael smiled, "and I'm sure Gaia will suggest it herself here very soon. Besides, if she or anyone else has a problem, tell them I told you to do it.

They can take it up with me."

Adrian looked shocked but contemplated Samael's suggestion.

"He's right," Azrael added, "this is not where your story ends. I'll do it if you will not."

"Azrael," Samael warned.

"No, you're both right," Adrian said, "I'll do it. I can put their energy to use healing things rather than breaking them, even if it's only a little. It's just such a loss, is all. Who knows what experience they could have added to the Agglomeration."

"Better to lose these Fractured than to lose you or the Agglomeration," Samael said.

"Right." Adrian nodded and steeled himself. "Well, I better see to it. And you both better get going. These Fractured aren't exactly coming in at a regular schedule, but the rate is increasing."

Samael and Azrael each nodded and faded from sight.

"Right. Right, right, right," Adrian repeated as he stared at the wraiths.

The dark stone hallway of Malakut stretched out in either direction from a grand table that was set centered between two of the endless giant pillars lining the walls. It broke the lazily flowing stream of water that it sat in and blocked the ripples generated by Azrael and Samael as they appeared. Each took a seat at the table, facing each other.

Samael rested his hands on the table and interlaced his fingers. He stared at them. Azrael placed his hands, palms down, flat on the table and watched his mentor.

"You're troubled. Beyond normal. Beyond the implications," Azrael broke the silence.

Samael looked at Azrael and offered a small smile.

"Azrael, do you know of any rogue celestials mulling about on Eorthe?"

"Lucifer. Malphas. The Virtues that hunt the Unholy," Azrael listed, rolling his hand.

"Malphas? An intangible? He'd have to possess a body to be material in that realm."

"Yes. He's attached himself to Thoth's host as her subservient. He took a body to do that."

"And the previous occupant's soul?"

"It became a Fractured and a violent one. Malphas does not possess the skill to extract a soul with the Animus intact."

"And so, you reaped it?"

"No," Azrael leaned back in his chair, "it poses little threat on Eorthe, and I saw no reason to damage the Agglomeration with it. It'll flail fruitlessly in the presence of Malphas and Thoth's host and, I surmise, will be a learning experience for the host."

"Hmm," Samael continued to think.

"What is it?" Azrael raised a brow.

"There was more missing from those wraiths than just their Animus. Tell me, think back; have you seen anything strange or unusual when reaping souls? Specifically, when you've seen Fractured."

It was Azrael's turn to clasp hands as he leaned forward onto the table. He thought deeply, going through his indelible memory.

"Mm, yes," Azrael said, "I have seen on occasion a gray-colored human soul in the vicinity of a Fractured. But I could not reap it. It flickered out of existence as if it had used up its energy instantly."

Samael's eyes widened, and he raised his brows as he leaned back.

"Oh, my friend, it is my unfortunate displeasure to inform you that you might have fucked up really badly."

"I don't follow," Azrael blinked.

"That gray soul is the one causing these fractures. It has to be. There's no other way that this kind of breaking can happen."

"You will have to elaborate."

"Those Fractured were missing whole pieces of themselves. Shards just gone. I haven't seen anything like that since before you replaced me, back when Min was still experimenting with mixing elements to create the first human souls. One of his attempts got out of hand and was pummeling its fellow souls, breaking them like I saw today. It absorbed the other's shards, becoming stronger itself."

"An Original Soul?" Azrael asked, "Adrian is an Original Soul, but I do not see that potential within him."

"I don't think Min abandoned his experiment like he claimed to do before the other Thrones," Samael said with a raised finger, gesturing a point, "I think he released all One Hundred, and this is something all gray souls can potentially do. You told Adrian of the path to become a Noden, so he changed into that. But this one? It's changing itself to become a predator. Consuming bits of Fractured as it takes over their bodies, sending the broken remains to the Agglomeration."

"So, then, we have a target—an Original Soul. But I lost sight of it somehow. It evaded me."

"Yeah," Samael said, "I'm not clear on that one. Min's One Hundred never had bodies when he was working on them, so maybe it has something to do with that. Maybe they violate something fundamental by taking a body they were not born into."

"Perhaps," Azrael pondered. "But the path is clear. I will respond to every new Fractured soul, whether or not it heeds the Agglomeration's call. I can determine those born Fractured from those newly broken and focus on those. If I am fast enough, I'll catch the gray soul and reap it."

"I don't think so," Samael responded, "there are a few

problems with that. It'll take too long to track. Too many Fractured could occur before you find it."

"We are tied to moments of death, you and me. That's the only feasible way of following the trail."

"I'm afraid my role is useless in this. These aren't suicides, I can't sense these deaths. And while you can, that means you can only track it from one body to another. You can only follow it while it gains in power."

"The power means little. We are Cataclysms. Any soul, Original or not, is subject to our control."

"True," Samael raised a finger, "yet not an option. If we find the soul in a body, not only is it hidden from us, but it's protected by Divine Law. We can't kill humans outright. And even if we caught it outside a body, we could only contain it. Sending it to the Agglomeration would compound the fractures as it and every shard it has taken would get absorbed."

Azrael nodded.

"And Original Souls are protected from destruction," Azrael said, tapping a finger to his chin.

"Right. Short of Raziel getting buy-off from every remaining Throne, that's not happening. Not with Gaia doing her best to fill in for Min. She wouldn't vote for that. Ever."

"Then I see only one way we can pursue this threat."

"You and I are in agreement, old friend. We need

assistance."

"We need Heaven and Hell to move on this."

Chapter Four

One year earlier...

Rook sat in the mocha and espresso-colored sitting room of Café Babka. He checked his watch. He wasn't impatient; he had been stalking this case for a while. He knew her routine, and she'd arrive at the café and order her usual in a few more moments. He pulled out this body's phone and unlocked it. Thankfully, it used biometrics and had no idea its owner wasn't themselves anymore.

Rook pulled up a news site and tapped on the second article it presented. It opened, and he set the phone on the table, leaving it on and unlocked. He wrapped his hands around the China teacup this venue was famous for using, savoring the warmth it gave him on this dreary London morning.

The scene is set, he thought. *I'm blending in.* Pretty easy to look lost in thought, likely over the article on the phone. And between him and a dozen others in the café, Helen would have no idea she was being watched.

As predicted, the tall, dark-haired woman arrived. She was dressed professionally, with a thin-rimmed set of glasses, a dark blazer covering a light-colored blouse, and dark slacks. If it weren't for her pink socks disappearing into her sensible black wedge work shoes, there would be nothing to note about her style. Around her neck hung a lanyard, and at its end, her identification as a historic librarian at the British Museum. Helen ordered a latte and sat near the window, pulling out her phone while waiting for the coffee.

Rook tapped his phone to keep the screen alive but watched the woman. Something was off. She didn't order her usual pastry. She wasn't settling in for lunch. Was she waiting for someone? Rook took a sip of his coffee.

Helen tapped her phone a few times and then put it away. She wasn't reading from it, another sign that something was different. Interest piqued, Rook cocked his head and waited. Her name was called after a few more moments, and she approached the counter to retrieve her coffee. As she picked it up, Rook noticed it was in a paper container—a takeaway.

Helen's hands were no sooner around her beverage when a man with messy, straw-colored hair and a slim build came up behind her and slipped an arm around her waist. He was dressed casually in a loose shirt with a faded band logo and worn jeans. He stood in stark contrast to Helen, who stepped out of his attempt at an embrace.

Ah, the boyfriend, Rook thought, *Mark*.

The couple turned and left the café. Rook rose and adjusted his Spector before heading for the door.

"Uh, sir!" A café patron called out. "You left your phone."

"Have it, mate," Rook replied, following his quarry onto the street.

Rook looked both ways and saw the couple making their way toward the museum. He shoved his hands in his pockets and followed behind, keeping a moderate distance, weaving through the busy sidewalk traffic to keep pace. Helen and Mark passed the museum entrance across the street and paid it no mind. They continued onward until they reached a parking garage, where they entered through a side door.

Rook caught the door before it latched, waited a moment, and stepped through. On the other side, he hung back, now able to hear the two talking in the corridor.

"You can't wear that to an interview," Helen said. Her voice was disapproving—a usual tone when directed at Mark.

"I know; I brought a couple of shirts. I don't have any nice slacks, though. I mean, I don't have anything," Mark said, shrugging.

"What about the outfit I bought you?" Helen was incredulous.

"I brought it. I'll get it out of the boot."

The couple crossed the garage to one of the parked cars. Mark took out a key fob and pressed a button, and the car trunk popped open. Mark reached in and pulled out a brown and black sweater and black jeans, both neatly pressed and on hangers.

"This will have to do," Helen sighed and grabbed the garments from Mark. She pulled the sweater off the hanger and gestured to Mark. Mark took off his shirt and turned to toss it into the trunk. Rook could see the elaborate tattoo work splayed across Mark's back. It consisted of a large outer ring and, within that, a heptagon. Within that was a heptagram. And within that, another heptagon. And, finally, at the center, a pentagram. All along the geometry were letters spaced singly and words in the negative spaces, all of which were in Enochian script.

The Seal of God, Rook thought. *But it's bollocks. Those ain't the right names.*

Mark turned back, took the sweater, and slipped it on. Rook turned away and leaned against the wall out of sight of the couple.

"Hurry," Helen said.

"Right here?" Mark protested.

"Come on, I have to be back at the end of lunch and need to introduce you. Get them on."

Rook could hear Mark rustle his jeans off and replace them. He knew they would soon return through this walkway and decided he'd seen enough from here. He pushed off the wall and left, exiting onto the sidewalk again. He pushed through the crowd to cover some distance as he waited for Helen and Mark to emerge.

That seal seemed legit, Rook thought, pacing as he waited. *But those names were from all over mythology. Who the hell would do that? And why the fuck would they ink it into their skin?*

Rook saw the couple appear through the crowd and hurry back toward the museum, crossing the street and climbing the stairs. Rook followed behind, using the thickly packed tourist groups as cover to stay close. When they reached the foyer, Helen and Mark broke off and headed toward the library. There, Helen stopped outside the administration office and turned toward Mark.

"You ready?" she asked.

"Yeah," Mark nodded, swallowing.

"Okay, because this is it. I don't know anyone else here that well. Even if it's just the mail room, it's better than the roadie bullshit you're doing now."

Mark sighed.

"If he offers you to work right away, take it. Maybe I'll see you here after work?" Helen said, attempting to infuse her directive with a hint of optimism but missing the mark.

"Yeah, maybe. I'll give it my best."

Helen brushed off Mark's shoulders and grabbed the card at the end of her lanyard. She pressed it against the sensor until the door unlatched. She placed her hand on his shoulder, opened the door, and guided him in, a motion that felt more prodding than guiding. The door clicked shut, and they were out of Rook's view.

Rook crossed his arms, leaned his shoulder into a wall, and waited. After a few moments, Helen reemerged and walked briskly back through the library. Rook followed her as she passed through the back gallery and headed toward the archives. Rook closed the distance. They turned down a hallway devoid of tourists, serving no one but the souls who worked the archives and the odd, poor tourist who was lost looking for the bathrooms, a set of which they passed as they neared the security door at the end of the hall. Helen stopped just after the bathrooms and listened. She heard the footsteps she had keyed in on moments ago stop a step after her. She turned around. Her expression changed from annoyance to fear when she looked at Rook's face.

"Employees only." Helen tried to sound confident and in control.

"Sorry, love," Rook said gruffly, closing in on her. "Got a bit lost, didn't I? But while I'm here, fancy a quick shag in the loo?" He twisted a smile.

Helen was enraged. She advanced on Rook, raising a finger and preparing to thrust it in his face.

"Listen here, you creep fuck-"

"Oh, fucking perfect!" Rook smiled as he grabbed her by the shoulders. Helen raised her arms and twisted away, ready to run for the door, but lost all sense of direction when she felt something slam into the whole of her from behind. Like a concussive force, she felt the blow through every inch of her body, and she coughed as her heart sputtered. In her daze, she didn't register that she was being guided toward the bathroom. She fell through the door and threw herself at the sinks, gripping them hard to keep the room from spinning.

"Wh-what's happening?" Helen sputtered, straining to see through her double vision.

"I don't like leaving marks," Rook said, closing the door behind him. He took off his shoe and jammed it under the door.

Helen turned to face Rook, pressing herself against the counter.

"What are you going to do? Th-there's no way you'll get away with it! Not here!"

"Get away with what?" Rook took off his Spector coat and hung it on the edge of a stall door. The fluorescent lights began to flicker and whine.

"I'm not going to fuck you! Get back! I'll scream!"

"Oh," Rook said as a shadow began to rise through his skin, glittering in the dying light, "you'll be screaming, alright."

Rook badged in at the archives door and pushed it open with his new, slender shoulder. The high vaulted ceilings of the museum's public spaces were replaced with a concrete slab that stretched across every inch of the back room. No tiles covered the exposed ductwork and wiring that sprawled the complex, and nothing braced the hanging lights that lined the lobby. Despite the industrial and spartan aesthetic, it was also clean; Rook noted that the air lacked any smell he'd expected to find in a closed-off library. It was dry, too. The humidity must be tightly controlled.

No one looked in Rook's direction. Though the employee count in this department was minimal, Rook knew he'd pass several of Helen's colleagues on his way to the historical archives. He was pleased he had profiled Helen correctly and saw that she got little notice as he took the memorized turns and pivots required to make his way back to her section. He stopped before a massive, reinforced steel door. Reminiscent of a bank vault, the six-inch thick door sat upon two riveted reverse hinges and contained a plexiglass viewing port in its center. Through that plexiglass, Rook could see a guard standing post on the other side, an older man with gray hair and a rounded physique.

Rook kept walking, heading for Helen's workstation. Rounding a corner and hugging the vaulted area, Rook badged through another door and entered the historical archive library proper. He passed the row upon row of ancient texts lining the shelves that filled the warehouse-sized storeroom, following the path he had practiced in his head dozens of times before. When he arrived at his destination, Helen's desk waited before him. Several books cluttered the workspace: a thick reference book that, at a quick glance, seemed to be about Mesopotamia, a dictionary on Mandaic, and a leaden scroll fully unraveled and in a plexiglass case, written in Mandaic, presumably. Other than the glance it took to notice the artifacts, Rook couldn't care less for the secrets that lay before him. But he took the seat anyway and hunched over the desk.

Helen preferred her computer to be set on a stand next to the desk instead of on it. It had wheels, and so Rook pulled it to himself. Tapping on the keyboard, the screen lit up and asked for Helen's password. Rook smirked, grabbed the lanyard around his new neck, and brought up Helen's identification card, inserting it into a card reader next to the keyboard. A second later, the password prompt on the computer changed, now asking for a security code. Rook froze, the smirk disappearing. He looked around the desk, moving papers and books, until he saw a small plastic device with an LCD screen on it. It had a string of numbers displayed. He entered them in and hit the Enter key. Rook smiled again as the lock screen was dismissed and Helen's computer desktop was presented to him.

"Well, well, well," Rook muttered in his new, feminine

voice as he took the mouse in hand. "Let's see if I was bloody right about you."

Rook looked for, and clicked on, an icon labeled *Employee Codex*. A window appeared, and featured in it was Helen's face and employee number. Several options were selectable for him, and he hovered the mouse cursor over each in turn as he read them off, until he found *Access History* and clicked on it. A log appeared showing Helen's recent interactions with the historical archives. The most recent entry was a line item with the reference number *132948*, a description of *thin lead scroll, originally rolled up; rectangular; lightly engraved on one side in Mandaic, margin ruled down each edge*, and the note of *110 and 88 lines; incantations against evil spirits*. He chuckled to himself.

Rook looked at the last heading of the line item, *check-out remaining*, and noted the value, *7d*.

"Seven days remaining," Rook said to himself.

Rook looked over the page until he saw what he was looking for, a toggle switch that turned this check-out history from *Archives* to *Restricted*. Rook clicked it, and the access log disappeared, replaced with a pop-up screen that blocked the log behind it. *Warning:* it said. *Authorised Access only. Restricted archives are subject to a 30-minute access period. Four-item check-out limit. All items must be returned or renewed every eight hours. Access logs are checked on a weekly basis.*

Rook clicked the *OK* button, and the pop-up slid from view, revealing the access log. Helen's log showed several line items, a dozen by quick count, each with similar information to the non-restricted items but lacking formal notation. Instead, they each had her own notes about the items she had checked out, detailing her findings with them.

"Ain't got nothing checked out," Rook grunted. "Good, that means all four are up for grabs. Let's take a gander at what we've got to play with."

Rook closed the window and clicked on an icon labeled *Archives*. It presented him with a search window. He refined his query to the restricted section, keyed in the keyword *enoch*, and clicked to search. Six entries appeared in the results window, each with a title, description, and location code.

"Aeternus Infernalis Breviarium," Rook read aloud, "description: Parchment, 16th century. Latin entitled, Enochian script throughout. Translation pending. Location: 6F, 4D, 387. Hm, promising."

Rook read further.

"Eosphorus. Vellum, 16th century. Greek throughout with Enochian subtexts; Enochian translation pending. Location blah, blah... Okay, maybe. What else?"

Rook looked over the others.

"Ugh. Fake. Fake, fake..."

He noticed one with no title. Instead, the archive showed a picture of the words on the cover.

"What's this?" he said as he peered closer at the screen. The image showed Enochian lettering inscribed on the book's front cover.

"VAOAN A-AI-OM," Rook read the words and then translated it in his head, "uh... 'Truth Amongst Us.' Description: Vellum, estimated 15th century. Enochian throughout."

Rook grabbed a loose piece of paper, scribbled down the location codes for the three books that caught his attention, and slipped the paper into his Spector's pocket. He then looked at the time on the computer.

Let's get to it, he thought as he closed the search window and pushed the computer away. Standing up, he walked back to the vault door.

Pressing Helen's badge against the scanner, a muffled buzz sounded through the plexiglass viewport. Rook could see the guard get an alert and check his computer before looking up and seeing Helen awaiting entry. The guard rounded his kiosk and approached the door. He stepped out of sight as he manipulated the locking mechanism on his side of the door. Rook could hear the clunking of the large, dense inner workings of the door security as it finally gave way and the door was pulled inward.

"Helen," the guard nodded as he opened the door for her.

Rook glanced at the guard's badge and read the name. He quickly thought about how she would respond to him.

"Hey, Gerald."

Gerald steadied the massive barrier and stepped aside as Helen walked past into the vault's temperature-controlled interior.

Gerald slid the door back into place and returned to his station next to the computer kiosk. Rook walked further into the vault and waited until he was out of the guard's sight before pulling out the piece of paper with the location codes. Every item in the vault was in a protective case, plexiglass, and tagged with a barcode. Rook frowned as he looked over the rows of bulky, cumbersome containers but continued until he found the first of his targets.

Pulling *Aeternus* from the shelf, he read the warning printed on a sticker along its edge: *Personal Protective Equipment required for handling*. Rook carefully tucked it under his arm and continued to the next one. One by one, Rook gathered the books and returned to the vault door, where he noticed Gerald was not standing in front of, but rather to the side of the kiosk. Rook looked it over quickly and saw a hand-held scanner attached to it. Guessing from the context clues, Rook surmised he had to scan these out to take them but didn't know what to do.

"Hands full, can you help?" Rooks said, gesturing toward the kiosk.

"Oh, uh," Gerald looked surprised, "not supposed to, you know. No cart?"

"I wanted to be quick," Rook shot back, emulating Helen's tone, trying to infuse just the right amount of annoyance into her voice.

Gerald stepped forward and reached out to take one of the cases from Rook.

"I got these. Just help me scan them in."

"R-right," Gerald said. He turned and grabbed the scanner as he tapped on the screen to bring up the check-out system. It requested more information, and Gerald looked to Rook for the answer. Rook looked and saw that it asked for an employee ID. The guard knew Helen. He'd have entered the name if that's what it wanted.

"One, five, three, nine, eight, eight," Rook said. Gerald entered that information into the kiosk, and it advanced to the next screen, waiting for check-out information. Gerald then took the scanner and pressed the trigger while pointing it at each of the cases in Rook's arms. Each time, it beeped and automatically filled the information into the system. Once all three were done, Gerald replaced the scanner and clicked *Confirm* at the bottom of the screen. After a moment, the screen read out that Helen was authorized to remove these items from the restricted area.

Nodding, Gerald hurried around the kiosk and to the door, beginning the unlocking procedure.

Rook said nothing, assuming Helen wouldn't have either, no matter the length of silence. Rook felt no sense of awkwardness but could read it on the guard's face when he pulled the door open. Rook nodded once and left the vault, heading back toward Helen's desk.

"Woah, where are you taking those?" a voice asked from near Rook's shoulder. Rook stopped and looked at the owner of the voice. A man, shorter than Helen and dressed with even less style in his business casual outfit than she did, addressed Helen with a look of amusement on his face. "Those go immediately to the clean room."

"Only when opened," Rook said, again attempting to match Helen's mannerisms.

"I know you like to work alone, Helen," the nameless face continued, "but I really have to report it this time."

Rook turned toward the man and read his face closer. It wasn't amusement; it was condescending, and this discovery made Rook's blood heat up. He felt his spirit rise in his arms and chest as he prepared to lash out, the lights overhead beginning to protest his actions. But, a moment before he would have attacked, Rook scanned the room and saw several cameras attached to the ductwork above, monitoring the hallways. Rook forced himself to relax, thinking of another way to handle the situation.

"Report it," he said, taking a step closer to the man, "go on."

Before the man could speak again, Rook shifted the cases to the side so he could get close enough to share a breath with him, Helen's eyes —Rook's eyes— staring directly into his.

"Report it, and let's see how tattletales are handled around here. Calling me into question? My record? My work ethic? You let me know if your report is worth shit compared to that."

"H-helen…," the man started as he stepped backward and raised his hands.

"I'm sorry. Is my name caught in your throat?" Rook persisted. "Then cough it out and let me get back to work."

Without a comeback, perhaps seeing something insidious in Helen's eyes, the man took another two steps backward and turned to take the first corner, quickly leaving the area.

Rook let out an exasperated sigh and pondered his choices. *Bloody hell*, he cursed in his head. *This could come back to bite me in the arse if these turn out to be useless, and I have to bloody come back here.* Rook shrugged and stalked back to his desk.

Setting the cases on the workspace desk, Rook inspected their locks and searched the desk, pulling open drawers and looking about the room. Seeing nothing readily available, he turned his eyes to the walls, seeing for the first time the awards and accolades Helen had earned framed and featured prominently on the wall. He already knew about them; his research didn't miss that detail, but only now were they in his view. One such decoration caught his eye, and he reached out to take it off the wall and looked at it closer.

"Nice," Rook said with a nod and then smashed the frame against the desk, popping out the long metal shaft that reinforced it. Discarding the rest of the award on the floor, Rook took the metal rod and placed it into the lock on one of the cases and, with a twist and flick of his wrist, leveraged the lock open.

A twang of pain ran through his arm, from his fingertips through to his shoulder. It caused him to drop the metal rod.

"Easy love," Rook whispered, "this is all mine now."

Rook picked up the rod and opened the other two cases. He then took his Spector off and wrapped it around the three tomes, folding the heavy coat to hide the bulk as much as possible. Once he was done, he checked the time on the computer, packed the coat under an arm, and left. No one he passed on the way out seemed to notice, and soon, he was on the other side of the archive's door.

Mark unlocked the door to the apartment he and Helen shared. He pushed open the door and walked in, his shoulders sunken and head low. He had expected Helen to ask about the job interview and then to tear into him when she learned he'd failed, but the car ride was entirely silent. Not that Mark often minded the silence, but it was unnerving this time. Helen had sat looking out of the window until they arrived and seemed to be in a rush to get inside the apartment. And now that they were here, Helen was more preoccupied with her bundle than him.

Rook cleared off the coffee table and unwrapped the books from his coat, setting the Spector aside, placing each book neatly on the table, and then sitting on the couch adjacent to the table. He touched each book, running his fingers over the text on the covers, feeling the grooves of the pressed lettering. He then slid *Aeternus* closer and opened it. He read the first couple of pages, flipped through several more, read on, and then sighed. Then he grabbed *Eosphorus* and repeated the behavior.

"So, I, uh," Mark began. He was standing opposite Helen. "I didn't get the job."

"Mmhm," Rook replied, flipping through *Eosphorus* with deteriorating care for the material, using his whole palm to shuffle through the pages.

Mark narrowed his eyes.

"Yeah, they said I wasn't a good fit for the 'sorting and toting' lifestyle." Mark dropped the 'r' sound from 'sorting' to mimic a rushed effect on the phrase. He watched for Helen's reaction.

"Why the bloody hell would anyone bother translating something *into* Enochian?" Rook sneered as he scanned the page. "Probably because it's a bloody ode to Lucifer himself? Written in bloody Greek no less."

Mark walked around the table, stood beside Helen, and looked at the book. It was old; he could tell that much. But the writing was foreign and unrecognizable. But, he could see what Helen was referring to written by hand in the margins next to every paragraph. The symbols were familiar to him.

"What's this?" Mark asked as he slid the book from Helen's hands toward himself. The gesture was meant to upset Helen and get a rise out of her so Mark could get some reaction. Instead, it caused an electric sensation to jolt through his skin and make him jump a step away.

Rook was, at first, annoyed by the interruption, but the emotion evaporated when he saw Mark's reaction.

"What happened?" Rook asked.

"I don't know," Mark said, placing a hand on his opposite shoulder and rolling his arm underneath it. "I got a shock just now."

Rook's eyes darted left to right as he thought, and then, as he leveled his eyes back on Mark, he slid the book back toward him.

"When you touched the book?"

"Yeah."

"Touch it again."

Mark looked at Helen and hesitated. He saw Helen urge him to try it, so he reached out and touched the book again.

"I guess it was static electricity or something," Mark said.

Rook reached out and took Mark's hand and touched his

finger to the Greek text and then the Enochian symbols. Mark jumped again when he touched the celestial writing.

"Ow, fuck!"

Rook smiled as Mark shivered off the second shock.

"What the hell is that?" Mark asked, backing away from the book.

"A rather slutty interpretation of Lucifer," Rook said, sliding back into Helen's speech pattern, "told by some Greek theist in the fifteen hundreds," Rook chuckled and then pointed at the Enochian script, "and then translated by a fallen angel who, apparently, both agreed and sought to correct the original author's opinions."

"What?"

"Ancient fan fiction," Rook said, lowering his eyes to the book, "but apparently some of it is real."

Mark reached his threshold of oddity and backed off a few more steps.

"Okay, what's going on, Helen? What's wrong with you?"

Rook looked back at Mark and read his face. He saw panic and confusion. He also saw an opportunity. He closed the book, setting all three aside.

"Mark, honey, sorry," Rook said, drumming up what he could guess as Helen's more affectionate side. "I've just been stressed as of late. Looks like you are, too."

Rook stood up, took off this body's blazer, and kicked off

its shoes. He reached up and removed its glasses, tossing them onto the coffee table. He then walked over to Mark and took his hands into his own. Mark tensed as Helen approached him but melted under her touch. He felt her thumbs rub over the backs of his hands, and he took in a deep breath.

"Yeah, I really didn't want to let you down," Mark started, "I thought you were going to be pissed that I didn't get the job."

Rook smiled and leaned close to Mark, sliding his hands out of their grip and along Mark's arms. He kissed Mark, pressing this body against him.

"I know just the thing to bring up our spirits," Rook said, sliding his hands under Mark's sweater and pulling it up and over his head, "I think we could both really use it."

Mark, dumbfounded, was enthralled. He offered no resistance to Helen undressing him. He didn't fight when he was turned around, and Helen placed her hands on his shoulders and caressed his back, tracing her fingers along the intricate tattoo work. He barely heard her speak.

"Besides, I think I've got an even better job lined up for you."

Chapter Five

Rook sat on Mark's couch, his new body thankful to be free of his Spector coat. A feeling Rook noted as a primary reason to abandon this body as soon as the next opportunity arose. In front of him was the worn book he had stolen from the bookstore, opened to a page showing a hand-drawn star chart that only contained four celestial bodies. Rook read what he could of the faded script, turning the pages over and taking in the other abstract imagery.

Mark stood across the living room before a credenza that sat in front of the only windows of the apartment. He flipped on a desk lamp to compensate for the lack of light coming in from outside. A collection of vinyl records sat to the side, which Mark began to browse through, nudging each one to cascade onto the last in the display rack that housed them. As he idly perused, his free hand reached out to power the turntable presented as the centerpiece of the credenza. This modern iteration of a relatively ancient technology popped to life, and an LCD display notated its attempt to connect wirelessly to the nearby speaker array.

"What's your fancy?" Mark asked, cocking his head to read the back of one of the album covers.

"Whatever," Rook replied, flipping a page and then looking at Mark. "No, wait, not that shite American Country, and nothing that'll make me want to slit my wrists. Which is the first thing I said." Rook returned his attention to the book.

Chuckling, Mark pulled out an album and slipped the record out of it. He inspected the vinyl on both sides before placing it carefully onto the turntable. He pressed a button, and another one of the modern, technical departures took over; the arm and needle of the player moved of its own accord to settle on the spinning media. The warm hiss of the record seeped from the speakers before the music began to play. Electronic percussions and synthesized tones filled the room, augmented by a deep, resonating bass line. Mark nodded in time to the beat as he adjusted the volume to a comfortable level.

"So, what's it say?" Mark asked, joining Rook on the couch.

"It's fucking odd," Rook said. "Sounds like it's talking about some damn realm of the dead. Or something that used to be one."

Rook flipped to a page showing one of the spheres as the focus of the artwork.

"Malakut is the name used," Rook said as he tapped the

sphere, "but that's a bloody odd choice."

"Why's that?"

"It's an Islamic word in the Arabic dialect. And it ain't prominent." Rook looked at Mark. "It's not generative. Nothing comes from it."

Mark blinked with obvious confusion.

Rook furrowed his brow and thought through a way to explain it.

"Okay," he began, "religions are bollocks. All of them. Not a single one of them has got it right, and as long as these devout twats keep pitchforking their opinions at each other, they're never gonna figure it out."

Mark nodded.

"We've barely scratched the surface of what's out there. These little moments in history where humans had run-ins with something celestial are scattered throughout time. You just gotta dig deep enough to find them. Sometimes it's a new word or phrase that pops up in their vocabulary, and they chalk it up to some supernatural force, like the blasted Genesis Flood."

"Genesis Flood?"

Rook smiled, excited to get into the details.

"Nearly every bloody culture for the past seven thousand years has a sodding story about some big arse flood. The Hebrews call it Noah's Ark, and it's in that Epic of Gilgamesh wank too. Even those Chinese blokes have their version.

North American Indians, Muslims—some one hundred and ninety different ways to tell the same bloody story: lots of rain, loads of people fucking dead, and a bloody rainbow at the end."

"Two hundred descriptions of a rainbow?" Mark asked, leaning in.

"It's all about perspective and interpretation. Different cultures have their own spin on things based on their biases, tech, and beliefs. One event can be twisted and turned into different tales, depending on when and where it happened. Even different *reasons* for the tale. But what about the little stuff? Stuff that's in one place? A small town hears of a strange occurrence, and whispers spread like wildfire. Some bloke turns water into wine, or some bloody beast munches on Norsemen. Or maybe Athens is saved from a plague because someone lit a few fires to cleanse the area. Shit gets real interesting then, doesn't it? But what happens then?"

"A religion is made to explain it."

"That's bloody right!" Rook grinned. "If there was one before, it'll bloody well be absorbed or become the new top dog."

"Okay, so you're saying 'Malakut' is odd because it didn't spawn a religion? I'm sure every religion has stories of places they gave names to."

Rook tapped the drawn sphere again.

"No, what's fucking odd is that it's written in fucking

Enochian script. You wanna tell the difference between the real shit and the bullshit? Look for recurring archetypes. When different sources all say the same damn thing, especially when they're not supposed to agree, then you know it's legit. Like Lucifer—he pops up in almost every goddamn religion. And get this—his name translates to something like 'light' or 'star' in nearly all of them. So yeah, he's a real fucker, and that's probably his actual name, assuming some changes over time."

Mark's eyes widened, and an understanding began to dawn. Rook continued.

"But a bloody realm of death? And its function, or here its *change* in function? There's no bloody clear connection to trace it back to a source. It might as well not even exist. And yet, here it is, written up in legit celestial scribbles. Malakut is real. But all these sodding religions have got it completely wrong. If it wasn't spelled out right here," Rook tapped the book, "I'd still be bloody convinced."

"Maybe because no one comes back from death?" Mark mused, "Not even you. You've never been to Malakut or any realm of the dead. No one who does comes back. So we've all just had to make it up to explain where we go."

"Maybe. Something's fucked about it."

Rook stood up from the couch, walked over to the credenza, and opened a drawer. He pulled a black marker from it and tossed it at Mark, who caught it with a questioning look.

"Do me a favor," Rook said, "take that and scrub out all the shite that doesn't fit with your seal. If your tingly reaction is as dead as Helen, strike it from the record like you should have done with that slag years ago."

Mark blinked once while looking at the marker in his hand. He was always caught off guard whenever Rook seemed to care about him or his past. He couldn't deny that he was much happier over the last year.

"Alright, sure." Mark scooted up to the book and closed it to see the cover, slowly running his finger over each letter and symbol until he didn't feel the electric buzz in his back. At each dead spot, he bathed the area in marker, hiding entire sentences behind a veil of black ink.

"Speaking of Helen," Mark said, "speaking of anyone you've taken over. How do you get away with it? How come the X-files haven't come for you yet?"

Rook turned and looked at the album cover Mark had selected. He hadn't really paid attention to the music until now, but it was strangely pleasant to him. It was much more modern than the medium it was playing from would suggest.

"Helen was a right pushover. I just waited until I got busted for swiping those old books from the archives. And wouldn't you know it, she 'died of a bloody heart attack' while in custody," Rook said, snidely mimicking quotation marks with his fingers. "No one suspected a thing, mate.

That's why no one's been up your arse since then. Just came to give you the heads up about the whole situation."

Mark nodded as he opened the book and continued hunting for and redacting mundane writing.

"As for the rest, I try to avoid cameras. They're a bloody pain in the arse. Always asking prying questions. That's why I usually switch bodies after I do my dirty work and take the new one far away from the one I left. Got it down to ninety seconds before I need to find a new one. Gonna keep pushing that limit, mate, so I can take my sweet time."

Rook picked up the album cover and turned it over in his hand. It was all black, with a depiction of a smooth stone or obsidian skull taking up most of the space. The band and album names were pushed out to the edges, away from the artwork, written along each edge so that you had to turn that edge toward yourself to read it properly.

"Matte b-l-v-c-k?" Rook asked.

"Matte Black," Mark looked up, "yeah, they're like my *favorite* darkwave band. Every song is so smooth, and they're not afraid to get out of the bassy low-end but make it stomp at the same time, too." He shivered as he spoke about the music, smiling. "Saw them live last year and had to buy the vinyl."

"It's b-l-v-c-k, not 'black.'"

"Oh, come on," Mark laughed, "didn't the Romans have 'v's for 'a's?"

"No, 'v's and 'u's were the same thing. So were 'i's and

'j's," Rook said dryly.

"Well, it's artistic expression, then," Mark retorted with a smirk as he returned to the book.

Rook pursed his lips as he listened, turning to watch Mark. Mark was in a groove, bobbing along to the music and dutifully carrying out his task. Occasionally, Mark would wince when he touched a mark or word, more than his usual reaction to true celestial writing. Rook walked over and looked at the dry and failing papyrus pages, seeing if he could tell what would cause the larger-than-standard reaction.

"It hurting?" Rook asked.

"Huh?" Mark looked up at Rook. "Oh, uh, no. It's just stronger. Almost burning instead of tingling."

Mark traced a word and demonstrated the reaction.

Rook looked at the word Mark was touching. He translated it to mean 'fused body' or 'conglomeration.' It was darker than the words on other pages and sat below a drawn depiction of a formless mass or void. He noticed that every page that had art drawn on it was similarly darker than the neighboring pages.

"It's like there's just...more," Mark said, "more of whatever triggers the seal."

Rook slid the book over to himself and flipped through a few pages. He saw where Mark had blacked out entire sections and, in a lot of cases, entire pages. He then noticed the change in papyrus type in these sections, as well as the degradation levels.

Mark looked up at Rook. "What is it?"

Rook flipped the book face down and pulled at the binding. He tore through the leather, exposed the twine and glue underneath, and snapped the fibrous tethers loose. The pages spread out, released from their captivity. Tossing the cover aside, Rook spread the pages out and tossed away those Mark had completely drawn through. What remained were the better-preserved pages, each appearing to have been cut from a scroll and then set as leaves in a book, as opposed to the ones he tossed, which were formatted pages. With that in mind, Rook tossed out the similar formatted pages that Mark hadn't looked over yet, leaving a much smaller pool of materials behind. Rook and Mark both looked over the remaining work. Each leaf was a section of a larger scroll, fitting together and written in the darker ink.

"Take off your shirt," Rook said. He splayed the pages out in a line across the table.

Mark did as requested, positioning his back toward Rook. He then reached out and touched one of the pages. The seal on his back responded, dimly glowing along the axes of the geometric shapes that made the line-work of the seal. But when Mark touched the writing, an entire section of the seal blazed alight. Rook watched as the light raised the edges of the lines and names that were written in a wedge, and for the first time, Rook could see the seal was split into ten such wedges, with the one now lit prominently placed at the top. The other nine sections remained dark, including the pentagram in the center.

"Woah," Rook said, "what in the bloody..." Rook hovered his finger over the largest name set close to the center, *Thoth*, and followed the wedge outward toward the edge, reading each of the names present.

"What?!" Mark asked, his breathing quickening, staring at his finger and wondering if he needed to pull it away.

"This bloody thing ain't just for telling you if something is celestial-made; it can even bloody tell you which sect it's from. But how the hell does that work?"

Rook grabbed the page from under Mark's finger, who was relieved to let it go. Rook held up the page to the light, turning the plane of the paper under it, trying to see if different angles would reveal anything. Frustrated he couldn't make anything out, he snapped his fingers at Mark.

"Phone. Where's your phone?"

Mark dug it out of his pocket and unlocked it before handing it to Rook. Rook tapped the camera icon and, after putting the papyrus back on the table, pointed the phone's camera at the lettering and zoomed it in. The image was blurry; the camera was not suited for macro imaging. Still, Rook grabbed the nearby lamp and held it close to the papyrus until enough light helped the camera sensor tighten up the image. He then clicked the shutter and stared at the image, setting the lamp back from whence it came.

While Rook strained to see anything of note in the picture, Mark picked up the papyrus. The familiar buzz consumed his back. He brought it to his nose and sniffed it, catching something odd. Metallic. He placed it back on the table and pressed his finger into the writing. Despite the buzzing becoming a burning once again, Mark pressed harder and then dragged his finger away from the writing, smearing the ink along the papyrus.

"Uh, Rook?" Mark said, grabbing at Rook's pant leg with his other hand.

Rook looked over and saw the marred text and that Mark was showing him his finger, a greasy black-reddish stain upon it. He took Mark's hand and brought it closer, smelling it. Letting it go, he touched the text on the papyrus and did as Mark had done, bringing his own smeared fingertip before him. He then put it in his mouth.

"Blood," Rook said, looking at Mark.

"Is this?" Mark asked, his eyes widening as he looked at the score of pages and all its writing.

"Bloody hell," Rook muttered, a hint of barely contained anticipation in his voice. "Char ink and blood mixed together. Still fresh as a daisy after all these years."

They both fell into silence.

The apartment window exploded, sending shards of glass into the living space like shrapnel, blasting the credenza apart and sending debris and electronic pieces flying. Rook and Mark turned toward the crash but shielded their faces with their arms out of instinct. As Mark fell to the floor, Rook turned to square the blast and stepped in front of Mark. As he lowered his arm, Rook could see a figure emerging from the window. Long, orange fingers, with fingertips down to the first knuckle stained black with claw-like nails of obsidian, dug into the windowsill and drywall. The hand pulled, and from the darkness, a second hand braced on the opposite side of the window. Stepping forth onto the bottom of the windowsill, a foot, orange and black, scraped its nails into the wood. A low, guttural, gurgling, slow laughter came from the figure as it birthed fully into the light, its head ducking low to allow its long obsidian horns to pass freely. It stood up fully, its demonic features accented by the business suit it wore.

"Have the mortals found a secret?" the bestial thing growled. "Have their feeble minds reeled from the possibilities?"

Rook crossed the distance. He swung at the thing, leveraging the bulk of the policeman's body in the throw. Rook's experience guided his hand, and he connected with a solid blow against the jaw of the demon, but the creature took the hit with a smile. Rook didn't hesitate, throwing another and another at the demon's center of mass, each hit colliding, thundering through the room. Despite the mass of this body, the blows did nothing to the demon.

It responded, backhanding Rook across the face and sending him back through the couch, splintering it. Laughing, it lunged after, sending the remains of the couch into the walls with a gesture before kicking Rook in the stomach and propelling him into the air. As Rook rose off the floor with the blow, the demon grabbed him by the neck and flung him into the wall. In a rush of movement, the demon pinned Rook by the neck against the wall with its forearm, pushing hard enough to restrict Rook's breathing.

"Time to go night-night," it growled.

Rook's face was bloodied; he could barely see the demon except for the bright embers of light glowing from its eyes. He focused on the light. What illumination that remained in the apartment began to flicker and dim. Rook's soul flared up through the policeman's skin, its glinting whirling bits expanding from his body. His own eyes, the eyes of the Anima that rose from the body, began to glow with a sickly green-gray as Rook let his rage consume him. He flung himself out at the demon, the blow sending a shockwave that collapsed the wall behind him, opening a gash into the neighboring apartment and sending the demon back several feet. Rook's body landed on its feet, and he receded back inside it, leveling his eyes at the demon.

"So, the broken one really does have a bite," the demon laughed, looking at his shredded suit. "Cael wasn't exaggerating after all. So, was he the one who fractured your soul?"

The demon braced as Rook charged at him again, but the attack was fruitless. Rook's well-trained strikes were useless against the celestial being. The demon grabbed Rook by the wrist and started crushing it, causing Rook to scream out in pain. With its other hand, it began to strike Rook in the face.

Mark lay frozen in place. He looked at the demon as it pummeled Rook. Beyond them, he could see his neighbors, a young couple and their year-old daughter, huddled together in the corner of their living room, blocked from getting out by the fight that now took up both rooms. He looked around his place, seeing his records and other band memorabilia in pieces strewn about the floor. He saw the shattered frames that had held pictures of Helen and himself as they were further smashed underfoot. But when he looked at Rook, a stranger's body but with a soul he knew, fighting with everything he had against the demon, Mark felt his heart seize in his chest. Despite Rook's ability, he wasn't winning this fight. It wouldn't be long before this beast-man put him down. Mark tried to think. Rook could jump into another body, right? What about his? What about the neighbors? No, none of the bodies here would be a match for this thing. Was there anyone else in the building? No, they'd be evacuating for sure. Rook's going to have nowhere to go. Rook's going to run out of time. Rook, his friend, was going to die.

Mark grabbed a shard of broken window glass and rose

to his feet. He looked on as he saw the demon raise Rook over its head and slam him onto the ground, denting the floor and snapping the wood. He took a deep breath, tried to steady his nerves, and gripped the glass. With a scream, Mark lunged for the demon and buried the glass deep into its side. Blood gushed from the wound, black, oily, iridescent ichor that drenched Mark's hand as he shoved the shard as deep as it could go. Mark's hand was engulfed in searing pain as the blood sizzled where it touched his skin. But he didn't have a moment to yell before the demon turned and grabbed Mark by the throat, raising him off his feet.

"Oh, the whelp," the demon grunted, the pain causing him to wince, "scarred with the blood of the Grigori upon its back." The demon spoke with clear disdain as if wretched vermin had bit it. Mark struggled but was helpless in the demon's grasp. The demon suddenly laughed and then looked to Rook, who collapsed onto one knee and leaned against the wall.

"So much you could have learned from your precious tool," it said, swinging Mark to hold him out between it and Rook. "But, alas," the demon clenched his hand, and the sound of Mark's neck snapping seemed to shunt all other sounds into silence, "I think I broke it."

Rook felt the snap. Despite this body being on the verge of failure, he gritted his teeth and rose, lunging at the demon. It was ready for the advance and flung Mark's body at Rook to bowl him back down. Finding his face against the floor, Rook tried to breathe through the pain and rolled his head over to meet Mark's lifeless, wide-eyed stare. He did not look away. The demon laughed again as he stepped closer to Rook and Mark's body.

"Oh, it's so rare that we get to come play in the Earth realm," it managed to say through its reverie, "and under orders, too! This is just too good!" It stood over Rook.

Rook's eyes remained locked on Mark's. He waited. And then he saw it. A black mist began to rise from Mark's body. His soul was freed from his shell. Unlike the ones Rook forced out, this soul remained spun tightly and intact. It resembled a shadow filled out with woven smoke. It hovered close, the wraith looking at its old residence and then, as if in a dream, at Rook.

The demon grabbed Rook by his neck and pulled him from the ground. Though the height difference was minimal, the demon's strength was overpowering, and Rook dangled, unable to touch the floor. Rook brought his hands up to the demon's, trying to pry it away enough to breathe. But he watched Mark's soul.

"I think we've had about enough," the demon said, the laughter having died to a gurgle.

"I...," Rook struggled to speak through the demon's grip, "I...know a secret."

"Oh?" The demon smiled and pulled Rook in closer,

loosening his grip just enough to let him speak. "And what's that?"

"You're a cunt. And I know where the bogeyman comes from."

"Eh?"

Rook raised from his body again. His fractured soul whirred into a cyclone as he lashed out with it like a whip. The demon raised an eyebrow and cocked his head to dodge the poorly aimed attack but turned to see Rook's true target. The razor-wire whip wrapped around Mark's soul and ripped through it, splitting the smoky haze with a force that drove a gash through its midsection. As Rook sunk back into his body, both he and the demon watched as Mark's soul began to crack and break, sending schisms through its form. Confused, the demon turned toward the fracturing soul.

"Sorry," Rook said softly. He braced his fingers against the demon's hand.

Mark's soul shattered but remained bound as if by magnetic force. The traumatic split sent the shards outward, but then they collapsed back in at the center of the form. The wraith began to agitate. It thrashed silently as the shards smashed and collided. In its eyes, a deep smoldering red began to glow. But instead of being set on Rook, as he had been so used to, the enraged and maddening stare was set upon the demon. The wraith transformed, its extremities forming long raking fingers, its edges serrated. The once tightly spun smoke was now completely replaced with glinting glass-like shards. It then engulfed the demon.

Rook was dropped. The demon screamed in pain as it attempted to bat away the wraith. It raised its arms to shield its face, but the wraith shredded its flesh, splashing its dark blood across the walls and floor. Though Mark was only an echo of what he was before, he remained relentless in his attack, flaying the demon's skin and splitting long gashes in its face.

Rook steadied himself but lost power in one of his legs and collapsed back down. He attempted again, but he was too weak. His labored breathing was no longer effective. His sight began to dim.

The demon roared, and a fel fire flared from his horns and exposed skin. The emanation threw the wraith back, and the demon focused the fire into a torrent that blasted the wraith through a wall and into the night sky. The demon dropped all pretense of a humanoid form, letting the fire burn away the rest of its clothes and twisting its legs into an inhuman shape. It turned toward Rook, who was struggling to keep his eyes open.

"Neat trick, Broken," the demon growled, "let it be your last." The demon raised its hand, long black nails lined in hellfire, and swung for Rook.

Something connected with the demon's hand in a blur and snapped it off its wrist. As it howled in pain, the blur slammed the demon back away from Rook. Rook, straining against his body, could see the blur drag the demon further away, smashing one of its legs in the process. Then, as the demon's motion came to a stop a dozen feet away, the blur settled, and behind the demon stood a monstrous new combatant. Towering over the demon was a larger one, with the same orange skin and black protrusions as its lesser, but with twice the mass, large orange-membraned wings, and a tail tipped in black bone. It reached across the chest of its lesser and grabbed its throat. In one motion, it ripped through the flesh of the demon's neck and splattered it against the wall. The demon's body erupted into flame and condensed to ash in an instant.

Rook scrambled; his failing legs tried to stand but only managed to jerk backward away from the massive demon. But, as he tried to move, the demon slowly approached him, its form shrinking and its features diminishing. It began to lose its orange hue, replaced with a more human coloring. It shifted and took on more human proportions, fingers turning fleshy and the nails turning clear. Before Rook stood a man of light skin and hair with blue eyes, and the shock of what he saw gave him a small wind.

"Nadir?" Rook exclaimed. "N-Nadir, h-how...?"

The man before Rook, the one he recognized as Nadir, knelt down before him.

"You remember that old name, my friend?" Nadir spoke. "Come on, we have to get you out of here."

Nadir reached for Rook and helped him to his feet. With blurry eyes, Rook took in his old friend from nearly five hundred years ago. Rook steadied against him but was tossed to the side when something hit him. He looked around the room and saw Mark's wraith, all reason since gone, attempting to pummel and slash at Nadir.

Nadir seemed unphased but still had a look of concern.

"Rook, absorb Mark."

"What?" Rook asked, barely thinking a coherent thought, let alone processing the command.

"Absorb him, Rook. Take in the Fractured. It is what you can do."

Rook looked back and forth between Nadir and Mark. When Nadir gave him a reassuring nod, as he had done so long ago, Rook knew he could do what was being asked. He relaxed his body and raised his soul to the surface once again. And as the wraith of Mark slammed against Nadir, Rook reached out with his soul and wrapped around it. Mark —what was left of him— struggled against Rook's spiritual embrace, but Rook bore down. The shards of Mark's form broke apart, and those shards of spirit glass joined the many others in Rook's swirling mass. Rook then returned to his body.

"Good, now, come on," Nadir urged. But Rook was no longer conscious.

Chapter Six

Clouds of purple, teal, orange, and blue, ever lit by their own radiance, floated over white-marbled buildings set in dark sand. The insulae were reminiscent of, or perhaps were the inspiration for, Roman and Greek designs and sprawled for a mile in every direction. The black sand lined the edges of the roads and footpaths that sprawled across the city, paths that were paved with more white marble. And the sand itself sparkled and glinted with inborn lights as might stars in the night sky.

Solid beings of elliptical white light, and those with far less of a glow but resembling people with angelic wings, walked through this city. For those who had them, feathers ranged from hues of blue to white to brown, with skin tones spanning the human spectrum. Many angels wore professional attire, informed by human culture and fashion, featuring three-piece or double-breasted suits.

Others wore armor of silver, some light with chest plates and shin guards, and others in heavier, fuller coverage, each forged and designed in exquisite detail. All of the armored wore swords bound to their hips. Scabbards terminated at ankle height, pommels of silver and gold polished to a shine, each was forged to the individuality of the bearer, and no two were alike.

A grand temple of marble took prominence at the center of the city and split the largest road in two as it circled around the building. Its forward was lined with pillars that spanned from edge to edge and served as the entrance into an enclosed, roofed courtyard. The open space was flush with black sand, combed into shapes resembling curved vines and round bulbs surrounding a massive fountain bubbling with clear, nearly invisible water. Beyond that rose a flat-top cylindrical three-story structure, the temple proper, that terminated high above the roof of the courtyard.

It was here that Azrael materialized. His dark, towering form was like a blot of shadow in the otherwise bright area, and he drew the attention of the celestials as they passed by. Azrael could see the veins of the marble react to the movements of the populace; the blue celestial energy contained within ebbing and flowing to the comings and goings of each passerby. They did not, however, react to him.

He stepped up into the temple, passing the pillars and entering the courtyard. He left no footprints in the sand as he marched forward. Those in front of him stepped aside and offered no resistance to the angel. When Azrael arrived at the temple doors, he reached out a slender, bony finger and gestured for them to open. They responded, swinging open to allow the harbinger to enter the facility.

A dais consumed most of the floor's surface in the room. The raised platform was circular and flat with a reflective surface. It projected above it a translucent rendering of Earth, slowly rotating and providing information on several locations of note on the planet. Though the Earth was portrayed in muted colors, the points of interest were bright, their white and blue markings highlighting the importance of these locations. The entire apparatus made Azrael diminutive in comparison. But he paid it no mind as he rounded past and made his way toward the rear of the building.

Lined up abreast, several angels stood at a large table, each in their armor, hunched over a projection of a map. Azrael recognized the town the map centered on, a port town in the Pacific Northwest region of the United States, and he recognized the area of focus that lay a mile outside its border. One of the angels, an olive-skinned man with a powerful build, short, dark hair, and a thick, black beard, looked up as Azrael neared and straightened out as he prepared to meet his guest.

"Azrael," the angel said, laying a hand to rest upon the pommel of his sword, "to what do we owe the pleasure of the presence of a Cataclysm?"

"Grave news, Sariel," Azrael said. "I bring an update to the state of the Agglomeration and ask that you might assist me in securing it."

Sariel looked at the other angels and back to Azrael, genuine concern on his face.

"Tell me, please."

"The Agglomeration is under siege. An Original Soul has discovered the power of possession and is taking new hosts at an increasing rate. It is sending Fractured to the Agglomeration with each new possession. It is nearing a critical threshold, where soon most new souls generated by the Agglomeration will be made Fractured." Azrael gestured toward the projection of Earth. "The resulting infection on Earth will be like a plague, and each turn of the cycle brings the Agglomeration closer to a catastrophic end."

As Azrael spoke, Sariel absorbed the information. Through him, nearly imperceptible lines of energy emanated outward, mingling and intertwining with those of the angels nearby. Each new bit of information he received traveled along these lines and into the angels around him. And from them to the others near them. On and on again until the entirety of the heavenly realm knew what Sariel knew.

"That does sound grave, indeed," Sariel said, "and what do you need from us?"

"I require help. I am unable to track the Original Soul until he kills, and we require a more active method of finding it if we wish to avoid more damage to the Agglomeration. I'd ask that your agents in the field not tasked against the

Infernal seek out aberrant trends in conflict and death and report them. You could detain it here and prevent it from rejoining the Agglomeration."

Sariel nodded but then shrugged.

"I see," he said, turning his eyes to the Earth slowly rotating before them. "But I don't think that we should interfere. It sounds like a human is doing what a human would with that kind of power, and it doesn't broker into our divine providence over the realm."

"You would not be in violation," Azrael urged. "Gaia decrees it."

"Be that as it may," Sariel turned toward Azrael, "we are all tasked as it is. The Infernal Sphere is rallying. They are probing the breach points and have already discovered that the barriers have failed. We're sending them back in droves."

As if on command, one of the areas of focus on the Earth projection flashed and changed from blue and white to red and orange. Sariel stepped past Azrael to look at it and then turned to his fellows at the table. He nodded to them, and one broke from the rest and left the room.

"I'm sorry, Azrael," Sariel said, turning back to the dark angel. "Even if the avatars of all creation are asking this of us, there's no one to spare. Not if the Thrones want a world at all."

Azrael looked to the Earth and thought for a moment. He watched as another marked area of the globe changed colors.

He then looked downward, his eyeless sockets motionlessly looking at the angels scrambling in response. He turned back to Sariel.

"You fight to keep the Infernal in their realm, but you do not fight for the preservation of Earth," Azrael said, leveling his gaze. "If you do not help in this endeavor, then the very thing you fight for will wither and die, and the Agglomeration will cease to be. Would you still fight to defend this dead husk when there is nothing more to gain from it? Would you defend it even as the Thrones unmake this failed experiment?"

Sariel's face darkened. He stepped toward Azrael, and despite Death towering over him, he still managed to appear matched in presence.

"Do not sermonize me," Sariel growled. "I command my legion of legions as I see fit. I don't deny your news is serious, and the problem is real, but do not presume to know the threat of the Infernal as well as I do. When I say that they are the true danger, I mean it to be understood."

Sariel walked through Azrael, passing through the Cataclysm's projected form.

"Besides," Sariel continued, "you mention Thrones and their decrees. What about the one on you? You're a Cataclysm. Add this one's blood to your hands like the countless nephilim you were charged with culling. Do your job instead of proclaiming I don't do mine."

Sariel unfolded his white wings and took to the air, flying through the dais and out into the city. Azrael remained still, aside from crossing his arms, as he watched the angel disappear into the light.

"The boss is a tough sell," a voice behind Azrael said.

Azrael turned back to the table. One angel remained; one of light brown skin, black hair that fell about his shoulders, and a narrow chin lined with a short, black goatee. "But I, for one, want to listen when Death has something to say."

"Virtue Cael," Azrael said, "will you not join your general's fight against the Infernal?"

"Oh, of course!" Cael laughed. "But, my role is more specialized."

Azrael noted Cael was laying his hands upon two weapons set on his hip. Instead of the customary sword nearly every angel received, Cael wore two dirks.

"And I think I can be of help to you," he continued. "I'm in reserve until Barons or higher start showing themselves, and we're still dealing with the lesser demon chaff. I can serve two masters for the time being."

"I thank you," Azrael said, his stoic expression lightening almost imperceptibly.

"It'll be fun," Cael shrugged. "And I think I know who you are talking about. I remember seeing a spat of Fractured wraiths a while back."

"Can you tell me what you saw?"

"Yeah. Seven decades ago, Earth time, I was waiting for an assignment in a church in England when a human entered with a dozen wraiths with him. I had never seen so many souls tethered to one human, and I didn't think he was aware of them. One wraith was enraged and attacked the man, and the man died as a result. I guess you hadn't collected these. Maybe you were busy."

"Go on," Azrael said.

"This is why I think I know what you're talking about. The dead human. His soul wasn't like the rest. When it left his body, he attacked the other souls, breaking them. He destroyed them. Nothing left behind. And when it was over, he disappeared. But I saw another human's soul leave their body, fracture, and go to the Agglomeration. And the body, it didn't die. The other soul went into it, I think."

Azrael remained silent.

"I called the murderer out," Cael said, a wicked grin crossing his face, "and I called him as such. He got angry, and he attacked me. He didn't know what he was up against, and I thought he should get a taste of his own hubris. I knocked him out of his body."

Azrael's demeanor shifted. Darkness drummed up around him, thrumming.

"You mean to tell me," Azrael growled, "that you fractured an Original Soul?"

"I-I didn't know at the time," Cael stammered, all sense

of mischievousness gone, "I just saw a few wraiths attacking each other and thought I'd sort them out. I didn't know that one of them was Original."

"You thought to do my job," Azrael growled, his presence darkening more, "by doing so, you have possibly condemned this realm to an age of horror before it is snuffed out like a candle's flame when the great engine ceases to churn."

"I-I said I'd help!" Cael paled and backed up. "I have a command; I'll take a unit out and cover the English area. We'll look for him."

"No, you must atone," Azrael said. "He must not be killed and found before such a thing happens to him. He is to be contained. His soul must never reach the Agglomeration."

"Yes, sir, I will do just that," Cael said, nodding short bobs of contrition.

Azrael's projection faded.

Cael smiled.

An empty, orange sky, swirling with streaks of black, expanded over a circle of seven stone villas, each with its castle-like towers extending into the endless sky. Gold was inlaid into and around every inch of the stone, branching out in lavish, rich design filigrees. Each villa faced the other around the circle, suggesting equal standing and community and that each should be watchful of the others. Sparse, purple grass struggled to poke through the black ground of the courtyard that was set central to the circle. Several lone white trees shaded the interior, casting no shadows over a stone heptagram that denoted the exact center of the courtyard set into the ground. Each of its seven points lined up with one of the villas. Cresting each point were carved words: avarice, pride, wrath, acumen, malevolence, lechery, and constitution.

Samael's projection formed from a haze and stood on the heptagram. He looked down at his feet and read the words. Looking at 'pride,' he turned and headed in the direction of that point's villa. As he stepped up the stone and gold steps, the doors opened, pushed out of place by a being of orange skin, bald with short, black horns. The demon wore a black brocade suit with a white frock shirt and stood straight-backed with an arm out to allow Samael to pass. He did not meet eyes with the looming Cataclysm, but with a slight smile and a nod, Samael crossed the threshold into the villa.

"Now presenting: The Cataclysm Samael, Harbinger of Misery, Patron Saint of Despair, Shepherd of the Sorrowed," the demon bellowed, looking off toward the foyer and grand staircase of the villa.

"Ariton," Samael whispered to himself, "Ruler of the North Cardinal Direction." He chuckled in his own amusement of repeating a title and smiled a small smile.

"Ah, Samael," a voice returned from the upper level of the villa, "I am glad I could receive you." A man of pale skin and hard-carved features descended the stairs. Despite being dressed in a black brocade suit edged in blood red, he appeared as an angel, with his stark-white hair pulled into an exacting ponytail.

Samael slid a side-eye to Ariton and waited. When no announcement for the gentleman was made, Samael laughed once to himself and looked at his host.

"Leviathan," he said with a slight bow, "who needs no introduction."

"A formality," Leviathan said with a smile as he reached the bottom stair. He looked up at Samael. "As is that I must receive you instead of Imperator Drake. He is otherwise engaged with matters of extreme import."

"Of course, though, I come with an important matter of my own."

"Indeed," Leviathan said, gesturing to a hallway to the side of the grand staircase, "I have taken the liberty of preparing a room for us to discuss this in. You will have my full attention, as you will of Drake's new general."

"Thank you," Samael said and walked in the direction given.

They passed through the ornate, polished, black oak foyer and hallway, stopping at a pair of double doors that Leviathan opened and pushed aside. Before them, the crackling of a fire spilled into the hallway, and Samael could see the villa's library revealed. At Leviathan's insistence, Samael entered and stood, hands behind his back, as he waited for Leviathan to secure the doors and join him.

The room was formed with the fireplace as the centerpiece at one end. The mantle of black rock inlaid with gold, framed the fire Samael had heard. A satin and velour couch sat before the fire, its red and black fabric accented by the light. To either side, the walls were lined with shelving in the same black oak and filled with books and tomes spanning many ages of human time. They housed an uncounted number of celestial works, as well, which Samael noted as he looked around the room. At the far end of the library sat a large, oaken writing desk, poised for any important work as indicated by the quill set neatly before its inkwell and a modern fountain pen placed to the side. Finally, the wall behind the desk was made entirely of a window lattice, square panes broken up by black wood molding, showing the fields of Hell behind the villa.

Another figure was in the room. A blond woman with eyes of blue, dressed in a dark leather bodysuit overlaid with black steel pauldrons, gauntlets, and a girdle that extended protection over her hips. The metal pieces appeared segmented, fitting together to allow movement, far more than the lighter armor of the angels. Their design work and the woman who wore them gave away that the armor was fit for a mobile, tactical fighter. Samael recognized the woman, and a look of mild surprise crossed his face. The woman met his gaze and narrowed her eyes.

Samael's concern for the woman passed as soon as it had appeared. With a shrug, he regained his pained smile and moved to the center of the room. Leviathan gestured to the sofa, and it shifted in place to face away from the fireplace. With another, the grand chair behind the writing desk leaped over it and slid across the floor toward them. Leviathan sat in the chair, offering the couch for Samael with an open hand.

"Thank you," Samael said as he sat. He looked toward the woman. She had pushed off the wall to join the other two but did not join Samael on the couch. She stood, hands on her hips, off to the side.

"Of course," Leviathan said, a courteous smile on his lips, "so what is it that brings a Cataclysm to Hell?"

"Frankly, we need your help," Samael's smile faded by half as he smoothed his red beard against his cassock, returning his eyes to Leviathan. "The Agglomeration is being assaulted. There is a soul on Eorthe that has learned the power of possession and is fracturing souls with each jump. It's sending most of those souls there."

Leviathan raised an eyebrow and steepled his fingers together on the knee of a crossed leg.

"Scarring? Is that the issue? Is there not a Noden busy at work healing those scars as we speak?" Leviathan asked.

"Yes," Samael nodded, "and he's doing wonderfully. But he is alone and is already nearing the end of his wick."

"Is the Noden considering sacrificing celestials already?" Leviathan smirked.

"Oh, no, no," Samael said, casually waving off the suggestion, "he is versed in Noden history and is well aware of what happened last time."

The woman stepped forward.

"This is a waste of our time," she said, "why do we entertain this like it's a problem?" She turned toward Samael. "More Fractured returning means more Fractured born into the world, and that's good business for us."

"Valor," Leviathan said, raising a hand just off his knee toward her, "if a Cataclysm is here to deliver the news personally, then there is more to it." He returned his eyes back to Samael. "Isn't that so?"

"And what, we should trust the word of the only Cataclysm to lose his station for getting too close to the mortals?" Valor growled as she hovered just over Samael's shoulder. "No longer the Angel of Death for loving a human. What's to say he's not got someone else to pine for now and wants to cover it up using us?"

Samael winced, though not from Valor's tone or proximity. He closed his eyes as he suppressed the pain. When he opened them again, he regained his wistful smile and looked at Leviathan.

"The problem is three-fold," he started, raising his fingers up, "you can take your pick on which is the worst. One, if the Agglomeration becomes too scarred, it will cease to function. Without Min around to fix it or make another one, human life on Eorthe will cease to be born." Samael looked at Valor. "Two, if this soul dies and is sent to the Agglomeration, it's likely it will completely destroy it. And in either case, if there is no Agglomeration, there is no great experiment. And if there's no great experiment-"

"Then there is no reason for us to be, and the Thrones erase us all," Leviathan finished the thought, looking at Valor. Valor frowned, not liking the exchange happening before her.

"And third?" she asked.

"Third," Samael continued, "it's an Original Soul. It has rewritten itself to be capable of this. It's been gathering pieces of the Fractured it's been creating, making them a part of it. As this continues, the scarring and the threat of a bomb going off in the Agglomeration both increase." Samael looked at Leviathan. "We are at a point that I don't think the soul is aware it has the ability to change itself. But that could soon change. Choose your doomsday; it either finds other Original Souls to teach this to and creates a storm of Fractured, or it figures out how to do something even worse."

"Min," Leviathan growled, "why would you leave such a glaring flaw in the First One Hundred?"

"What would you have us do?" Valor asked, the iron in

her voice softening as the situation sunk in.

"Azrael and I are on the case, as it were," Samael's pained smile returned, "but we're not as equipped for soul hunting as much as we are soul reaping. We need eyes. And I could think of no one better to help with that than you," Samael gestured to Leviathan and Valor, "especially now, with Valor being Hell's new general." He chuckled. "Congratulations, by the way, I apologize I didn't start with that."

Valor placed her hand on the back of the couch and leaned on it, looking at Leviathan. Leviathan looked between them, brought his steepled fingers to his chin, and tapped his lip.

"You were right, old friend," Leviathan said, "your missive said I'd find this troubling. Azrael's on this, too? I assume he's off to speak with Sariel about this." He slid his eyes to Valor when he said the angel's name and watched as she began to seethe silently.

"Yes," Samael nodded, "and I'm willing to bet it's going about as poorly as you could guess."

Leviathan rose.

"Well, we are nothing if not friends to humanity," Leviathan said, "and we will, of course, help you in this endeavor."

"Of course," Valor said.

"I will brief Drake on the matter, and Valor will contact our agents in the field. We will be your allies in this and help you contain the threat."

Samael rose and offered a small bow.

"Thank you for your time, my friend," Samael said. "I'm ever available for your summons should you find anything." He turned toward Valor. "Congratulations again."

Samael took a step back and faded from sight.

"What an opportunity," Leviathan said, letting his features break into a smile as he turned toward Valor.

"What's the play?" Valor asked.

"Let's kill a dozen birds with a whole lot of stones, to molest a human saying," he said as he gestured for the furniture to return to their previous positions. "Alert our forces. This soul is to die. And be dragged to the Agglomeration if we must."

"Sir?" Valor's brows raised, alarmed at Leviathan's turn.

"Samael's in pain and constant misery. I wouldn't put it past him to exaggerate the issue, whether he knows it or not. I doubt the damage would be as extreme." Leviathan's smile turned dark. "But more importantly, I haven't seen a better way to take a jab at the Celestial Empyrean like this in a millenium. What better way to make them swallow their own hubris than to make sure such a devastating act happened on their watch? After being warned by a Cataclysm?"

Valor began to share Leviathan's smile.

"And what better way to fuck over my father," Valor said, "than to bring the experiment to the brink of failure while he was charged with protecting it?"

"I think this calls for a drink," Leviathan said, stepping back and opening the doors to the library.

"This is going to be fun," Valor said as she bounced on her feet and passed Leviathan, leaving the room with him.

Chapter Seven

1524...

Rook looked through the duo-chromatic clarity of his detached senses. A spectrum consisting of only shades of gray and blue gave Rook enhanced sight, able to cut through the darkness of his chamber as though he was seeing it through the shade on a sunny day. It was midnight, or as close to it as he could know from the last bell that rang through the monastery, and the room was pitch black. But to Rook, the dark held no secrets.

He looked back to his bed, a simple set of wooden planks hammered together to hold a sewn mattress and woolen blankets. His body was on top of them, dressed in a black cotton night coat that left his linen-hosed legs otherwise bare, reclining with his hands clasped over his stomach. He was peaceful, breathing steadily. He'd be mistaken for sleeping if anyone checked on him. Only he would see the silver, shimmering line rising out of his chest, originating from somewhere near his heart, that drew a direct line to where he was standing now, infusing into this form. Only he and his abbot.

Rook looked himself over. He was a mirror image of the fifty-one-year-old man lying in the bed painted in oily gray and blue hues. He was translucent, shimmering. He chuckled at the fact that he was in his drawers, and focusing on his form, he willed himself to appear in his daytime cloak and accompanying attire. With a nod of approval, once the clothing manifested, he turned and left the room, walking through the wall as if it wasn't there.

Rook passed through the halls of the monastery. Most of the other monks were in their chambers, though he floated by an odd novitiate or two as they cleaned or tended to maintenance tasks in his path. Rook entered the library and looked over the wooden tables and stone walls that were cluttered with scrolls and tomes. Several monks of the night station sat hunched, scribbling with quills or charcoal sticks, working in silence except for the endless, whispered chanting coming from the attached chapel. One monk was holding up a rosary, inspecting it closely, as he notated the details of it into a small leatherbound journal. Rook, despite being dozens of feet away, could hear each scratch, each breath, each wipe of a brow, and each holy word with distinctness. In this form, the sounds resonated unimpeded through him and were perfectly perceptible.

"Father Maison," came a voice that rang clear over the din, carrying with it a strong Middle German accent. Rook saw another translucent image of a man pass through a wall not far from where he was now, his cord spiking back through it behind him. He saw this man appearing late into his seventies and in his elevated attire, depicting his status at the monastery.

"Abbot Vogt," Rook said, bowing his head in respect.

Though the two spoke at a non-hushed volume, none of the monks seemed to notice.

"Shall we?" Abbot Vogt asked.

Rook nodded, and they both lifted off the floor. In an effort that took some concentration, they rose upward through the ceiling and through the remaining levels of the monastery until they broke into the night sky. They ascended higher, crossing each other's paths and circling, enjoying the freedom of movement that astrally projecting offered. When they reached an impossible height, and the monastery wasn't much more than a large, dark blotch on an otherwise twilight-infused German countryside, they hovered and took in the expanse around them.

"I live for these nights," Rook said, "we rarely get to do this together anymore."

"I'm sorry I haven't had the time or energy like I used to," the abbot said, "since taking over for Abbot Lauderman, God rest his soul, I haven't had too many nights I didn't leave work to be done by the last bell."

"You know I'll help where I can."

"You will, my friend. I intend to confirm you as my second. The bishop has already sent back his blessing. It's only a matter of time now."

Rook smiled as he looked around at the countryside. He still marveled at how well he could see when like this, all the way out to the water's edge a distance away and the occasional wandering wraith that dotted the lands. Rook's smile faded when he saw the few hovering about the monastery graveyard.

"What is it?"

Rook looked at the abbot.

"I wish there was more we could do for them," Rook said, gesturing toward the spirits.

"They're absolved," the abbot said, "they are clean before the eyes of God. We did that for them." The abbot's face withdrew. "But they are stuck, you know that. They have to let go on their own."

"I feel like we could do more, somehow, Cristof," Rook said, looking back at the abbot, "we have this power, and it feels like we're still missing something we can do with it."

Cristof thought a moment and then looked back at Rook.

"Even though God gave us this ability, he didn't send with it knowledge of his intentions. You learned everything I had to teach you, and you and I have both pushed the limits, seeing what more we could do." Cristof smiled softly at Rook. "God himself would have to tell us more. But I am sure we have made him proud and haven't squandered his great gift."

"Hm," Rook uttered as he looked back at the ghosts repeating their limited series of actions around the graveyard.

"Rook," Cristof chuckled, "do you remember when we first met? Your parents were terrified. They thought you were possessed, talking of walking outside of your body and knowing things you couldn't know. You couldn't even control it, a boy of 8 seasons given to the church to protect themselves from your communion with the devil. They were sure you'd bring evil and ruin."

Rook looked at Cristof.

"Lucky for me, you knew better," Rook said.

"No, my friend, Providence. God guided me to that English village some forty years ago, guided me to you. To hear that you had such a unique and incredible gift, that you were selected by God himself, just as I was, I knew I had to teach you all I knew and see you rise to greatness in His name."

"What greatness?" Rook interjected. "We're no different than they are," Rook said as he pointed down to the monastery, "it is we few ordained that have power over sin and soul, not just us two, because we can leave our bodies and fly about, seeing ghosts when we do. What has this," Rook gestured to himself, "given us that the others don't have?"

Cristof frowned in concern for his friend.

"All this has been inside you, my friend?" he asked. "Why haven't you told me of your concerns before now? Does your faith waver?"

"No," Rook said with a shake of his head, "how could I doubt God when he made us closer to Him than all others? No, what I am concerned about is that even as we are so close to Him, we cannot soothe those suffering or in pain any more than we can in the flesh. I don't doubt that there's greatness for us; I doubt that we've already obtained it."

Cristof nodded and looked out over the countryside.

"We have time yet to discover God's true purpose for us, my friend. We-" Cristof cut himself off, floating past Rook to look at the nearby village.

Rook turned and looked as well. He saw the village alight in a glow, appearing blue-gray through his astral projection vision. He looked to Cristof, who returned his concerned expression. Together, they agreed to move and flew toward the village as fast as their projections could travel. They touched down in the center of the village, seeing the source of the light was a raging fire that had already consumed most of the village.

Rook and Cristof could hear the cries of the villagers, some calling out for missing loved ones, others crying for the losses of those they found. They could hear the screams of anguish as injury and trauma took others down. Rook went to the well in the center of the village and saw people scrambling to douse as much of the fires as they could. He could hear a scream from inside a burning, thatch-roofed house, one of the many targets for the water bails.

Rook rushed into the house and saw the people inside. He saw a man and his child huddled as far away from the flames as they could, but they were surrounded, and the fire was encroaching fast. Rook ran over and tried to grab them, but his hands went through them as though they weren't there. The two gave no reaction to his attempt, unaware of his presence.

"Rook!" Cristof yelled, his voice cutting through the wall of noise and clamor like a direct transmission. Rook stood, looking at the man and child once more before tearing himself away to rejoin his friend.

Cristof stood at the far end of the village, watching a band of men armed with long blades and torches brandishing them at the villagers and setting a new fire. One of them slashed out at one of the residents, cutting him down and spilling his blood across the cobblestone. As the man bled out, Cristof ran over to him and knelt, watching his body.

Rook arrived to see the man die, his body relaxing and his eyes losing focus. He watched as Cristof waited for the man's soul to rise and then speak to it.

"It's over now, young man. Your fight is over," Cristof said to the dark form manifesting over the fallen body, "let go of your earthly concerns and walk with God." Cristof made a gesture in the sign of the cross and began to pray. "*Christe qui lux es mundi dator vite eleyson. Arte lesos demonis intuere eleyson.*"

The wraith hovered, looking around itself. It saw its own body and then turned to see its comrades being sliced down as well. It gathered on itself, condensing, thickening. Rook seized on this critical moment.

"No!" Rook said as he put himself directly in the line of sight of the wraith. "Do not give in to your anger and despair. God's light cannot warm you if you become stuck here; heed His call and return to Him."

The wraith looked at Rook, as did the abbot.

"Go," Rook said sternly, "you are absolved of your sins and are welcomed into the kingdom of God. Return, lest here be your purgatory in the cold forever." He kept his eyes fixed on the wraith's. "Return."

The wraith relaxed, letting its form spread out again. It turned away from the fighting and drifted from it. A moment later, it descended, pulled away, and out of view. With the wraith gone, Rook and Cristof looked toward the other villagers, freshly dead.

"We have to do something," Rook said.

"Keep performing the rites," Cristof said, "guide as many as you can."

Rook froze. A looming, eight-foot-tall skeletal figure,

dressed in the holy black robes of mourning and bearing a harvesting scythe as tall as it was, moved through the village. It came before the spirits of the dead, those who refused to move on, and touched them, absorbing them into its skeletal hand and swirling their essence along its arm. The spirits that had turned feral and violent he attacked, swinging his scythe and splitting them into wispy halves that then gathered around his weapon. It turned toward Rook, and with smoldering pinpoints of light instead of eyes in its dark sockets, its gaze met Rook's. The reaping angel was here, and Rook was chilled to the core.

"Rook!" Cristof yelled in an attempt to get his attention. He looked up at Rook and then slowly stood, seeing the figure for himself.

"Azrael," Cristof whispered.

"What do we do?" Rook asked, backing up.

"That's the archangel of death, Rook," Cristof said, turning away and looking at the people who were still fighting, "he's here for them, not us. We don't interfere with his work."

Rook turned, his eyes attached to the archangel until the last possible moment when he looked at the attackers. He took in their details; there were seven of them; they all looked to be in their mid-twenties to thirties, and they were all men. Aside from each carrying a sword and torch, they were also all wearing cloaks bearing a sigil of a cross at the center of a heart surrounded by a simple rose and outer ring embroidered across their backs with the words "Post Tenebras Lux."

"Light After Darkness," Rook whispered.

"Lutherans," Cristof spat, "looters, killers. We need to get back to the abbey. They'll be coming to tear it down and take everything."

"What?!" Rook said, turning toward Cristof.

"Rook, we need to move now!"

Cristof took to the sky and receded along his tether, moving as quickly as he could. Rook stood, watching the looters continue to ransack the village and Azrael claiming the souls that dared linger. After a moment, he followed Cristof back to the monastery.

Rook bolted upright in his bed. Adrenaline, coursing impotently through his veins for the last twenty minutes, suddenly found purchase and electrified his muscles. He leapt from the bed and slammed the door to his chamber wide open as he rushed down the hall.

"Arise! Arise, brothers!" Rook yelled as he entered the cloister surrounding the inner courtyard. "We are under attack!"

Rook found the rope to the warning bells and pulled hard. The bronze rang out, clanging their alarm call across the monastery. As Rook pulled the rope again and again, Abbot Vogt burst through an adjoining door and joined the gathering of monks flooding into the cloister and courtyard.

"Why do you rise us from our rest?" a monk asked, rubbing his eyes and looking around at the others. A murmur began to crawl across the mouths of the gathered.

"Father Maison speaks the truth. We have seen it from the bell tower. Niedam is burning. Lutherans are coming!" Abbot Vogt said, holding his hands out toward the direction of the village.

"Lutherans!" several of the monks gasped. Others murmured, "God preserve," while others stuttered and stammered over several prayers.

"We must protect the relics," the abbot said, "we cannot let them claim them for their own."

Several of the monks dispersed, but most remained.

"What would you have us do?" a monk asked.

"The Codex," another exclaimed, "we could never move it!"

"Bring all the artifacts and relics to the Codex," Rook said. "We will gather everything there and barricade the door from the inside."

"We can't all fit in the reading room!" came a protest from a monk and, with it, a clamoring of similar objections.

The abbot raised his hands.

"Do you fear your duty?" he yelled out, causing the

monks to fall into silence. "Do you lack the faith to do what you must do? Have you forgotten what is most important?"

He met eyes with the congregation, his stern countenance commanding their obedience.

"You will gather each and every holy piece and place it in the reading room," he continued, "and you will also bring to it your faith and conviction, for I will bar the door and brace it from the inside."

Gasps broke out through the monks. Rook looked at his abbot aghast.

"Cristof, no..." Rook said.

"It is the necessary thing to do, Father Maison," Abbot Vogt said, pulling on the shoulders of several monks to spur them on their tasks, "you guide our brothers in doing this and then take them to safety away from here."

"I cannot," Rook started, but the abbot cut him off.

"It is your duty, Rook. Carry it out."

And with that, the abbot turned and left the cloister.

Rook watched his old friend leave, envisioning the potential outcomes of the night's events playing out in his head. His mind's eye overlaid the horrors he had seen in Niedam onto imaginings of Cristof's body on the stone floor of the reading room, and he shook his head to be free of the flashes of his slit throat or bludgeoned head. He took in a breath.

"None are so like Him than us..." Rook said. He then

pushed forward.

Rook entered the hallway and ducked into the chapel. He took off his night cloak and fashioned it into a makeshift bag, filling it with as many holy items as he could. When he was sure he had left only the lesser blessed things and those of no worth behind, he re-entered the hallway and passed the library. He saw monks gathering books and making similar decisions about their holy values. While they discarded many, others were chosen and handed off to brothers to be ferried to the reading room.

Rook entered the abbot's quarters. Though this room was technically a part of the dormitory wing, the abbot's room had no door that allowed entry into it from the rest of the living chambers. It was larger than theirs, too, and was home to many of the most sacred relics that weren't to be displayed in the chapel without cause. Rook stood and looked over the reliquaries and other holy containers. He grabbed the ones said to house pieces of the True Cross and others that held bone fragments of several saints. In his rush, he could no longer tell which was which, so he grabbed them all and stuffed them into his cloak. At capacity, Rook had no choice but to return to the reading room with what he had.

As he bounded down the hallway, he stopped on his toes, catching sight of something out of the corner of his eye. Between the refectory, where they gathered to eat, and the kitchen was a narrow passage that led out behind the monastery. The cooks once used it to access livestock pens, but it had been out of use for ages. But Rook saw two monks desperately trying to leverage the iron grating barring the passage free, using one of the many bronze crosses as a pry bar.

"Brothers," Rook called out, "what is this?"

The monks froze and looked back at Rook for only a moment before they dug back into the bars with the cross.

"We'll not die here with you, Father," one said, putting his weight on the cross and bending it without much to show for the effort.

"Are you mad?" Rook asked. "You abandon your faith and station in our greatest time of need? Do you have any idea what happens to deserters?"

"Apostasy?" the other barked back. "You can have your communions with the Lord when you die here, Father. I'll ask forgiveness when I am alive later."

Rook was floored.

"Your souls will die adrift for your sins, brothers, even if you are forgiven for deserting us now. I pray of you, stay and help us, and I'll make sure we all get out together as the abbot ordered."

The gate popped open, and with hardly a look back, the monks dropped the deformed cross to the ground and escaped out into the night. Rook looked at the empty passage for a moment, closed his eyes, uttered a prayer for them, and then resumed his dash back to the abbot.

Rook dumped out his haul in a corner of the reading room. While the monastery, on paper, was built around the chapel and focused on it as its most prominent feature, the true heart of the abbey was the reading room. It was a large space carved from the solid stone of the hill the abbey was built around and was the only space not to be built by brick and mortar. It was the true center of the monastery. The room was lined with thick, woven rugs and tapestries of red and gold, serving both to keep the cold of the stone away and to depict the creation of the Codex in their artwork. Along the walls were sconces, groupings of small candle holders that were chosen to benefit from a quantity of flames rather than larger candles to cast light.

And in the center was the Codex. It was a Bible, the largest ever written, measuring an arm's length in breadth and width. It was as heavy as a stout man, which necessitated its permanent place on the gold pedestal upon which it was mounted. Its pages were vellum, and the depictions on the tapestries suggested more than one-hundred sixty young cattle were sacrificed to create them. Other tapestries denoted its conception as a written work, encompassing the Old and New Testaments, every chant of consecration, every incantation of adjuration, and every rite of exorcism. And, prominently over the Codex itself, was an illustration of an unknown monk working alongside a winged devil, creating two such books, suggesting one of them resided here in this room.

Rook turned to see Cristof directing other remaining faithful to place their collections in the corners of the room. Despite its size, the natural cave was quickly filling up. Rook guided a few more monks to deposit what they had but then moved them out of the room. He looked at Cristof as he inspected the door to the reading room and made ready a heavy bar to barricade it.

"It should be me," Rook said, a hand grabbing one of Cristof's arms.

"It most certainly should not," the abbot said, "I'm older than Lauderman was when he died. And I am twenty years your senior."

Cristof patted Rook's hand.

"Don't worry. Once we seal me in here, it'll take a Protestant miracle to break in."

Rook and Cristof shared a tense stare.

A scream broke through the silence between them. From beyond the hall, several men cried out. Some came from a few monks, but the other cries neither Rook nor Cristof could recognize as their own. Rook moved to the door as Cristof picked up the bar.

"They're here," Cristof said, "go now, get our brothers out of here."

Rook nodded and stepped outside. Cristof slammed the

door shut, and Rook could hear the scraping of the retaining bar as it slid into place. Rook followed the yelling and emerged into the cloister to see the men bearing the embroidered rose sigil enter it from the other side. He counted a dozen of them as they poured in and spread out.

Rook counted three of his brothers lying in the courtyard. He could not tell if they were dead, but the man who cut them down paid them no mind as he stepped over their bodies to enter deeper into the monastery. Rook turned to run down the hall toward the living chambers and refectory when he saw a spilling of fire roll along the floor. More of these men entered from the narrow passageway the deserting monks had pried open, rolling barrels that ablaze and kicking them into the walls, spreading tar and fire where they splattered. A wall of flame blocked Rook.

Behind him, the Lutherans had already set the chapel on fire, and Rook could hear more screams as more monks were discovered and slaughtered. The only other paths left to Rook were fighting his way past the men to try and to make it outside, or returning to the reading room. Rook tried to think, but he was panicking. He'd start to move in one direction but feel the flames. He'd try another to see a sword cut through a brother. He backed up, the feeling of being cornered and hunted welling up inside of him. He moved backward along the wall, touching the stone with his hands, until he felt the reading room's door.

"Cristof," he whispered as harshly and forcefully as he could, trying not to give his location away. "Cristof, let me in!"

The door groaned and then opened as Cristof unbarred the door. He reached out for Rook and pulled him in, pushing the door closed again and resetting the bar.

"W-we're surrounded," Rook said, panting, "a dozen, maybe more. More than in the village. They have tar." Rook broke down as the images flashed in his mind. "They've killed all of us."

Cristof's hand touched Rook's shoulder.

"Pray for them. And for us," Cristof said. "There's nothing else we can do."

"Isn't there?!" Rook yelled, staring Cristof in the eye. "There must be something we can do. Something-"

A boom rocked through the door. Rook and Cristof could hear the men on the other side of it slamming something heavy against the wooden barricade. Though he couldn't make it out, he could hear them talking. Rook backed away from the door.

"I lied," Cristof said.

Rook looked at him.

"I lied when I said the door would hold. I knew it wouldn't."

Cristof looked at Rook.

"I had just hoped it would have bought you enough time

to get out with the other monks.”

The door boomed again, and the stone around the hinges cracked, sputtering dust into the air.

“We had no chance,” Rook said, looking at the door.

“No,” Cristof said, stepping closer to Rook, “we were dead as soon as we saw Azrael.”

The door boomed again and for the last time. The hinges disintegrated, letting free the impediment that came crashing to the floor. Behind it, men bearing the marks of Luther stood, a heavy stock in the hands of the two up front, who tossed it to the side now that it was no longer needed.

“And there it is, my friends,” said one of the men, gesturing to the Codex.

As several of the men entered, Rook and Cristof backed up.

“And, look, they gathered all of the relics for us.”

“Stay back,” Cristof demanded, stepping forward and raising a hand. “God will deliver unto you retribution should you desecrate these holy remains.”

A man stepped forward, unsheathed his sword, and slashed it across Cristof’s neck in one motion. He spat on Cristof as the abbot fell to the ground and clutched his neck, gasping for air.

“Your old scare tactics won’t work on us, old man. Your God no longer favors you.”

“Cristof!” Rook yelled. He threw himself to the floor to

scoop the abbot up. Cristof's blood spurted down Rook's arms as he held the dying man.

"You. Secure the room," one of the men said, pointing to another. "The rest of you come with me." All the Lutherans, except the one, filed out of the room and disappeared into the monastery. The one left behind glowered down at Rook.

"Alright, that's enough," the man said as he kicked Rook in the side, sending him to the floor and Cristof out of his arms. Rook watched his friend's eyes grow distant as he fell away, and when Rook came to rest on his back, he looked up at his assailant.

"You are the Devil," Rook growled.

"What?" the man said, cupping his hand around his ear in a mocking gesture of not hearing Rook.

"You will pay for this," Rook said, straining to get up, "I call upon God; make them pay for this."

The man laughed and kicked Rook again.

"Your God isn't here. Haven't you heard?" he laughed. "Your coffers grew while the faithful suffered. Your God abandoned you the moment you Catholics abandoned us."

"If we are so like you," Rook said through gritted teeth, "then help me."

The man looked confused and cocked his head. As he tried to sort out what Rook was talking about, Rook rolled up to his feet and lunged at the man. But the man was quick and strong, and he punched Rook in the stomach.

"I think you've lost it, old man," he said, "this is a kindness."

The man punched Rook again and then slammed his fist across his face. Rook collapsed to the floor. He was pushed flat on his back and then felt the man's hands grip his throat and push. Rook struggled, trying with all his strength to wrestle the man off of him, but he couldn't do it. He was just too weak and the man too heavy. He flailed his legs and clawed at the hands around his throat with his nails, but the grip didn't let up. Rook couldn't breathe. And soon, he saw the room darken.

No, no! Rook thought. *This cannot be it. This cannot be how everything ends! I won't allow it!*

Rook closed his eyes and cleared his mind. In spite of his body wracking as it wanted to cough and breathe, Rook kept his eyes closed and forced his dying body to lie still. When the pain in his head began to give way to a feeling of euphoria and detachment, he willed himself up and out of his body, rising as his astral projection. He looked around and saw through the familiar gray and blue again. He saw Cristof's body, and over it, his wraith, watching back.

"Waiting for me to join you?" Rook said with a small smile.

Rook looked at his body and his attacker. He waved his hand through the man, and when it passed effortlessly, he sighed. He waited.

With Rook no longer fighting back, the man was able to get the angle he wanted and pushed down hard. Rook heard the snap and watched as his body's neck popped out of place and his head fell to the side. But a slow horror set in when Rook also saw his silver, shimmering cord snap free from the body and dissolve as it fell away from him. He was severed, no longer tethered to his physical shell.

Rook jerked backward, feeling a pull from inside, attempting to drag him down. He looked at Cristof's wraith and saw it was fighting the same sensation, fluttering and pulling itself higher to resist.

Rook felt the pull again. Horror turned into panic.

"No! No, no, no, no!" Rook said, holding his chest and looking around the room.

The pull came harder, and Rook slid across the floor on his feet. He looked to Cristof just in time to see his resistance fail and watched as the wraith was pulled down and out of sight.

"No! No, I refuse!" Rook screamed.

The pull came constantly now, pulling him through the floor up to his waist, stopped only by Rook's hands as he clawed at the stone to stay in the room. He gripped and crawled and pulled himself across the floor toward his body. He dragged himself onto it and tried to settle down into it again, but it wouldn't have him. He strained, his form sinking by a finger's width into the floor as the pull intensified. He watched his killer stand, wipe his brow, and turn to walk away.

In a blind panic, Rook lunged and threw himself at his murderer. Instead of passing through him, Rook slammed against something. It was solid. Something in the man blocked him. And Rook watched as the man reacted, clutching his chest and letting out a deep cough.

Rook charged at the man again and again he collided with something solid. The man reeled, flinging a hand out to steady himself against the wall. He coughed again, a wheeze coming from the bottom of his lungs.

Rook felt as though he could resist the pull no longer, and with all of his will, he threw himself at the man again. This time, whatever solid thing that had kept Rook at bay gave way, pushed out of his body by Rook's force. Rook occupied the space with the man, who now sunk to his knees and collapsed against the wall. Rook saw the thing he had dislodged, a humanoid shape made of smoke and mist: his spirit, his soul, his ghost, his wraith. But something was wrong with it. It was missing a portion of its lower torso. A hole that, as Rook watched, began to crisscross jagged edges from the cavity that traced lines all throughout the wraith. Rook saw the wraith shatter, like glass, into innumerable pieces that came back together and loosely hung in place, like clumps of rock held together by magnetism.

Before Rook could process what he saw, he felt a new sensation. Like a vortex had opened in the man's body, whose space he still occupied, Rook felt himself being sucked up. It was a wholly different sensation than the pull of death. It was warm and electric. So Rook accepted it and dove in. He felt his spirit fill the empty space, feeling parts of his essence disseminating throughout the man's chest, then arms, and then legs.

Rook screamed. An intense pain completely obscured every other thought Rook had. He had never felt pain like this before, as though every nerve was being pulled through his skin. He wanted to flail, but he couldn't. This body wasn't responding. Every attempt at movement reinvigorated the pain, but not attempting to move felt almost worse, as if he were dying again. Rook screamed and screamed, and finally, his body responded, and he could push himself off the wall to lay out on his back on the floor.

Rook opened his eyes. His eyelids stung. His eyes hurt. Blinking felt like he was grinding sand into them. But he forced his eyes to open and look. He saw the reading room's tapestries above him. He could see the smoke filling the room from the fires, fires that he could smell, fires that were burning throughout the monastery. As he slid his eyes around the room, he saw a form, dark and with sharp edges, for just a moment before it was gone.

Rook rolled over onto his stomach. The act shot fire down his arms and legs, and Rook coughed a stifled yell. The pain was subsiding, but it was still debilitating. He exhaled and let his head rest on the floor.

He saw the dark form flicker back into view again. And then it was gone. He blinked, and it was back, coming closer. He blinked again, and it was gone. Then, as he concentrated on keeping his eyes open and focused, he saw the form fade into view again. He saw the wraith of the man who killed him, now somehow broken and wrong, hovering just out of reach. As he watched, the wraith began to condense, constricting on itself. It heaved as though it was breathing. In its eyes, Rook could see pinpoints of light, like small embers recently cast out of a burning fire. They were growing in brightness and intensity. And as they did, the body elongated, its hands forming into long, demonic-looking claws. It began to seethe with visible anger at Rook. It started to close the distance. Rook felt fear rising up in him again and tried to move away, but his body only responded with pain. The wraith jerked erratically and then charged at Rook.

A scythe's blade swung through the air, slicing the wraith into two. A skeletal hand braced against the frame of the reading room's door as Azrael stepped into the room. Rook watched in terror as the Archangel of Death, in full color and vibrancy, stood before him, pulling the shards of the wraith from his scythe and inspecting them closely. Azrael looked at Rook, the pinpoints of light in its dark sockets appearing almost purple. But the angel did not linger. It turned and left Rook on the ground.

When the specter of death had gone, the room filled with noise as the Lutherans returned. The men entered the room and surveyed the scene.

"Isaac, are you alright?" one of the men asked, coming to Rook's side and helping him to stand. Rook could only respond in a grunt of pain when he was moved.

"Guess that old monk had some fight in him," another said, "get him back to church."

Another man came to Rook's side and, with his comrade, both picked Rook up and balanced him between them. As they started to walk him out, the pain was no longer enough to keep Rook conscious, and he went limp as he passed out.

Firelight flickered beyond Rook's closed eyelids. It buffeted his consciousness, forcing his brain to come alive. It sent shocks along his forehead and then down his spine. When Rook tried to open his eyes, the lids fluttered but did not open and his head hurt for the attempt. Rook tried again, and light passed through the slits of his lids. It burned him.

But his brain fought back. It denied him. It shut down. Darkness replaced the light.

Something opened Rook's eye. He felt pressure against it, pulling on it. Though it was open, Rook couldn't see. Light came through, but his mind couldn't register it. It refused to.

The poking made Rook try to pull away. He couldn't form a thought, but instinct compelled him. He felt the shock of pain travel from his eye to his neck, then to his shoulders, the sensation telling his brain that he had moved and passing the information to Rook. This caused a jumpstart in Rook's consciousness. He became aware of it, just for a moment, before his consciousness became aware of something else.

Rook felt claustrophobic. He felt like he needed to escape. That wherever he was, he needed to get out. He felt displaced, alienated from something so fundamental and elementary that fleeing was the only option.

Rook tried to give in to the feeling. He tried to awaken, to move. His primitive instinct to fly from this place shifted into fear when his body didn't respond. The fear became an overwhelming panic when every urge to flee came up impotent to Rook's twilight consciousness. The panic caused him to thrash, and though his physical body didn't respond to the turmoil, Rook's spirit did, and it rose from the body.

Free from his shell, Rook's mind crystallized into clarity instantly. He could see around himself, see himself hovering over his body, and that he was surrounded by unfamiliar people in unfamiliar garb. A woman was leaning over his body, covering his face with her hands and prodding at it. He saw the dress of the men that lay in other beds near his, and he saw the embroidered Lutheran rose upon them. Rook's soul spun around to see that he was in a church, ransacked and occupied by the looters. Rook looked down, fearing what the woman could be doing to him, and hovered closer to see.

The woman moved her hands, giving Rook the first clear sight of his face. But Rook saw the face of his murderer lying before him where he had just been.

Rook's mind reeled. He couldn't understand it. He looked for his body —his real body— but it was nowhere near him. He looked down at himself, looking for his astral cord, but it was not there. The fear that had permeated his body before saturated him still, and when the pull of death thrummed through his form anew, he gripped at the body to stay in place.

The body's heart became erratic and slowed. Rook could feel it while his hands were buried in it. He felt the electrical impulses in its nerves fire less and less, carrying less strength. It's breathing shallowed and then stopped. He felt the body cool. Rook felt the body dying.

The pull gripped him again, yanking him from the body, leaving only his hand to clutch its leg while the rest of him passed through the woman who was attending to it. He slammed against something inside her. He watched the woman, who had been desperately trying to rouse the body in the moment before, clutch her chest and turn away, placing her will to live and her body's reaction to very nearly losing its soul at the forefront of her concern. She coughed to compel her heart to stabilize. She wanted to live.

As did Rook. But he could see that the body, an empty shell, wanted to die.

The pull gave Rook no other choice. He clawed back toward the body. He traveled up its leg until he could grip it with both hands and then pulled himself over it. Looking down at his killer's face, Rook felt revulsion, frustration, and anger but could also feel the parts of him that sunk into the body become free from the otherworldly call while safely housed inside. Rook made the determination, and he pulled. He descended into the body.

The body hated him, but it could do nothing other than accept him. Joined once again, it took from Rook his clarity. His thought. And Rook sank back into only darkness.

Rook's eyes fluttered open. The pain had subsided. He could open his eyes and look around himself without the act shooting sparks along the nerves, but his eyes were still refusing to focus. Rook could see shapes, light, and darkness but could not tell where he was or who was with him. The voices he heard sounded foreign to him; he could tell the accents were various German, but the words sounded other-worldly. Wrong. Unnatural.

He blinked and tried to move his head. It responded by falling to the side, only tangentially related to what he was attempting to do. But it caused those around him to touch him. They righted his head, pulled on his eyelids, and grabbed his arms. Rook used the sensations as something to focus on. He chose one shape, one person that was moving and talking, and zeroed in on them. Slowly, the image began to sharpen, and the words started to sound less and less bizarre.

"Isaac? Isaac," the voice warbled through his brain. More, mostly unintelligible, words followed. Rook could make out "hear," "okay," and "out" in the German tongue. He could also tell the voice was feminine.

The shape moved and darkened the area over his eyes, and Rook suddenly felt a biting cold shoot through his forehead and down behind his ears. A cold cloth was placed on him, he surmised. It was so very near being painful, but also soothing. He was being cared for. But when he relaxed and let the sensation sink in, others quickly overshadowed it, and Rook could not keep them all at bay. Lights flashed all around his sight, a sour-bitter taste filled his tongue, and his pain was replaced by sheer numbness. He felt a storm swelling in his head. He could feel the body taking his lack of focus to rebel.

Rook jolted and contorted as his body convulsed. His spine moved in opposition to his arms and legs, and his head smashed the fabric underneath it repeatedly. Rook's brain fired every synapse it could at once, sen him into a seizure, causing him to thrash. The people around him rushed to his sides and tried to hold him down, but Rook could not tell if they were successful. All he could see, hear, or feel told him that his body was doing its best to reject him.

Yet, Rook could think. He thought back to the last moments he could remember before waking up. How he left his body and how he shoved the soul out of this one. Of how he took up residence inside it. He could hardly believe it, but it was the only explanation that made sense. This had to be the power God intended for him and Cristof, the power to guide the flesh with their immortal souls.

If only Cristof had resisted longer, Rook thought. But then Rook remembered this body's soul and how it broke when he pushed it out. The anger and hatred he could see in it. But Rook couldn't let himself believe that was because of him. He pushed that thought from his head. *Your soul was fragile because you were evil*, he thought. *Your fate was sealed in sin.*

Easy now, Rook thought, directing it at the body. *I am not here to hurt you. I will guide you. You will live.*

The body did not respond to him. The seizure had reached a fever pitch, and he could tell he was in danger of permanent damage if he didn't regain control.

I compel you, Rook thought. *I command you to heed.*

Rook forced his will upon the body. He bore through

its resistance, feeling the junction point where his soul met the body and pushing through it. As though he was opening a door wider or breaking through a levee meant to stop a raging river, Rook's essence flooded the body, and it finally responded. The thrashing stopped, and the body relaxed. Its heart was beating rapidly, but the rest of it came to calm. Rook could feel the flood of pain and strain fill his senses again.

Rook leaned back against the back of the bed. He looked down at the three-by-three grid on his lap that already had several Xs and Os drawn into it. He reached out for the charcoal stick that was being offered and tried to take it. His hand shook with small tremors as he commanded the muscles to close, but he could and soon possessed the writing instrument. He brought it down to the wooden plate and marked his move, an O that connected three in a row. He then drew a line, crossing them out, and smiled.

"You win again."

"You're letting me win, Vivian," Rook said, smiling at the woman sitting with him.

She was young to Rook, somewhere in her twenties, with dark hair pulled back into a tail and dark gray eyes. She wore a gown that was reminiscent of a Catholic nun but altered to honor her newly chosen faith. The black robe was opened in the front, and under it was a white, laced bodice whose collar framed her neck. She smiled at Rook as she took the wooden board and wiped off their game with a cloth.

"You think you could try walking again, Isaac?"

Rook heard the name and was reminded he didn't appear to them as he knew himself.

"I think so," Rook nodded.

Vivien placed the plate on the side table and pulled off the covers that were over Rook. She then stood and came to his side, pulling on his legs to help him swing them over the side of the bed. She took his hand and braced for him, nodding to him that it was time for him to try to stand.

Alright, Rook thought, *we're in this together—you and me. We can do this.*

Rook pulled on his muscles. His legs tensed. Wobbly, jerky, but responding, Rook's body rose out of the bed and ascended to full height. He gripped Vivian's hand tightly as he steadied himself.

"Okay," Vivian said, "now walk."

Rook took a step. The movement took full concentration, commanding nearly every muscle to work in series until he got his foot placed on the floor before him. He then rocked his weight onto it, his knee threatening to give up but holding as he placed his other foot forward.

Rook, with Vivian's support, walked in a small circle until

he was back to where he started. With the walk complete, she guided Rook to sit back down on the bed and then sat next to him again.

"So much better!"

"It's you, really," Rook said, only partially lying, "I don't think I would have recovered without you."

Vivian smiled at him, and then it faded as she looked into his eyes.

Rook's smile faded as well, replaced with concern.

"What's wrong?" he asked.

Vivian shook her head, and her smile returned.

"Oh, nothing," she said, "you're just progressing so well, I think you'll be back to normal very soon."

Perhaps it was Rook's age and wisdom, or perhaps this body knew something Rook hadn't yet figured out, but he could tell she didn't say her whole thought. He gripped her hand and patted it with his other.

"What is it? I cannot have spent all this time with you for you to keep your concerns from me now."

Vivian hesitated. Rook waited patiently.

"You really don't remember anything before that night?" she finally spoke.

"No, not really," Rook said, lying through his teeth, "I can remember being dragged out, but that's it."

"Oh," Vivian said, her smile waning again.

Rook said nothing, watching her, waiting for her to say

what she was feeling.

"Maybe it'll come back to you someday."

"Perhaps," Rook said, "but what is concerning you? Or is *that* what's concerning you?"

Vivian shifted how she sat on the bed to face Rook more directly. She took his hands into both of hers and looked at them.

"You don't remember us," she said, "how we met or..." She met his eyes again. "Or why Luther's words were so important to us that we left the old church together?"

Rook's mind tumbled through all of the differences between Catholicism and Lutheranism that he could think of. Ceremony? Status? Wealth? That was a big one, he knew. Lutherans didn't like how the church hoarded wealth. But that wasn't it.

"Were we to be married?" Rook asked, his voice threatening to stick the words in his throat as he felt a pang of shame.

Vivian didn't respond at first. She only let her eyes drop back down to their hands. Rook let the moment continue, both for himself as well as for her.

"You are different now," she said. "You ask for beer instead of wine. You wait for me before you eat. You *sound* different—you talk like an Englishman sometimes."

Vivian returned her gaze.

"You don't look at me like you used to. You're so-"

"Different," Rook said, his eyes falling away from her.

"Nicer," Vivian said and then gripped his hands.

Rook looked at her.

"I'm afraid that's all going to change again," she said, her eyes misting over. "It hurts right now that you don't remember us, but I-" Vivian wiped her eyes and then continued. "But I hope you stay like this. Get better like this."

Rook blinked. He felt a terrible sadness for Vivian and could not fathom what she was going through. He was confused as to why she would so willingly let go of her past with Isaac and support what was essentially an impostor in his place. He also felt a tinge of fear and uncertainty at what else he didn't know beyond this room. As he looked over Vivian's face, he reached up and, with a tremoring finger, wiped a tear from her cheek.

"I don't remember anything about us," he said, "but I will remember you right now, like this. It will get me through. And maybe, on the other side of it, we can connect again."

Vivian smiled at him.

"Alright," she said, wiping her eyes again and standing, "enough of that. Let's get you some food."

Rook smiled at her as she turned and walked away.

With a broom in hand, Rook swept along the floor, trying

to get dirt and leaves into a central location. It was no longer a matter of getting the body to respond; he and it were now perfectly in sync but more of a matter of negotiating the debris to cooperate. The dirt was one thing, falling in line more-or-less where he had shoved it with the broom bristles; it was the leaves that were vexing him. The church the Lutherans had converted into a base of operations was drafty, and the frequent comings and goings of the so-called "missionaries" brought in a lot of turbulence and filth, making the leaves jump and dance.

The nave of the church had been converted into a personnel space. Though Rook had observed the Lutherans worshiping and revering Christ on the cross, the church had no real room for them to live and store their stolen relics other than where the pews had once been. They had long since been ripped out and re-purposed elsewhere, and this area now housed beds, trunks, and crates.

As Rook cleaned around the crates, he noticed a ledger sitting on one and picked it up. It was written in High German and denoted rough descriptions of the items the Lutherans had acquired and where they were sent to. Rook didn't see anything from his own monastery on the list; the ledger was too new for anything that was acquired months ago, but he could tell what they were being used for. Most were being sent to other Lutheran centers across the region, while a few were being directly fenced with buyers. In those cases, a value was written in and presumably collected. Rook's stomach sank as he looked through the ledger and put it down, trying to contain his disgust.

The doors to the church opened, and the raiding party returned. Several men, a few Rook recognized from the raid on his own monastery, entered carrying sacks and with handfuls of loose paper in their hands. Once they crossed the threshold, men and women who inhabited the space came to relieve the raiders of their loot.

Vivien walked up behind Rook and reached past him to grab the ledger. She met eyes with him and smiled as she took it and fished a charcoal stick out of her cloak. She then hurried over to where new relics were deposited. She began to mark new entries into the ledger and dig through the items.

Rook held his breath and bowed his head, counting the seconds until his emotions settled. Gripping the broom handle a bit too tight, he resumed his cleanup and turned his back on Vivien to focus on a new area.

"Listen up," one of the men called out, "we come with news." He began to hand out a sheet of the bundled papers to each who came up to him, and as he walked past, Rook was handed one as well. He took it and looked it over. It was printed, which was something of a marvel to Rook. Rather than being hand-written, some machine made this copy, and presumably all the other copies being handed out. He looked up at them all, trying to reconcile the feat in his head.

"Luther denounces the uprisings," the man said, holding up his copy, "says that those who take up arms against other Christians are protestant to his and their goals."

Rook put down the broom and looked back at his copy. It had a title, *Against the Murderous, Thieving Hordes of Peasants.*

"He says we are sinners and that we cloak these terrible and horrible sins with the gospel. That we are the worst blasphemers of God!" The man said as he passed out a few more.

Several of the others gasped and whispered amongst themselves. Rook, who saw the man's paraphrased words in writing on the paper in his hand, read it over twice more before he looked and spoke up.

"So, we are to stop all this?" Rook asked. Vivien gave Rook a nervous look.

"What? No!" the man said as he snaked an arm around Rook's shoulder. "Luther just publicly denounces us. As he should."

Another of the raiders laughed and chimed in.

"Are you kidding, Isaac? We're funding the Reformation."

Rook looked between the men and back down at the paper.

"Luther has to denounce us," the man holding Rook said, "it wouldn't benefit the movement to back the revolts forever."

The man looked out at the people around them.

"Though," he continued, "we are not too fond of the fact he's siding with the aristocracy so quickly, but he's got to make a show of it."

"And that does not bother you?" Rook asked.

"Why should it? He's no saint. He's not Christ. Says it himself."

"But, does not he lead us?" Rook asked.

All eyes fell on Rook. He stammered, panic rising in his chest.

"I-I mean, do we not follow what he says?"

"Isaac," said the man holding Rook as he took his arm away, "you haven't been quite right since that old man got the better of you. I guess it's expected that you get confused. But on this?"

Rook's mind raced. He searched it, desperately trying to conjure up some thought, image, or miracle that could get him out of this.

"Right, no," Rook said, clearing his throat, "what I meant to say was: does Luther writing this change things for us?"

The man smiled and patted Rook on the shoulder.

"No, not really. This is the job until the Catholics start sharing their wealth and realize Grace belongs to the people." He turned and faced the crowd. "As Luther says, 'the destruction of the world is to be expected every hour,' and so we should be ready to face it. To go before God knowing we did all we could to let the people know His Word."

The people, the ones here at least, agreed and said as much, taking their copies of Luther's words and returning to their duties. Rook looked back at the one in his hand and read over more of the words. *They are starting a rebellion, and are violently robbing and plundering monasteries and castles which are not theirs*, he read. Rook gripped the paper.

Vivien brought Isaac's boots to Rook. She placed them before him as he was pulling his outdoor cloak over his head. Smoothing out his hair, she sat beside him on the bed.

"You don't have to go with them," she said, a look of worry in her eyes.

"I think I do," Rook said, reaching down to fit on a boot.

"It's time," a man said, walking past them to join a posse that was forming. He stopped just long enough to narrow his eyes at the two and speak. "Issac's been with you women folk for long enough. He needs to get back out there and work for the church."

Rook put on the second boot and looked at Vivien.

"It's all work for the church, Otte," Vivien snapped back, but Otte had already left.

"It's alright, Vivien," Rook said, touching her arm. "I

need to prove my worth again."

"You could just stay unwell," Vivien said, "say that you are never going to recover and need to stay here."

"I think that if I don't rejoin the raids, I will be kicked out. And you with me if you stand beside me on that." He gripped her arm. "It's okay. I can do this."

Vivien nodded and leaned in to kiss Rook on the forehead.

"Be careful? Please?" she said.

"I will."

Rook rose and turned away. He adjusted the cloak and walked over to the rest of the raiders. There, Otte handed him a sword and scabbard, and a torch. Rook fastened the scabbard to his belt and took the torch. Otte looked him over.

"No more seizures, right?" Otte asked, not really caring to hear the answer.

"Not for months," Rook responded.

"Mmhm. Your sword hand better be good. If it's even the same one."

The doors to the church opened, and Rook could see a gathering of horses on the other side. Otte patted Rook on the back and then shoved him forward, forcing Rook to step outside with the rest of the raiders. There, he was handed a horse, which he mounted when he saw the others doing the same. He steadied it as best he could, being out of practice with the animal, but he managed to get it facing the same direction as the rest.

Otte mounted his horse and maneuvered it to the front of the pack. With a quick glance at the rest of the group, he reared his horse up and then galloped down the path away from the church. The rest of the posse followed one by one. Rook along with them.

For hours, they rode. They crossed the countryside and followed the well-worn trade routes that lined the coast. As they traveled, Rook tried to piece together where they were, but the lands seemed unfamiliar. The signs, too, were also no longer his to recognize; the Middle German town names were replaced with High German, and with new names altogether. Though Rook had lived in Germany for decades, he never had cause to leave the monastery, and his lack of knowledge was showing.

They arrived at a village, remote and set near a northern stretch of land where the air was always cold, and frost touched everything. The water of the sea nearby carried the cold from the north, and Rook could see that the village's main harvest was fish from the abundance of nets and spears. With no harvesting tools or grain sheds, Rook guessed that this village depended on trade to survive.

Otte stopped at the outskirts and dismounted. The others followed his lead, with Rook following up and doing the same. Otte handed his horse off to Rook, who looked at what the others were doing with theirs. He tied his horse off to a hitching post along with them. Otte took out his torch and lit it. Rook did the same, as did the rest of the party.

"Someone keep an eye on Isaac," Otte said, turning toward the village. "It's our brother's first time back in nearly a year." He looked back over his shoulder. "Let's not keep them waiting."

Otte rushed in, torch raised, and dashed toward one of the closest thatch-covered housings. He pressed his torch into the dead leaves, and though the cold plant matter resisted the flame momentarily, a fire soon caught and spread over the roof. Rook saw the rest of the group fanned out to do the same, each choosing a new building or helping a brother with any not catching straight away.

Rook's torch burned, but he couldn't bring himself to light anything. He followed several of the Lutherans as they pushed deeper into the village, but he was in shock at what he was seeing. He heard an alarm bell ring out and looked to see where it was coming from. A stone church sat in the far reaches of the village with a friar pulling on a rope just outside the church doors. But between Rook and the church were the people of the village, emerging from their housings to take in the burning of their entire lives. Rook's hands shook as he saw some of the Lutherans pull swords and slash at the residents. Just like before, Rook relived what he saw in Niedam.

Cries filled the air as the Lutherans pressed on. Though their target was ultimately the church, they were sure to take the fight out of the peasantry before they reached it. They set alight nearly every structure in their path and cut down any who revolted against them. Though a few villagers denounced the Catholic church and thus were spared, none were trusted, and all were forced to retreat and huddle in what buildings the Lutherans saw fit to leave standing.

Blood pooled in the divots and depressions of the dirt roads. Rook could see the reflection of the fires in the cooling sanguine streams. Stumbling, Rook reached out to steady himself against one of the buildings, forgetting that it was ablaze, and nearly threw himself into the flames. When he looked inside the building, he could see the remains of a family inside, roasting into ash under the fire.

Then Rook saw the impossible. He saw, mingling with the white smoke of the fire, dark wisps of mist rising off the bodies. He watched, clutching his chest with one hand, as the spirits of the dead rose from their bodies. He shook his head in disbelief. But as he looked out over the village, Rook saw the same apparitions starting to appear, coming out of homes and filling the streets.

"Why, God?" Rook whispered. "Why do I see them now? When in the flesh? When I can do nothing?!"

Rook threw up and fell to his knees. At this moment, it wasn't his body rejecting him; it was him rejecting everything he was seeing. He tried to rip off his cloak and tear off his sword, but with the bloody dirt on his trembling hands, he couldn't work to get them off. He heard more cries as the screaming intensified, the Lutherans facing their biggest resistance as they neared the church, and the sound caused him to weep.

The blazing heat suddenly felt cold to Rook. The copper in his nose was replaced with an earthly scent. He shivered to the core. When he looked up for the source, he witnessed the arrival of Azrael. Gliding in on black, feathered wings, the angel of death touched down at the edge of the village. He brandished his scythe and began a slow march forward. As inevitable as death itself, Azrael walked through fire and flame to touch the spirits of the dead, absorbing each in turn. He paid no heed to Rook as he passed him.

Rook scrambled to his feet. He followed the angel as it made a path in the wake of the destruction the Lutherans had caused. Azrael touched the wraiths that lingered on, absorbing them into his hand. He gestured and pulled in those that were a distance away. He passed his hand over the ones that were disappearing or sinking into the ground. He ignored the ones that departed immediately. And, rarely, he slashed his weapon at the ones that turned rabid and sought to attack each other or the living.

Azrael stopped before a building, turned slowly, and stepped inside. Rook could see through the deteriorating walls the angel approaching a body writhing on the floor. The man had been stabbed and had been burned to char along most of his body. There was no possible way for him to be still alive, and yet, he gurgled out screams of pain as he refused to die. Azrael towered over him and knelt. He reached out, his skeletal hand passing through the charred flesh until he took hold of something. Pulling his hand back out, Rook could see Azrael grasping the soul of the man, which was then let go. Azrael seemed to wait for it to make a decision, and when it decided to give up and descend, Azrael stood and resumed his journey to the church.

Rook ran after. As Azrael entered the church, Rook followed, but the was nowhere to be seen. The church was simple. It was not a grand cathedral like he had seen in England or Munich. It was smaller, just a nave and altar and a room off to either side. What struck Rook was the cross on the altar. It was metal, thick, silver, and black. It stood taller than himself and looked as though it was forged, much like a container to hold something. Rook looked around the church and found no sign of Azrael nor of the Lutherans. Instead, he only saw the friar and a couple of the villagers huddled just off the altar in a back corner of the room.

As Rook approached, the friar held up his hands and pleaded.

"No, please," he said, the villagers clutching his robes, "we have nothing. We collect no coin, keep no gold."

"Ah, there you are," Otte's voice came from over Rook's shoulder. Rook turned to see him covered in soot and blood, his blade crusted with both.

Otte looked Rook over and judged the dirt, smoke, and blood on him to be acceptable of a raider.

"I was afraid you'd suffered another beating by an old man," Otte chuckled, "good to see I was mistaken." He pointed his sword at the friar. "Finish them off so we can get this reliquary cross out of here."

Rook looked at Otte, his hand shaking as he reached for his sword. He looked at the friar, the cross, and then down at his hand.

"Why hasn't he taken me?" Rook said to himself.

"Taken you where?" Otte asked.

Rook unsheathed his sword and looked at the friar. He turned toward Otte and slashed at him, slicing through his neck and sending blood splattering into the cross. Otte clutched his throat and fell to his knees, his own sword falling uselessly out of his hand.

Rook watched Otte choke and bleed out. He dropped his sword, raised a finger, and made the sign of the cross.

"Oh, Lord," Rook muttered, "forgive these sinners, for they know not what they do in your name. Forgive them for sending these faithful to your embrace."

"I-Isaa," Otte coughed as he fell forward, the hand steadying him quickly coated in his own blood.

"And forgive me, Heavenly Father, as I take his life. I do it to stop his evil, and I give myself in return for my sin."

Otte collapsed. Rook backed up. He watched, waiting for Otte's soul to rise from his body. He glanced at the friar and two villagers as they remained stunned into silence but returned his eyes to the corpse when he saw the black smoke beginning to rise. When it had fully formed and hovered over the body, Rook approached it again.

"Don't go. Don't you dare go," Rook said, challenging the wraith to defy the pull.

"Come! Come Azrael, we await you!" Rook yelled, turning and pointing an open hand at the wraith as if in offering. "Take us!"

The wraith hovered for a moment longer but began to sink. Rook reached out for it, but it passed through his fingers and descended into the ground. Enraged, Rook kicked the body and smashed through the candles and ostensorium that were placed on the altar. The friar and villagers took advantage of the break in Rook's focus to run out, fleeing through the burning side room near them. Rook ignored them. He grabbed the communion chalice that remained on the altar and shoved it into Otte's body, scooping up his blood. Spitting in it, he flung the contents onto the reliquary box, covering it in muck and blood. He then flung the chalice at it, and when it bounced harmlessly off, he raised a leg and kicked the altar.

The reliquary cross toppled from the altar and smashed onto the ground. Rook straddled it and pried it open. Inside it was a dried, mummified hand. Rook took his torch and stuck it against the flesh, which blazed almost instantly. Backing away, watching the holy flesh burn, Rook looked around the church.

"This is not a gift," he yelled at the ceiling, "you gave me false hope! False power! Lies! Come take them back!"

Rook looked around, stepping over his own feet.

"Is this not the power of God?!" he screamed. "Or is this Lucifer's work?"

He gestured to the burning hand.

"Peccatum mortale! I Sin Unto Death! Come! I invite the wrath of God!"

Rook panted. He looked across the ceiling, waiting for his inevitable end, to be struck down by God himself for his blasphemy. But nothing happened. He turned to each of the corners of the church, arms outstretched, but none held an angel or demon to take him. Even the angel of death had been gone for a while and had not returned.

"Isaac!" someone yelled. Rook turned to see several of the Lutherans enter the church and survey the scene. Rook dropped his torch. The Lutherans drew their swords. Rook bolted for the burning side room, hoping the friar knew something about it that had let him escape earlier and would do the same for him now. Thankfully, he was right, and the room was mostly stone, a kitchen, and nothing impeded Rook from breaking out into the night air.

Rook ran. And he did not stop.

For weeks, the hinterland regions bordering the North Sea served to keep Rook out of sight. The harsh winds and unpredictable storm tides that plagued the area regularly washed out roads and settlements that braved the coastline, and so only the most stalwart people dared to claim the land. For Rook, this meant the chances of coming across a Lutheran or anyone who would know Isaac's face were low enough to be safe. What Rook didn't account for was how he was going to survive in the unforgiving landscape.

Forced to subsist on the dead things that washed ashore or the livestock that broke free during a storm or were lost under hardship during travel, Rook managed to stay fed, though just barely. What food he could secure was tainted or diseased, and how to clean such things was a knowledge beyond his own. Shelter consisted of hiding in broken homesteads or abandoned livestock sheds, often using his Lutheran cloak as his only source of warmth. Soon, Rook began to feel the blight that pained his stomach and blotched his skin seep into his joints and dully ache in his body. When Rook developed a cough that produced a sickly discharge from his lungs, he knew he could no longer risk staying out in the cold, barren lands. He could only hope to reverse his sickness closer to a dryer, populated area.

The town of Husum was the closest permanent city to where Rook was. It carried with it a promise of food and shelter that Rook began to feel desperate for. He weighed that against the potential of being caught. But the time away from the Lutherans and his progressing ailment both dulled his fear of them, and Rook chose to set himself inland and pressed on toward the town.

As he closed in on the city and found a road to ease his travel in the final miles, Rook discarded his cloak and sword to the elements and stumbled ahead until his legs couldn't carry him any further. Rook fell to his knees just inside the city border, coughing up sick onto the dirt street. He was ignored as he crawled, dragging himself as much out of sight as he could down an alleyway. The people of the town barely registered the newest vagabond to join the rest.

However, Rook was not invisible to all eyes in Husum. Across the square from where Rook had crawled stood a man atop a makeshift barrel stage. Dressed in a brocade houppelande of white on red, red-hosed legs terminating in black, leather boots, and a black circular cloth hat, an aristocratic man of light skin and hair with blue eyes saw Rook disappear in between the buildings beyond the crowd that had generated before him.

The man's speech on Martin Luther and the Protestant uprising had drawn to him a gathering of war-minded individuals. He didn't speak out for or against the Protestant Reformation but instead for the merits of the unrest itself.

"Complacency," the man argued with authority, "is tantamount to facilitating the advancement of all that is evil in the world. The war rages on around us, and its effects have already begun to take hold. To ignore them is to invite destruction into thy heart! Make sure ye stand ready to fight for whatever cause you believe in. For know this; no Godly force will ever be able to forgive those who do not fight in His name."

The crowd was riled, and the man had accomplished his goal of stirring them up even more. But, when he saw the curious, out-of-place individual cross his eye-line, the man decided he had spoken enough and stepped off the stage. Shaking hands and nodding thanks to those in the crowd, he pushed through them and followed the wretch into the alleyway.

There, he saw Rook curled up and wedged against a building, coughing up phlegm and infection onto the dirt passageway. The man looked at Rook, a puzzled look on his fair-featured face, and approached him. Crouching beside him, the man reached out and touched Rook's back. Rook pulled away with a start, staring at the man he had only just became aware of.

"You are on the precipice of your demise," he uttered with a silky timbre, his words as inviting as nectar. "The contagion has taken over your lungs."

"Stay away from me," Rook wheezed, waving the man away. "Let me die in peace."

The man raised his eyebrows.

"If you had sought a solitary death, I surmise you would have abided on the shore."

Rook shielded his face and head from sight with his arm, but he stared at the man from under it. In return, the man peered closer, lowering his head to meet Rook's eyes. He smiled.

"I can help you."

"I-," Rook started, but then coughed hoarsely into the dirt, "I don't need it. Don't deserve it." He lowered his head more.

"Now, why would you say such a thing as that?" the man asked. He pulled up his houppelande from his leg and revealed a small pouch. He watched Rook as he took from it a strip of dried meat that he held in his hand.

Rook saw the meat, and, despite his sour stomach, he craved it. His eyes darted from it to the man's face and back again.

"You can have this," the man said, offering the meat. "It may not be a remedy for your current condition, but I expect its consumption may provide some respite, however brief, from your plight."

"What do you want?" Rook asked, suspicious.

"Only to talk," the man said. "Here." He handed the meat over to Rook, who shoved the whole thing in his mouth, grinding it between his teeth, keeping his eyes locked on the man.

"What is your story?" the man asked.

The meat did just as the man said. Though it was only a morsel, having it in his stomach eased his queasiness and even seemed to dull some of the pain. Swallowing the last of it, hands still at his mouth, Rook looked at the man and felt no less suspicion.

"Story?" Rook asked. "Why bother? I'm an outcast. Dying a deserved death."

"More deserved than the last one?"

Rook jolted away, pulling himself from the man who merely raised his hand away as Rook left his touch.

"Easy now," the man said.

"What do you know?" Rook asked, unfurling enough to look both ways down the alley and press himself against the building.

The man smiled again.

"I am well-versed enough to know that you are a devout one, is that correct? That your faith has waned? As though the Lord has rendered his verdict against you."

The man finally sat. He eased down onto the ground with his hands and then wiped them clean, appearing displeased with the dirt. But, he measured the movement to show Rook he wasn't there to pursue him. That he really did intend on just talking. He looked at Rook, who did not ease his tension.

"I know that your death is inevitable," the man said, gesturing at Rook, "and there is no future for that body." The man's smile widened ever so slightly. "You should acquire a new one presently."

Rook's eyes shot open. He fumbled over himself, trying to drag himself away from the man. He uttered a prayer out of habit, calling for a higher power to preserve him, but the words were only harsh whispers that made the man chuckle.

"Steady now, steady," spoke the man. "Yes, I am aware of your hidden truth. That you are a foreigner in this vessel of flesh. But I have no designs to press upon you. I simply wish to understand how you came to be allied with it."

"H-how?" Rook asked, forced to remain in place as his body failed any meaningful movement.

The man looked at Rook a moment.

"I've always had a special connection to the divine," the man said. "It allows me to peer into the depths of your being and behold the secrets you keep hidden from everyone else. You fascinate me more than any other I have come across, for I am positive that the spirit within you is not this body's own."

Rook thought about the man's words. He thought back to Cristof and how rare he thought the two of them were. But Rook had to admit that, while the two of them never came across another with their abilities, they had spent their entire lives sequestered in a monastery. There might have always been more like him. He just had not crossed paths with them. This eased Rook's fear, and he allowed himself to settle his nerves and lay his suspicions down for the moment.

"You don't want to know this," Rook said, "it's a blasphemous twisting of God's gift. I am shunned for it. Not even the angel of death sees fit to deliver me."

The man's eyes widened.

"You have seen the Tobit?"

"The-," Rook coughed a new sputtering fit, "the what?"

The man dismissed the question.

"What makes you think what you did was so sacrilegious?"

"How could it not be?" Rook asked, his chest burning. "God gave me the gift of walking among the dead, to commune with them and offer them absolution when no one else would be able to." Rook, having not spoken so much in weeks, strained to keep his breath in check to continue. "And I used it to steal life. To trade my death for another and live on in his skin. I am an abomination!" Rook spat out the word and fell into another bout of coughing.

The man waited for the noise to subside and offered a serene look as he turned toward Rook.

"What is your name, friend?"

Rook clutched his chest.

"Rook."

"Rook, let me tell you something that I think you need to hear," the man said, leaning his head down more to Rook's level. "That is not blasphemy. In fact, it is a clarion call from on high."

"How...how can you be so sure?" Rook asked, his body sliding along the wall to rest on his elbow as he continued to hold his chest.

"You are extraordinary, Rook. So incomparably special. If the Lord had not desired for you to inhabit this body, He would never have enabled it." The man's lips turned upward at the corners. "It is His divine intention, then, and it shall be your salvation, in due time."

The man turned his head to look down the alleyway at the people who passed the gap.

"And," he continued, "if you were to replicate the feat again now, it would simply serve as confirmation."

"No-n...no," Rook struggled to say as his eyes fluttered closed. He took in a deep, rasping breath. "I'll push their soul out... Send them...to their death."

The man looked back at Rook.

"Then, may I ask, are you not performing the divine labor? Do not all the souls displaced by your noble pursuits ascend to Him, perhaps even when they would have otherwise failed to do so?"

"M-m..." Rook could only mutter.

"Death is blissful, Rook," the man said, returning his gaze

to the passers-by. "For them, it is their purpose."

The man turned and got to his feet. He took Rook by the arm.

"It will be blissful for you, too, should you choose the path of death," he said. "However, your fate is to remain in this world." He propped Rook upright and knelt before him. "Reclaim another form, and so live on. If you would do this...," the man smiled again, "I will bestow upon you all knowledge you seek."

The words sunk into Rook's brain even as it was dying. Rook felt the cold creeping in and felt the euphoria rising like he did when he was so close to death before. That blissfulness terrified him, making the man's words ring even more true to Rook than he could deny. He felt his body take its last, labored breath and finally shut down, but Rook didn't drown within it. He released himself from it, rising through it and above it to watch the body collapse.

Free from the body, Rook could see again and saw the man speaking to a woman whom he had beckoned into the alleyway with him. The man pointed to Rook, and when the woman saw the dead body, she rushed over to administer aid. The man turned his back to the opening of the alley, facing the woman, and placed his hands on his hips, effectively blocking anyone from looking in on them. He looked up at Rook, who was shocked that he could be seen and could only reason that the man was telling the truth.

Rook felt the pull of death only a moment before he seized upon the woman, coming down upon her from above and sliding along her inner core. Unlike before, when Rook took a body out of panic, Rook, this time, wanted to ease the woman's transition and tried to pry her soul out gently. This only caused the woman to flail violently as every inch of her tried to reject the parasitic embrace. Rook realized his folly and changed his tact to break her out as fast as possible, sending her soul from her body beside them. Rook then looked for the remaining shard of soul that was the anchor to the body and seated himself on it, making the connection.

Rook screamed, pain wracking through the woman's body and mingling with his own consciousness. He felt the pain coming in waves as each inch of her body that he commandeered sent a fresh crash of agony on his soul. He felt her collapse, and he with it, as the muscles each lost control, one by one, as he tried to wrest it back. He remembered what happened when he lost focus before and refused to back away from completing his melding with the body. And, as if responding to his intent, the body allowed him to make the necessary connections to keep it alive. Rook breathed in a new breath after the scream subsided and lay in the alleyway as he slowly recovered.

The man watched, doing little to hold in his astonishment at what he was witnessing. He could see Rook's soul interacting with the woman's flesh and marveled at the thought of it. When he saw Rook break off the woman's soul, his eyes widened, and he took in the sight of it floating free from its body. When Rook's new lungs swelled up, the man raised a hand and stopped the sound of his —her— scream from reverberating beyond the alleyway. When the process was complete, he approached Rook, waving off the wraith like discarding trash, and grabbed the body from under her shoulder.

"Truths have a penchant for being unearthed when the ground is shaken and burned," the man said, whispering into Rook's new ear, "maybe a little fire of your own is in order."

The man pulled the woman up and flopped an arm over his shoulder to brace her on her feet. Her eyes slowly opened. She groaned. As if answering her, the man smiled.

"You can call me 'Nadir.'"

Chapter Eight

"The years have not been kind to you," Nadir said, lowering Rook down into a chair, "it is fortunate I came along when I did."

"Not that you'd fucking know," Rook grunted, spitting blood onto the ornate, lacquered hardwood floor that surrounded him. "You're fucking immortal? A cunting demon? Christ, after learning from you for five goddamn years, how the fuck did I miss that?"

Rook sat in one of a pair of large, Queen Anne chairs set before a grand inglenook marble fireplace. Gargoyles, grotesquely carved into the surface, stared down at him, judging. Mahogany was the color of choice for the room, the wood walls behind a grand array of Renaissance paintings being made of it, the marble colored to match it, and the paneling in the walls and ceiling both cut to resemble and resonate with it. What wasn't golden brown was dark red. The upholstery of the Queen Annes was a deep ox blood. The Persian rug the chairs sat upon was the color of dried blood. Even the fire in the fireplace seemed to burn with the darker brown and red tones that matched the Old Fashioned cocktails in the glasses Nadir held, one of which was offered to Rook.

"You could not have," Nadir said. "I am nothing if not skilled in managing information."

"Lying, you mean," Rook snapped, taking the drink with an arm that ached and fingers that could barely hold the glass.

"I have never," Nadir said. "That is below me. Everything I have ever told or shown you has been the truth, even if you could not accept or process it at the time." Nadir sat across from Rook in the mirrored Queen Anne and sipped his drink.

"Like your name? 'Nadir?' 'The lowest point.' How bloody daft was I not to catch on sooner?" Rook growled, gripping the glass. "No, pretentious, that's what it is! I couldn't see it through all your cunting pretentiousness."

Nadir sipped his drink again.

"I can see we will get nowhere until we address this, so go on, Rook, say it. Call me by any name that suits you so we can get on with the real, important matters at hand."

Rook attempted to adjust himself in the chair but found that one of his legs had been broken. He gritted his teeth through the pain, leveraging that anger against his companion. He sucked down a gulp of the whiskey, savoring its burn.

"Satan. My mentor in bloody body-stealing was Satan

himself."

"Not one of my favorite names, but yes."

Nadir's form shifted. Like the pulling of a veil from a corpse, the visage of Nadir fluttered away, revealing a face that was alien to Rook but was much more modern and contemporary in style. Nadir appeared as a man in his mid-thirties, with short, black hair, trimmed facial hair, and of mixed heritage, almost as if to illustrate how different from his previous form he could choose to be. Yet, the man was still beautiful.

Rook noticed something else, as well. Though he had never seen it before, in all his time with Nadir, he could see it now; an aura, just barely visible, surrounded him. It looked like a sunset radiating softly through his skin. Orange intermingling with red surrounded the body before him, and it did not change, even as Nadir's form did.

"I prefer Lucifer," he said, "though I am sure you know that. You were always quite good with your research."

Rook looked at his hand, searching it for an aura as well. What he saw wasn't orange. Instead, he emitted a hazy, gray color. It reminded Rook of an overcast morning sky. He slid his eyes back to Lucifer.

"Fine. Let's go with that. *Lucifer*."

"Great," Lucifer said, taking another sip of his drink before setting it on the arm of his chair. "With that out of the way, we can discuss-"

"What in the bloody hell?!" Rook interrupted. "What the actual fuck was that? A literal bleeding demon comes knocking to stomp my shit in, and my long-lost, silver-tongued 'mate' pops up and rips its throat out?! Just an hour ago, I was pouring through Enochian shite trying to find a trace of your bloody existence, and now I find out we were mates five hundred years past?"

Lucifer sat forward, crossing his hands in his lap.

"Rook, if you would let me-"

Rook threw his drink to the floor, interrupting Lucifer again.

"Mark's fucking dead," Rook growled. "If anyone deserved to be saved, *old friend*, it should have been him." Rook's words dripped with venom.

Lucifer looked at the broken glass and spilled reserve and then back to Rook.

"Rook, please."

"Go on, Lucifer," Rook said, leaning in as far as he could, sneering as he slowly spoke. "By all means. Answer my prayers."

Lucifer drew in a breath.

"You are being hunted," he began, "by both the Celestial Empyrean and the Infernal Sphere. They have taken notice of you and your unique ability. More so, they have noticed the damage you are causing when using it. They fear that if they do not stop you, you will destroy the one thing that keeps us all here, bound to this universe."

"Fucking right," Rook said, half in disbelief, "I threaten the universe. So, I'm the villain in your twisted tale?"

"Not mine, Rook," Lucifer said, raising an eyebrow as he sat up straighter. "Our goals are not so unaligned. When I met you in that ancient era, I knew you would one day upset the balance. You just needed to live and continue on in this world until you gained power enough to do it."

"So, I'm your bloody pawn now, is that it?" Rook snarled. "You played me. You're poison. In my ear when I was too much of a git to see it. And now you're here because I've strayed from the path you carved for me, and you think to set me back on it?"

Lucifer growled. His eyes changed. For a moment, Lucifer's irises shifted into snake-like slits ringed in orange. Rook saw this change and smirked, tilting his head forward and locking eyes with him.

"Go on, Lucy. Tell me I'm wrong."

Lucifer flicked a finger, and the broken whiskey glass mended itself, along with restoring the splattered liquid. He gestured and sent it back into Rook's hand. Though the act seemed, on the surface, to be benevolent, Lucifer did this while his body continued to transform, inviting the shadows of the room to blanket him as his skin lost its color and became translucent, his hair fled from him like smoke, and his eyes emitted a fiendish light. As Lucifer pointed, shoving the glass into Rook's battered hand, he smiled, the tip of his finger elongating into a blackened, sharp tip.

"You are wrong," Lucifer said. "If there was such a thing as a kindred spirit, Rook, you just might be mine."

Rook frowned. He scanned Lucifer from head to toe and back, noting he could still see his aura, and took a drink from the repaired glass.

"Calling the kettle black, eh? Forgive me if I don't swallow the bullshit of the King of Pride and Vanity," Rook spat, mocking Lucifer with a tipped glass in his direction.

"I am here," Lucifer said, his voice resonating deeper within him, "because you would not have survived that attack otherwise. And I will not have you condemned to eternity in a cage to be dissected by the Empyrean to cover up their mistakes, or have you thrown to the Agglomeration in some petty attempt by the Unholy to punish the Divine for their hubris."

Lucifer picked up his glass and looked at it, rotating it in his fingers before turning his attention back to Rook.

"I am here," he continued, "because none of us know what you are capable of, Rook. And to a system that was designed to control every one of us from inception to demise, not knowing is tantamount to chaos. Every agent beholden to the system, celestial or otherwise, fears you. Fears us. Together, we can pick it apart."

"I ain't working for you," Rook said, taking another

drink. "I can barely stomach being in the same room as you. What makes you think I'd want to throw my lot in with you?"

"It is already done. There is naught else for you to do but exist and grow stronger. I am not offering some deal or exchange to entice you; I do not proclaim to own your soul. I will merely inform you of your situation, give you some advice, and then sit back to watch you wreak beautiful havoc. We both know you ultimately want to burn the cosmos down, Rook. I offer nothing more than the opportunity to do just that."

Rook's broken leg reminded him of its state. It caused Rook to inhale through his teeth sharply. He took another sip, polishing off the Old Fashioned. He placed the glass purposefully on the arm of the chair.

"Alright, mate. Inform me."

"No doubt you have seen that Divine cannot track you when you take a new body," Lucifer said. "This is true for the Unholy, as well. They are not built for it. Their laws and their roles, it is like trying to find a lump of burning coal by listening for it to sizzle. They will not learn to look for the glow until it has already caught the wood on fire."

Lucifer helped Rook up out of the chair. He touched Rook's leg and took from it the pain, but he did not mend it. Rook grunted as he stood, nodding to Lucifer to acknowledge his words.

"You can stay here until ready; this house is warded, and nothing within these walls, including your presence here or the knowledge we exchange, can be detected from outside. But you must go soon, and you should take a new body at your earliest opportunity."

"On that, we both agree," Rook huffed. "Won't even heal my leg a little bit?"

Lucifer shook his head.

"I am afraid that is a cantrip too far. Influencing mortals leaves no trace; we are free to do that as we wish. But to impart a physical or mental change to one crosses into the realm of deal-making and leaves an imprint. The moment you leave this refuge, all it would take is for one celestial to notice that imprint and report it. Once all of the spheres become aware of it, a line will be drawn between you and me."

"Time and knowledge, they flow faster in the other spheres," Rook said. "Best not revealing your cards too soon."

"The lesson here is to manage the knowledge," Lucifer said. "Use it to your advantage. Do not reveal what you are capable of until you are sure you can leverage it. Send a message, but only when you are sure you are the one controlling the narrative."

"Right," Rook said, "so everyone knows what went down at the flat?"

Rook looked around the room and through a nearby window. The sun was high, illuminating the lawn out front. He could see a wrought iron fence and gate surrounding what had to be a larger estate that he could only see the corner of. Of more concern to Rook was that the sun was shining. It was just past midnight.

"If it was revealed, yes. Though that demon did not know I intervened, he will most assuredly tell of how you damaged him and your clever use of Mark's wraith. He will not know what killed him, but he will suspect you accomplished that somehow. Secrets exist, but knowledge transfers at the speed of light."

Rook hobbled toward Lucifer's liquor cabinet and opened it. He looked through the offerings of high-end labels and settled on pulling a bottle of Johnnie Walker Blue. He poured out a double into a glass tumbler and then downed the whole drink. He gasped as the burn hit him.

"Speaking of which," Rook said as he turned toward Lucifer, "there's this new trick I can do now."

"Oh?"

"But this stays between us."

"Absolutely."

"Good. Because I don't know how I got it." He gestured with the empty glass at Lucifer. "I can see your aura. Kind of."

"Aura?" Lucifer raised an eyebrow.

"Yeah. You're all orange and red. I got this gray." Rook

raised his hands and looked at them, tracing his aura along his arms. "Can't see it unless I really focus, but ever since you brought me here, it's been there."

"Hmm," Lucifer thought. "We call the Original Souls 'gray souls' because we can see their color as such. It is how I knew you were not in your original body when we first met. Humans are black, normally." Lucifer shifted his appearance to a fully human persona. "But if you can still see it now, then this means you can see the Infernal in me and potentially see the realm of origin of any celestial."

"Yeah, but how'd I get it?"

"When you absorbed Mark."

Rook paused for a moment and then set the glass down on the cabinet shelf.

"Right."

"His power added to your own, which is why you must absorb all the wraiths you can—even the ones who have long been dead. Do what the Tobit carelessly chooses not to do and reap them into yourself. Each will elevate you, and whether they impart on to you a new power or you achieve them through sheer accumulation, this will be the key to your ascension."

"Right. Let's go."

Lucifer walked over to Rook.

"Are you sure?"

"More than sure," Rook sneered.

"Where would you like me to take you?"

"Take me back to the flat. You forgot my coat."

The midnight black of the cold night air filled Mark's ruined apartment. The wind kicked up, billowing out what remained of the curtains that once framed the apartment's windows. This rush of invisible force peaked, and as though riding upon it, Rook emerged from the gaping maw in the apartment wall and stepped onto the carpet. Lucifer pulled himself through just after, his giant, leathery, orange wings receding into his back and from view.

Rook took slow steps about the room, looking at the tossed debris and overturned furniture. He looked at Mark's body and the blood that covered it. He saw the welts upon it that did not have enough time to form bruises before he died. He saw how the eyes were still open, looking lifelessly out at nothing. Rook turned away and set himself to the task of looking for his coat.

Lucifer gazed at Mark's body and then over to Rook, watching him pull at the overturned remnant of the couch that stood as a barrier to the closet door. Rook's body, as conditioned as it was from the police officer's efforts, was in too poor a state to leverage the strength needed to move the blockage. Lucifer approached and, with barely a motion, shifted the mass by telekinetic command, enough for Rook to get through. Rook opened the door and retrieved the Spector. Despite the chill, he folded it over his arm.

"I am sorry for your loss," Lucifer said as he knelt beside Mark. He reached out and closed his eyes.

Rook stepped over Mark's body, passing Lucifer. He returned to the section of the living room where the table had been, looking around at the torn and scattered remains of the ancient scroll and the other old books. Rook bent over and picked up a section Mark had blacked out partially and turned it over in his hand. He touched the text Mark had reacted to before and felt nothing.

"Anything worth knowing in this mess?" Rook said, his back to the body.

Lucifer looked at Rook and stood up. He looked at the scroll along with the other works and shook his head.

"Nothing relevant to your quest, no," he said. "Malakut is no longer the realm of the dead. Nothing written there is current." Lucifer studied Rook again. "Nothing in that text, nor Malakut, can repair you."

Rook tossed the scroll fragment before him. It fell lazily to the floor and settled next to the Matte Blvck album cover that had somehow made it across the room. Rook picked it up. He looked for and found that the record was in pieces, only this sleeve was still whole.

Lucifer's ear twitched, and he looked toward the door to

the apartment.

"Mortals approach. Emergency crews. I will take you to the ground level."

"No," Rook said, staring at the album cover. "Do something else for me."

"What would you like?"

Rook turned and handed the album cover to Lucifer.

"Put him where he can hear this music, just like Mark loved. Don't let him rot in some hole."

"There is nothing in this shell-"

"I know," Rook said, looking at Lucifer, "please."

Lucifer nodded as the album cover faded from his hand. As Rook turned away and headed for the broken wall between the apartments, Lucifer knelt and took up Mark's body.

"And we ain't done, you and I," Rook said over his shoulder.

"I know," Lucifer smirked. The Unholy one flickered from sight, taking Mark's body with him.

Rook laughed to himself and shook his head as he knelt and then lay prone with his back on the floor. As he positioned himself to appear as crumpled and tossed as he could, he thought back to a similar moment.

"It's like being back in the war," he said.

Rook relaxed and fixed his eyes on a point on the wall. He remained motionless as he heard the crew shouting at each other and barging through doors along the complex's hallway. When he heard them getting closer, Rook let his body go and pulled himself from it, rising above and floating toward the ceiling. Almost instantly, the body began to die, Rook's sheer will no longer sustaining it after it would have given up otherwise. Subconsciously, Rook began to count the seconds.

1, 2, 3, 4...

The door to the apartment burst open, splinters of the frame shooting outward as the lock shredded the wood from the impact. Two people, dressed in fire protection gear, pulled back on the handles to their battering ram, settling it between them. One of them let go of the tool and entered the apartment. The other hefted the weight back up and moved down to the next door.

9, 10, 11, 12...

Rook hovered close to the firefighter as he walked through the entryway, surveying the scene. The firefighter pulled on the closet door, looked inside, and then went into the kitchen area. When he entered the living room, he looked through the missing wall out into the night sky. He reached up and squeezed the communication device strapped to his shoulder.

"Located the source of the impact," he announced. "Twelve twenty-one. Proceeding inside."

The radio crackled a response. The man turned, saw the hollowed-out wall between the apartments, and squeezed his radio again.

"And twelve twenty-three."

The firefighter then saw the battered policeman's body.

"Civilian spotted," he said into his device as he ran over. "Appears unconscious. Send in medical, administering first aid."

26, 27, 28, 29...

The firefighter knelt next to the body and looked it over, checking for obvious breaks or any indication the body couldn't be moved. His helmet-mounted torch illuminated the body's gnashed leg and bruised neck, and the firefighter reacted by reaching for his CPR mask and bag and positioning it over the body's mouth.

"Sir, if you can hear me, I am going to provide CPR until the paramedics arrive. Please give me any indication you can hear me." He then squeezed the bag, forcing air into the lungs of the dead man.

Rook slowly willed his hand into a long glittering whip. He watched as the firefighter worked on the body, but Rook focused on seeing the man's aura. Through his gray-and-blue spectral sight, Rook could see darkness suffused throughout his form, wisps of it blending into the air around him like a shadow on a moonlit night. It was distinctive to Rook, blending a shade of black he could never see before in this form.

Rook couldn't focus his vision on the aura. Despite seeing

it, it was still formless, and he couldn't use what he saw to pinpoint where the soul was, as though it was an optical illusion that defied scrutiny. But Rook didn't need to see it to know where his quarry was. He reached back and flung out his hand, wrapping a length of the whip around the man's body. Unlike when Rook lashed at the demon, he didn't will the shards of glass to be on edge like razor-wire. Instead, he made his weapon smooth this time, allowing it to pass freely through the man's flesh to lasso his spectral core.

45, 46…

Rook wrenched back his arm and ripped from the man his wraith. Without a cough, without even an added breath, the fireman's body collapsed on top of Rook's old one. But, despite being as clean and quick as Rook had ever forced a soul out, the wraith immediately began to crack and buckle like all the others. Rook wasn't concerned; he didn't smoothly execute the man to preserve his wraith somehow. He did it to be efficient.

As the wraith broke and fractured, Rook expanded his form and retracted his arm, reeling the wraith into Rook's grinding, saw-toothed mass. He devoured it, like he had Mark's, and shattered its pieces to mingle them with his own, the glass becoming indistinguishable among the rest of his shards.

Rook felt his power swell. He felt it like an increase in mass, weightless as it was, as though each new shard carried potential energy, just waiting to be released, multiplying with the rest. With two full wraiths consumed since his last attempt, Mark's and now this fireman's, Rook wondered what this next part was going to feel like as he looked at the fireman's body.

60...

He dove into it, forcing himself through its limbs and attaching himself to the Animus. He locked himself in place and began his usual procedure, dominating the body's rejection response and restarting its heart and lungs. Within moments, Rook screamed, seizing control and melding with the body faster than he had ever before.

The merging wasn't immediate, but it was fast enough now that by the time the firefighters had breached the neighboring apartment and found him huddled over his old body, Rook had enough control to jerk his new body into following basic commands. He could reach for and replace the CPR mask onto his old body and squeeze it. He could stuff his Spector under his arm. He could stand and brace himself against the wall when the paramedics arrived. And he could lumber down the hallway and flights of stairs into the throng of emergency responders. He moved like a man fatigued, which no one saw as strange.

Firefighters, police, and paramedics had flooded the streets around the apartment complex. The flashing lights of their vehicles were dwarfed by the construction lights they had installed along the sidewalk, aimed up at the hole in the side of the building twelve floors up. Rook looked up to see the damage from his fight with the demon. He wondered how the story would be spun by local media. As if reminding himself, Rook looked and saw no reporting outlets or obvious cameras on the scene yet. He took it as an opportunity to blend in with the other firefighters until he could stash his Spector under a sidewalk trashcan and make it to one of the fire engines, open the door, and get inside.

Rook left the body. The firefighter slumped forward in the cab as if he had fallen asleep, and Rook passed through the metal of the vehicle out into the night sky. He marveled at his speed, able to cross a distance faster and with less effort than he ever could before as an untethered wraith. Within a moment, he had crossed several London city blocks and, in another, had left the neighborhood entirely. The commotion of the apartment building was far beyond his enhanced sight or hearing.

Rook slowed and looked around at the facades of the modern corporate buildings in the area. He had entered the business sector, and it was mostly deserted. Several unhoused individuals lie with thick blankets tucked in the nooks and corners of a few buildings' alcoves, but the population, as far as Rook could see, was fewer than a handful. He came in close to one of these individuals and looked them over. Though Rook couldn't smell, he assumed the worst of the individual and turned away. In the back of his head, the seconds had ticked by, but Rook felt in no hurry to claim a body that he felt was unworthy just yet.

Something electrified his remaining senses. Rook could hear a crackling, almost tearing sound that came from the end of the street, more than a block away. He looked and watched as the space just above the street warped and stretched. It contorted upon itself into a convex shape and then split as three humanoid figures emerged through the fissure. Behind them was an alien landscape. Clouds of red and purple swirled above the intruders, a field of black sparkling sand and blue billowing trees behind them. Two of the figures appeared masculine, one feminine, but all wore the silver armor of their divine station. These three were dressed for reconnaissance, the silver covering only their chests, forearms, and shins. At their sides, instead of swords, they had attached silver hilts without blades.

The rift behind them closed, knitting together seamlessly. With the brightness of the other realm obscured, Rook could see the figures more clearly, the humanness of their faces. He almost believed they were human until he could see the flair of their auras, a shimmering azure like a clear summer sky. They spotted him despite his lack of a body. They had merely scanned the roads before them when they pinpointed him.

"There!" the woman shouted.

The three brandished wings, white feathered expanses,

and took to the air. They rushed directly toward Rook.

"Look how he glistens!" shouted one of the men, who overtook the others as he closed the distance.

Rook turned and fled. He didn't pick a direction, just away from them. He shot like a bullet, flying through buildings in his way and the open spaces between them so quickly he could no longer hear his pursuers' shouts. He changed directions, no mass stopping his choice of trajectory, and flew as fast as sound across the city. When he looked back, he was shocked to see the angels on his trail no further than they were before, their pursuit homing in on him.

Rook bolted through another residential neighborhood. Passing through the buildings and dodging the people, Rook tried to evade the angels. Though the buildings provided barriers they had to avoid, their speed eclipsed Rook's, and they were quickly back on his trail at any open space. They, too, had to dodge the people, but the angels were too agile to be concerned.

Rook fumbled. Watching his hunters caused Rook to misjudge the distance between him and a human. He clipped one, a fragment of his wraith slicing through their soul. The collision knocked Rook to the side and caused the person to drop to their knees before they were out of his sight, but the contact caused the angels to shriek and slow, covering their eyes. They lost sight of Rook and shot up into the sky to regain their bearings.

Rook began to feel a pang of panic. He had been out of a body too long. He no longer had any idea of how many seconds had passed. He felt a pressure working against him, tugging him down and slowing him. It was light but noticeable, and it signaled something worse. Rook had to find a body now. He had no time to weigh options.

"There! That Fractured," a male voice from above shouted, "it's him!"

"*Allar Cocasb!*" the female yelled.

Rook turned, hoping to choose another escape route, when he saw the third angel behind him. Before he could process what he was seeing, the angel screamed and strained his body, his every muscle twitching from the sheer tension. It dawned on Rook just a moment too late what the female said as she commanded this angel to burn his own life source to slow the passage of time for Rook. The male angel's eyes gushed with blue blood, splattering the ground under him as he gritted his teeth to maintain the spell Rook understood to be "bind time."

Rook could not wrench himself free of the enchantment. He was slowed, but the pull of the underworld tugged on him even harder; it was all he could do to hold himself in place and not succumb to it. The other angels landed on either side of Rook, their commander removing something from a pouch. She unfolded a semi-solid mesh square and tossed it into the air. She pointed at it, and it unfolded more, glowing blue, forming a net.

"The Agglomeration is pulling on him," she said, "hold."

The angel raised her finger, and the net hovered over Rook. As she lowered her finger, the net descended.

Rook let go and sank to the ground. He let the pull take over for just a moment, enough to drag him to the earth, enough for the net to flop onto the concrete. He steeled himself again, knitting his form tightly, balling up, and stopping his fall. The pull didn't cease, but he defied it. It was enough to allow him to move again, and he pushed himself forward and from the earth. He jetted into the air again, making a dash for the nearest warm body. The angels dashed along with him.

The commotion brought the curious out of their homes, and Rook targeted a group that had gathered. They were stunned at the sight of these winged creatures, motioning the sign of the cross and not thinking to run. In the second that was allowed to him, he chose one at random, a woman near the center of the group. He smashed into her, ejecting her soul, grabbing it, and taking it into himself as he anchored into her body. He devoured her soul, dismantling her while taking over her body.

The angels dove into the crowd, driving them all to the ground with a buffet, but then yelled in frustration again. They covered their eyes and turned their backs to the group. Rook's act of predation somehow blinded them, and they reeled from it. Something about them couldn't process the soul's destruction before them, and their celestial bodies wholly rejected it. When they could see again and looked into the crowd, they couldn't see Rook's wraith anymore, nor could they see any other indication of where he was. All the humans had fallen prone on the sidewalk, writhing from the impact, moaning, screaming, and lamenting the coming of angels for their sins.

The angels began combing through the crowd, picking up a human each and inspecting them. The angels uttered incantations on each they touched, causing them to fall into a deep sleep, terrifying those who witnessed. They couldn't scramble to their feet fast enough to evade the angels, who brought the wrath of God down upon them, at least in their minds. Rook relied on the distraction the other humans provided, using the seconds they gave him to lock in his control of the woman's body. He waited until one of them selected him, grabbing him by the neck and pulling him from the sidewalk.

As his new body rose into the air, Rook fell from it, appearing like a ghostly afterimage of the body in motion. The angel raised the body up, seeing a moment too late Rook's wraith partially hovering outside of it. It registered this just before a blast scorched his face.

Remembering how he had concussed the demon before, Rook whipped up his shards into a frenzy and flung them forward. But, unlike that impactful blast in the apartment, the power unleashed a torrent of spectral energy and glass that spewed like a fire hose, slicing the angel's face. The eruption of power startled Rook but also debilitated the angel, who had to drop the woman and hold his face as he screamed. Blue blood gushed from his wounds as he stumbled away.

The other male angel advanced, lunging forward and striking out at Rook. He dodged the fist but let his Anima lash out a whip that wrapped around the angel's arm and raked broken glass along it, opening up gaping wounds and spilling more blue blood. The angel reeled back, clutching his arm and yelping in pain.

Rook turned toward the female angel who drew her silver hilt from her waist. She gripped it, activating a long, slender blade that extended impossibly from within it. As she brought it to her side, the edge of the blade began to glow with a blue energy that ignited into blue flames.

"Give up, broken," she said, squaring off. "Your actions are pointless. Your fate is inevitable."

Rook readied opposite her, circling the angel and her companions that drew in closer. His eyes darted between the three of them. He could see the wounds he had inflicted beginning to knit, their celestial flesh healing.

"Is it, mate?" Rook growled. "I kicked that demon's arse back to Hell. Don't test I can't send you cunts into the light, too."

The angel sneered.

"The beast sought to kill you. We will only contain you," she said.

"You ignored me," Rook spat, his voice dripping with venom. "Then, you turned your back on me. Then you fucking broke me!" Rook's Anima flared, rising like glittering mist above his body. "And now that I'm bloody well relevant, you cunts seek to kill or lock me down?"

The other angels drew and armed their weapons.

"You don't matter," the female scoffed. "You are just the fulcrum upon which the balance can tip. You will be removed, that balance restored."

"Balance?! What a load of bollocks. You're defending something that doesn't give two shits about you, Acolyte. You're even more useless than you claim I am."

The angel roared and charged at Rook, who dodged and whipped her side as she passed. She gasped in pain as she landed, but the other two angels bounded in to fill the gap. One raised his weapon and swung it downward at Rook while the other aimed to slash from the side. Rook responded by whipping down at one of the sleeping people, making contact with their Anima, and sending another invisible shock wave out, stunning the angels.

Rook jumped to the side of one and lashed out with both arms as whips, each wrapping around one of the angel's arms. He then retracted his whips, shredding the flesh and tearing it off both of the angel's arms. He fell to his knees and looked in horror at what Rook had done to him.

The female flew in from overhead, her wings blotting out the moonlight as she descended at speed. Rook raised his arms and instinctively willed his soul to expand out beyond his flesh again, the shards of glass taking the impact of her attack, shattering the fragments that blocked her into infinitesimally small, burning embers that flickered out of existence.

Rook welled his soul up inside him and then unleashed it again, rising out of the body and up into the air. He expelled another torrent of energy that began to shred the female's shoulder, to which she brought her wings down to block the attack.

Just then, the other male appeared, flying in from the side with his sword poised to run Rook through. Rook moved out of the way, only barely, again extending his arms into ropes and winding them around the angel's neck as he passed by. Using both his momentum and Rook's own will, Rook retracted his arms as fast as he could, with as much force as he could, slicing through the angel's neck like the whips were razor wire. The angel landed on his feet. And then his head landed next to him, gurgling blue blood upon the concrete.

The other angels cried out. The remaining male stammered and backed up, his eyes wide as he looked between Rook and his fallen brother. He watched as the angel's flesh burst into bright, blue light and then faded, leaving nothing behind. He took another step back and then another. His hands shook as he looked at his remaining companion.

Rook returned fully back into his body. He breathed hard. He didn't exert a lot of physical stamina, but his soul ached. He no longer felt the power he had before, feeling like he had spent a reserve of it. But he steeled his face and body, determined not to let that show.

"Shameless!" the female yelled, tears of fear in her eyes. "You risk it all! You risk undoing it all!"

"You better scurry back to your bloody masters," Rook snarled. "And tell those spineless bastards that this is their punishment for keeping quiet all these years." Rook flared his soul again, kicking up a whirlwind of glass around the body, spectral arcs jolting across the shards.

The angels backed up, trying to calculate their next choice. They looked to each other and then to Rook. Then, they turned on their heels and leaped into the air, fleeing as fast as they could, piercing the veil back into their realm.

Rook let his shoulders slump and breathed heavily. He panted, clutching his chest, though the pain was much deeper than the flesh. He looked around at the sidewalk and street, now deserted except for the few people the angels had forced asleep. He then looked at his hands, raising his soul through the flesh. He could feel, and now see, the greatly reduced density of his form. He gripped his hands into fists.

"All that for this, eh? They won't make that mistake

again."

Rook looked at the sleeping people and turned to face them. As he lowered his arms, he let his soul rise again.

"If they want a bloody spectacle, I'll give them one to remember."

Chapter Nine

Azrael gripped the ancient stone parapet before him. His fingers were tight, and his knuckles tensed upon the waist-high wall. He leaned on his hands, angled forward, and hunched. He looked out across the still waters of Malakut.

Samael walked up the path that stretched out behind them, joining his friend and pupil out on the precipice. His hands were clasped behind his back as he journeyed, eyes upon the dust-covered stone walkway. He moved as if carrying a weight upon his shoulders.

When Samael reached his companion, he came to a stop and regarded him, taking a moment to comprise the words he wished to use.

"I confirmed that the Fractured have stopped arriving," Samael started. "Adrian is no longer in danger of burning away. For now. He's making progress on the remaining scars."

Azrael did not move and did not answer.

"And you were right; the Unholy have spit on my request of them. Something about paying the Empyrean back for the expulsion of their agent on Earth they sent to collect the

Original Soul."

Samael stepped up next to Azrael and looked at him before turning his eyes out to the waters.

"They have little room to complain," Azrael said. "It appears the broken one is capable of repeating that impossible act."

Surprised, Samael looked back to Azrael.

"He expelled an angel, too?"

Azrael's grip tightened.

"Three were sent out from Cael's legion. Two returned. Until the third completes their reformation, we only have the report of the others."

"So, it's true," Samael said. "But they were only Acolytes. I doubt he has the power to harm a Seraph, much less a Deva or Virtue." He shrugged as he said his piece, looking back out at the water.

Azrael's head bowed.

"It is worse than that. No mortal soul should have ever been able to challenge a celestial, let alone dispatch one. Yet, even as a Fractured —incomplete— he has done so twice."

Azrael's head raised again, his body straightening, his shoulders tensing. Then, he continued.

"We are reaching the point of no return. Had we dispatched the soul when we first learned of it, the damage might have been manageable. But now," pinpoints of purple flared in Azrael's empty sockets, "he is beyond. He is an inevitable causality of our mistake. My mistake."

"Azrael," Samael said, looking back to Azrael and reaching out to touch his shoulder, "you can't think like that. We can still manage this. We just need to-"

Azrael pulled away from the parapet. The movement was sudden, cutting Samael off. But Azrael still looked outward.

"I cannot track him," Azrael said, the statement a fact. "He now consumes the souls. They are torn and destroyed with no death in between. There are no moments near death for me to follow."

Though Azrael's tone never rose, Samael could feel the anger rising in him.

"My friend, do not let this get the better of you. The legions are still combing the realm. We will find him, and we will bar him from returning to the Agglomeration. I'm sure the Unholy will recognize the threat and," Samael cut himself off with a small, dark chuckle. "No, no, they won't." He shook his head. "I can't believe I am saying this, but I think I miss Lucifer..."

Samael looked up with a smile, expecting Azrael to meet him in his commiseration. Instead, he saw Azrael turn and recognized the look that had formed on his face. Azrael stepped forward and began to walk down the path away from the edge.

"Azrael, you mustn't."

"I am done waiting," Azrael said in a grave and low

rumble. He looked back over his shoulder with cold determination in his eyeless sockets, the air crackling with electric energy. "I will do this myself."

A cold wind blew through the dark streets of the London suburb, threatening the coming of rain, as Azrael set foot onto Earth. He set the shawl that framed his gaunt, pale face and turned his eyeless sockets toward the blue light that intermittently illuminated him. The flashing of police lights broke through the night air and signaled to him where he would begin.

Under the cover of darkness, he walked toward the crime scene, each step measured with purpose. He could see the growing number of concerned neighbors coming from their homes, covering their mouths at what they saw now that the commotion had subsided. He could see a number of police personnel barring the civilians from entering their hastily defined perimeter. And, he could see the first responders kneeling beside and covering the bodies with nondescript, heavy cloths as they readied gurneys nearby.

"Stop."

Everyone froze. The paramedics. The police. Even the onlookers. On his command, all slowed their movements until they moved no more.

Azrael walked up between the police officers in his way. He walked up to the paramedics who hovered over the bodies. With a languid motion of his hand, Azrael called a force to remove the cloth covering the nearest body as he stepped closer.

He looked them over. He looked with eyes that were not there for something that, similarly, would not be present. He passed his hand over a body but could only coax out a remnant of energy that poked through the chest. It appeared severed and cracked as if something larger had been sheared off at this point. He looked at the other bodies and could only see the same.

Azrael lowered his hand. He stared at the corpses. At the corners of his eye sockets, a faint blue light crept in. Along his crow's feet and the wrinkles near the bridge of his nose, the light sunk into the cracks. There, it shifted in color, giving up its blue hue and sliding into purple. The light then set into his sockets, snaking like veins across the bone. Azrael shifted his perception from Animas and Animuses to that of dead things. Before him, the soulless, empty husks of the dead people became vibrant in his sight. And all around him, the other dead became known to him, from the ancient forgotten burials in the ground under this neighborhood to the fresh ones in the cemetery just outside it.

He grabbed the body as he kneeled and pulled it toward him. Slowly, he breathed deep over it, taking in its scent.

He lingered on it, committing it to memory, drawing in familial essence shared between the dead before him. Then he dropped the body and turned his nose to the air, working through the cacophony of scents until he found the one he wanted. Stronger than expected, sweet and salty, similar to, but different than the ones here. It led away, down the road. Azrael stood, and as he walked out of the perimeter, the lives of those he left behind were allowed to resume once again.

Azrael followed the scent to its conclusion. The body of a woman lay on the carpet of a modest home's living room about a mile away. The house was otherwise unoccupied; no other bodies, living or dead, were in the premises other than this empty shell, but Azrael could sense fresh death nearby. He followed his sight into the backyard of the home and looked upon the cooling remains of five more people splayed out in the grass. They were barely dressed, nightgowns and sleepwear for some, nude for the rest, and arranged as though they were moving as a group through the yard, perhaps running. Running away from danger.

Azrael grabbed one of the bodies, jerked it to him, and inhaled deeply. But when he let it go and sampled the air around himself, he could not detect a scent that those lying here in the grass wouldn't account for. No body was taken here. The Fractured only consumed them, moving on.

Azrael's body tensed. With a sudden movement, he unfurled his massive, black feathered wings and took to the sky. He rose above the buildings and put his back toward the moon, scanning, with his necromantic sight, all the buildings, yards, streets, and alleyways that spread out before him. Bodies, warm and alive, dotted the landscape. There were no more that were recently dead. The trail had gone cold.

Azrael seethed. He raised one of his hands. His long, almost skeletal fingers were already wreathed in a static blue charge. He faced it, palm out, to the world before him. Then, he slowly turned his hand, closed his fist, and tugged.

A woman carrying her early-morning coffee fell face-first into her tiled kitchen floor. A man, standing behind the cash register ringing up a sale, tilted forward and smashed his head into the open till on his way down. His customer, someone on their way back from an all-night shift, watched in confusion as the cashier plummeted to the ground just a moment before they would join him on the other side of the counter. As Azrael pulled on the souls, the sky behind him crackled a warning of his abuse of power; a lick of lightning thundering through the clouds urged the angel's caution. Families in their beds, people in their vehicles, men, women, children, and everyone in between—all souls heeded Azrael's call to sleep. All but one.

His head turned, and he locked on to the one soul that defied his command. He flexed his wings and dove for his target, crossing the span of the suburbs and carving deep into the heart of London. He came down atop the steeple of All Saints Church, landing on the delicate slates of the spire without disturbing them. He looked down to the street level, where he saw a man standing over the sleeping form of another. Azrael watched as the man looked the sleeping person over, nudged them with his foot, and looked around.

Screams broke the silence of the night. Dozens of screeching voices passed over Azrael's head. He looked up to see the wings of demons soaring through the clouds and diving low through the streets and alleyways. A clap of thunder and a flash of light revealed to him their bodies as they swarmed, and he watched as they landed in the street and pursued the man. Despite their black and red brocade suits, the demons ran on all limbs, snarling and baying as they neared him.

Those weren't the only wings Azrael could hear. Turning his face skyward again, he could see the many eyes of others reflected in the night, others that were landing atop the rooves and building facades surrounding them. With another flash of lightning, he could see a mass of angels watching the demons press their attack in the streets below.

The demons reached the man, one of them lunging for and tearing through the man's arm and sending his blood onto the street. The man fell, and the demons descended upon him, their beastly maws opening to gnash upon the body. They piled over him, ripping and tearing at his flesh like dogs.

A boom rocked the demons. Shards of spectral glass shot in every direction, slicing through demonic flesh and sending them flying. The power of the blast sounded like a bomb, and it shook the street. A gray light, nearly blinding, quickly dimmed as Azrael saw the Fractured at the center of the explosion. It fell into its host body once again and, despite the bleeding wounds and missing arm, stood up and faced the demons. Azrael saw no fear in the man's face as the rain began to fall. Instead, he wore a look of dark delight streaked with blood and rain.

The lowly beast demons rushed at the man again, but he turned and brandished his bleeding stump of an arm and exuded a long vine of spectral energy through it. The tendril was lined with spectral fractures, thousands of shards that the Fractured used like a whip and lashed at the demons, splattering orange blood along the walls of the church. But their number was too great, and the man found himself pressed back. As the demons, backed by the thunder and lightning of the tumultuous sky, closed in for a second time, the man laughed, and from under the street came up a wave of fractured shards that contracted like a trap to rake the demons from behind. Sliced, like cross-sections, the demons were flayed by the spectral rake that drug across the battlefield, spreading gore along the street and down into the storm drains. Though the surprise attack was devastating, it wasn't enough to kill the demons, and they were left to suffer in pain.

"Biah uniglag!"

What was left of the vanguard halted their attack. Those who could stand up did so and straightened their collars and their clothes, doing as they were ordered. They backed away, letting their commander through. Unlike the orange-skinned, hornless beasts that they commanded, the unmistakable drapings of the Baron caste emerged. Four of them stepped up to the man, and all four let their human glamours dissipate to reveal their hairless orange skin, long, black cranial horns, and steeped black fingers. More black filled out their clothing, with damask cloaks billowing over their exquisitely pressed brocade suits, each lined with silver hemming and pinned with platinum broaches and buttons.

All color had left the Fractured, his body rapidly nearing a death Azrael could see. Despite the terminal blood loss, the man somehow kept the body from expiring and kept that determined, even demented, expression on his face. The man looked the Barons over and then through them to look at what was waiting next.

"Come on, you cunts!" the man shouted, raising up his nub arm and flexing a spectral hand to raise his middle finger.

The Barons loosened the collars on their exquisitely tailored shirts and bared their claws, the black bone heating up and glowing orange hot, fizzling the rain that fell upon them into steam. Within a moment, the claws dripped with molten slag that sizzled and melted holes where the drops hit the concrete.

The angels could bear to wait no longer. On the other side of the Fractured, they descended from the rooftops and began to approach. They drew their swords and imbued in them a blue fire. Azrael could see a few Acolytes among their ranks, but it was the Seraphs that concerned him. They were not looking at the Fractured as they neared the front line.

The Barons charged. Faster than the lower demons, they moved like blurs across the distance, slashing through the man's body in a blink of an eye. The man couldn't defend against it, losing an entire leg and the other arm and suffering a gash across his gut. The molten claws cauterized the skin. No blood seeped from the man's steaming wounds as he fell in the middle of the street.

Smug with satisfaction, the Barons laughed at their conquest, posturing to the angels that stood just a few feet away.

"We did what you could not!" one Baron said with a boastful laugh, but it subsided when he saw the angels readying themselves. He turned back toward the man, whose body had succumbed to his wounds and lay dead in the street. But also saw the Fractured rising from it, its form a mockery of the human shape, stretched and distorted, whirling with the shards of stolen spirits and gleaming with eyes of sickly green. The Barons all turned and ran toward the Fractured, but were almost immediately blasted back by an explosion of shrapnel that embedded deep into their chests and faces. Like blasts of a shotgun, the Fractured unleashed a volley of shards at each Baron, eviscerating their flesh and exposing the black bone underneath. The Barons screamed in pain, and the rest of the demonic detachment backed away from the specter.

The Acolytes, too, retreated toward their commanders as the Seraphs moved forward. Unlike the raw, animalistic patterns of the demons, the angels moved with all the coordination of a well-trained military. The Acolytes didn't retreat; they took up stations before their commanders, brandishing shields that materialized like projections from bangles around their wrists. From between the gaps in the shield wall, the Seraphs pointed their flaming blades. In their other hands, they retrieved squares of netting that began to glow blue as they readied them. They moved as a unit, marching toward the Fractured.

"Under the order of the Celestial Empyrean, you are hereby ordered to surrender," barked one of the Seraphs. "Comply or be compelled."

The Fractured hovered over its dead body, seemingly sizing up his opponents as they made their slow approach. He shot out a shard, watching as the angelic shields harmlessly deflected it. He turned, seeing the Barons already nearly healed, but otherwise did not move. It did not run.

"Comply or be compelled," mocked one of the Barons, the last of his flesh mending, allowing him to sneer a grin at the angels. "I don't think he's listening. But don't worry, we can take care of it." The Baron nodded to his kin, and each removed a Coptic jar from their belts, each adorned with infernal symbols glazed into the pottery. They poised, ready with their hands on the lids.

"This is our realm to protect, Unholy," a Seraph yelled back. "Your presence threatens the treaty between realms! Disperse and return to Hell!"

"Ha! You hear that?" another Baron yelled, looking back to his contingent as he gestured toward the angels. "They think to remind us of our place!" He looked back at the angels, staring down the Seraph who spoke. "How quickly they forget that they rely on us to get around the Celestial Laws. You couldn't kill the Fractured, Boy Scout. You needed us!"

"And your obstinance served us well, Fallen! Now be gone with it!"

The Seraph in command gave the order, and the unit moved forward at full march, stomping in perfect rhythm through the gathered pools of water in the street. The phalanx covered ground, closing in on the Fractured that retreated to maintain some distance. The angels on the ends of the formation unfolded and initialized their nets, straightening them out and forming a large boundary that closed off the Fractured's means of escape to the sides. On the roofs above, more nets were cast out, cutting off aerial escape, as well. The

Fractured looked back to the Barons.

"I fucking knew it," came the voice of the Fractured, a sound like static and grinding stone. "You cunts *are* the shitfucks of creation." He laughed, sticking out his hands and flipping them off. "Failures when it matters most."

The Barons roared in anger, each in turn uncapping their Coptic jars. As the symbols on the pottery lit ablaze, a massive vacuum formed before them. Each jar was designed to capture and contain spiritual energy, which, in concert, formed a gale-force wind that sucked the Fractured toward the demons. The Fractured resisted, attempting to fly away from the negative pressure, flying at full speed only to gain an inch of ground.

The angels charged. Fearing their quarry lost, they retracted their shields and threw their nets. The ephemeral fabric was similarly tuned to the capture of spirits and thus was also subject to the jars' pull. The nets flew toward the Fractured, only to be sucked overhead and into the jars. A net or two was contained within the jars, but too many were caught and tangled, sending masses of ethereal threads to gum up the jar openings.

The Barons were enraged. Tossing the jars, their claws ignited once again, and they charged at the Fractured. The angels, too, raised swords and dashed forward, yelling cries of war and claims of birthright as they charged.

In the middle of it all, the Fractured struggled to stay

in place, not giving nor gaining any ground from right where it wanted to be. As the forces of Heaven and Hell came to collide upon him, the Fractured lashed out, striking at what everyone, even Azrael, had forgotten about in the chaos. Rearing up and throwing out a tentacle across the distance to the other side of the street, the Fractured struck the still-sleeping, soaked, slightly roughed-up man on the sidewalk, causing a shockwave of blinding, deafening force to tear through the block. The angels and demons reeled from the shock, screeching in an agony they'd never felt before. Even Azrael had to cover his face and bear the flashbang. To him, it felt as though a raw nerve was touched. Like an electric shock ran through his body. Like reality itself abhorred the act and desperately tried to tear itself away from it.

When the static and pain had passed, the body was gone, and so was the Fractured. The angels and demons pulled themselves up from the road, sidewalks, and from the rooftops, looking around to understand what had happened.

"Impudent, petulant beasts!" the angels yelled, pointing the tips of their swords at the demons.

"Hubristic conceited cowards!" came the reply.

They charged at each other, claw clanged upon shield and sword upon black bone. They swiped and slashed at each other, devolving into a brawl, spilling orange and blue blood into the streets that flowed along with the rain into the gutters.

"Enough!"

All the celestials stumbled and fell to their knees—the flames, whether fel or holy, quenched to sizzling steam. From within each of their bodies rose their essences, floating to the tops of their heads like rising heat, and each felt the chill of death replacing their life force. Azrael stepped from the alleyway and into the middle of the fray, his hand raised, wreathed in blue, with pinpoints of purple light floating in the center of his darkened sockets.

"F-forgive us, Azrael," stammered one of the Infernal, "if it were not for the interference of the Divine-"

"Stay your tongue, wretched beasts. We're the only ones following orders!" retorted an Empyrean.

"I said, enough!" Azrael barked, pulling his hand down, sending every celestial to the ground to shiver with a cold that rattled them to the core. They watched as strings of their essences left their bodies and floated through the air to Azrael as if he had called them to their rightful home. Azrael held their life suspended in the air and turned toward the angels.

"You, begone! You failed in your task. Let it be known that the fate of all reality is to be laid at your feet."

He twitched his hand, releasing some of the captured energy, returning it to the angels, and letting it sink into their skin. When the infusion finished, they stood and picked up their fallen swords and shields. Shaking in terror, they said nothing more and, one by one, phased out of Earth.

Azrael then turned to look at the demons, still held to the ground and shaking under their unbearable chill.

"And you..." Azrael said, drawing in closer. "You were given a simple task. Same as the Empyrean. To apprehend the Fractured. To bring him before us. To save the very reality you so desperately claim to love."

"W—we were only.... f-f—following orders," one of the Barons said through chattering teeth.

"Orders?" Azrael asked, tilting his head at the demon. "Well, then, let me be clear. The only order you needed heed in this endeavor, was mine. The only way for your petty squabbles, your precious balance, to matter beyond this moment was to listen to my warning."

Azrael clenched his hand. The lower demons felt their essences extinguish, their forms flaring in a flash of burning flame and then cooling into inert embers gathered in the puddles on the street. He then looked to the Barons.

"Take this back to Leviathan. Take this to Drake if you must. But should the Agglomeration die, should the universe stall, should the Thrones unravel all creation and us with it, then let it be known it was you who failed them."

Azrael released his grip. The Barons gasped for air.

The Cataclysm was gone.

Rain fell like a sheet in front of Azrael. Thick clouds and violent lightning did nothing to obscure his vision of the world below. His massive black wings, absorbing the lightning when it flashed near him, were spread out and fixed. They did not beat or fold, yet the Cataclysm remained aloft. His eyeless sockets scanned the city before him, piercing through the miles of mists and rain, looking for his prey.

Not letting the Fractured have the same advantage again, Azreal released his hold on London, allowing the people to regain the sliver of their souls he had locked away. They slowly began to rouse and then set to managing the new problems their brief, forced, dreamless sleep had caused them. Through the growing movement of souls, Azrael watched the city wake up, looking for any aberrance that he could use to follow the Fractured.

From the edge of his vision, Azrael noticed something disappear. Something that was once there was now gone; he was certain of it. Turning his head to the north and bringing it into view, Azrael saw a large mass of dead and grave dirt spanning some thirty acres of land nearly four miles from where he was. As small as it was from his vantage point in the center of London, Azrael knew the true size of this graveyard and of the numerous wraiths that remained there. And, as he watched, he saw again what he thought he saw a moment earlier. One of the resident wraiths disappeared.

Azrael tore through the air, cutting through the rain like

a blade as he crossed the early morning sky. Moving like a shadow, he crossed the distance and set down at the edge of the Victorian cemetery that he knew well. He entered the necropolis, passing by the sign that bore the name of it, *Highgate Cemetery*, and gazed out over the grounds at the two hundred thousand graves that filled it. Azrael could see through the years the death in this place, seeing the dead in a state of decay that corresponded to their internments. Many were fresh, or as fresh as could be, where some flesh, hair, and bones remained in their resting places. Most, however, were old. Long forgotten and many since unmarked, these dead were little more than grave dirt, nothing left behind of their mortal vessels beyond the dark soil they turned into.

Above the graves, the necropolis had a different population. Wraiths existed here. Numbering in the hundreds, the souls of the dead that refused to —or could not— move on lingered on the land. Souls of those who were interred here roamed mindlessly or were locked into a never-ending, repeated dream among the gravestones and mausoleums. Still, more wraiths were attracted here over the centuries, some from before the formal rites of burial were ever performed here, and others seeking out more of their kind, but all in their final glimpse of sentience before fading enough to succumb to their twilight.

The wraiths seemed to sense Azrael as he neared. As if wakened, even if only slightly, some of the spirits turned their faces —or the voids that were once such— toward the Angel of Death as he passed between the graves. Fewer, still, found his presence enough to gravitate toward him, following in his wake like flotsam caught in his current, roiling toward him under a power that was more his than their own. These wraiths, as evanescent as they were, still were whole and intact. None exhibited the broken and shattered lines of a Fractured, devoid of any hard or sharp edges or any glass-like semblances. Even if limbs or whole extremities had long ago faded away as their energies waned, these were never broken souls. They were all merely unreaped.

Azrael moved slowly through the burial grounds. He passed his sight over the graves and pierced through the mausoleums and sepulchers, looking for anything out of place. Though he was sure the wraiths he saw disappear were once here, he did not see any evidence to prove that fact. No signs of struggle would be seen here, no spectral fight would be had feeding among the senseless, and so Azrael had to look for a different means of tracing his foe's movements. As he entered the Circle of Lebanon, Azrael instead focused on the ambiance of the cemetery, feeling for energy left in the place, attempting to detect a soul whose power outshone the rest.

Azrael leaped, crossing a distance more than his height, to perch atop the mausoleums at the Circle's center and looked out over the Egyptian Avenue. All was quiet here. Only the rain beat upon the stones and along the ground. Not even the wraiths in Azrael's tow disturbed a single leaf of the tangles of vines and thick trees of the courtyard, though they bunched up around and passed through the ancient stone monuments. Nothing felt off, overabundant, or singularly sharp to Azrael's senses. If the Fractured remained, it either knew a trick to lower its presence or, Azrael surmised, it must have expended its stolen power when it faced the celestial hunt.

This left Azrael with few options left to ferret out the broken soul. A fact that angered him further, something he couldn't let the Fractured control any longer. If he would hide and feed among the wasted, then Azrael would take from him the false safety of being a wolf in sheep's clothing. He would make the Fractured know the power of the Cataclysm of Death, and he would make him know the fear of it.

Azrael pulled his weapon from the darkness, raising aloft his reaping scythe and brandishing it before him. He gripped it in one pale hand and willed it to manifest a power. Lining the edge of the blade, silhouetting the macabre tool, a line of purple energy crackled into existence. Subtly at first, the energy spread across the blade and then down the tang and shaft of the scythe, cloaking the instrument in necrotic power. The wraiths, lit by the dark light of Azrael's manifestation, quivered and receded from him, a primal fear awakening from within them.

Gripping the scythe in both hands, Azrael reared it

over a shoulder and squared his feet. He swung with the weapon and, from it, with the sound of a deafening void opening faster than sound itself could travel, projected a blade of deathly amethyst light that was impossibly vast to pass over the entirety of Highgate in a single motion. Through every grave, every monolith, every columbarium; across every crypt, sarcophagus, and tomb, the blade passed, slicing through every wraith both above and below ground before terminating where it began from within Azrael's scythe.

The blade did not destroy or damage the wraiths it touched. Nor did it cut them down or knock them away. It instead imbued within each of them a touch of Azrael's power. It imprinted on them just enough of their lost essence to energize them, granting them a small measure of their missing sentience and will. As if waking from an endless dream, all two hundred wraiths and more awoke in unison and saw for the first time, for some in centuries, the cemetery surrounding them and the dark angel who gazed down at them from above. The horror of their sudden consciousness took root in them all, each just above the threshold to feel it, as panic washed over them. They were dead —they only now knew it— and they only now felt the coldness of their deaths that had ripped from them their memory of the lives they had lost or the pain and loneliness they felt as it radiated from the center of their souls.

A cry of anguish and mourning rolled through the wraiths. Many called out names of those they barely remembered or admonitions to enemies also long since dead. Others cried in deep, weeping sobs for pains they couldn't fully comprehend. And still, others roared in anger, cursing the dark one above them and the shadow of death that ensnared them, calling for their release from their prisons and sentences that were unjust or unfair. All of these cries were heard by the angel, who allowed his scythe to lower at his side as he watched the turmoil and strife welling up. But Azrael heeded none of them. Instead, he lifted his other hand and faced his palm toward himself, closing it into a fist and then flinging it toward the earth. The seeds of power that Azrael had sewn within the wraiths all blazed alight at once. Purple motes of energy at the centers of each spirit burned suddenly bright, and the screaming stopped. Each wraith felt a pull from within them, and the suddenness of it robbed them of their chance at prescience, dragging them into a ground that offered no resistance to their fall. Each, illuminated by the light of Azrael's touch, was reaped and fell toward the Agglomeration. In as quick as it was to awaken them, they were gone, never to be who they were again and fated to mix with the soul stuff of others and dissolve away entirely.

Azrael looked over the now quiet cemetery, seeing it as empty as the living do, devoid of the dead. He had expected to reveal the Fractured in the mass reaping, seeing it struggle to resist or watching it panic and consume the others as its doom closed in. But no such thing happened. But that was not possible. Could he have escaped Azrael's notice, somehow slipping away before the culling? Or was he never here?

Azrael gripped his scythe tightly, pressing the grooves of his grip into the preternatural wood. He swiveled his head back and forth, searching the grounds and the lands beyond but not knowing what exactly to look for. Rage began to blind him, and he took to the air, tearing the wind as he ascended. He reached an apex, unfurled his wings, and then roared into a sky that had dawned a sun obscured by the black rainclouds.

"Having a bit of trouble, there, Tobit?" came a voice from behind Azrael. He growled but did not look back at the man who spoke.

"Move along, Beast," Azrael said, his shoulders heaving as he looked over the world below.

"Now, now," Lucifer said, floating forward to hover next to the angel. "It is rare to see the ever-stoic Azrael lose himself in a fit of rage, let alone to any emotion. What kind of friend would I be if I did not help one in need?"

"I do not need your assistance," Azrael spat, turning to the man who would be otherwise unassuming if not for his hovering so far above the Earth. "No doubt you have something to do with my inability to find the Fractured. Maybe you are even the cause of the problem."

"Careful," Lucifer said, raising a single, black-tipped finger, "one could mistake that for an accusation." Lucifer smiled and placed his hand behind his back. "I am, in fact, not aiding Rook in his effort to elude you. That is something he is accomplishing all on his own. I am here because you are so dangerously close to losing yourself, and I would hate not to be the reason you are finally pushed over the edge."

"So you come to mock me?" Azrael let go of his scythe, the weapon dissolving into silvery mists and dissipating.

"No, Tobit," Lucifer said, lowering his head slightly, "I am warning you. The entire universe is aware of that stunt you pulled earlier last night. Though I am sure Raziel is immensely appreciative of your actions in preventing an almost guaranteed holy war, I do not think he will overlook you endangering the millions of human lives whose protection is a part of your oath of office."

Azrael turned away sharply, returning his sockets to the world slowly turning beneath him, rejecting Lucifer's words.

"I assure you," Lucifer continued, "I am very much aware of the danger Rook poses to us all. I can help you find him. Give you what you need to track him unerringly."

"You, offering *me* a deal," Azrael said, turning back to Lucifer. "I refuse. And don't think to offer it to me again, Beast."

Lucifer sighed and floated around Azrael to hover at his other side.

"You misunderstand," he said, "I am offering a conclusion. I agree that this must come to an end. Quite soon. The resolution of this chapter is rushing toward us at a pace that I am afraid even you cannot see."

"And yet you continue to speak nothing and offer less," Azrael said, "I don't expect much from our interactions, Beast, but I know when you have a hand to play. So, get to it or leave me be."

Lucifer chuckled, "You two are not so unalike."

Lucifer turned toward the Earth and gestured with his hand.

"You cannot find Rook because you are not looking for what he is."

"A Fractured?" Azrael scoffed. "You jest."

"No," Lucifer gestured again to get Azrael to look, "he is one of Min's creations. An Original Soul. Stop looking for a wraith and start looking for what they were made for. What they have that all other souls lack."

Azrael looked out over the world again. He gazed out and thought upon what Lucifer had said. What would someone as good and pure as Adrian have in common with a serial killer like Rook? What do the other Original Souls, those who recycle through the Agglomeration intact and those who had given themselves in service to it as the Noden of the past, share in common with one another? Slowly, it dawned on Azrael.

The first souls, the First Hundred, were created with the

ability to alter themselves. To grow, adapt, and change. When they were used as the blueprints for all of the souls that would power the engine of life, these qualities were transferred as well. But while all normal souls can only change themselves, the Original Souls retained their ability to change the souls of others. To heal fractured souls, to mend the Agglomeration, Adrian had to learn how to use himself to gather the entropy and disorder of broken souls and heal them. Set them right. And the Fractured? He learned to use himself to dismantle that order, break it down into chaos, and compel it under his own control. It was that power that allowed Azrael to find Adrian wherever he might be. It was a lesser form of the very same power he commanded. That all Cataclysms commanded. It was the power to manipulate souls.

Like a beacon of light, Azrael could see the Fractured in the city below. The rest of the world fell away, and only the Fractured remained. He shot forward like a streak of lightning toward that light and, in an instant, propelled the Fractured and the body he was in into the ground, coming to rest kneeling before the prone parasite, slowly rising to his feet.

The Fractured rolled onto his side, clutching his ribs under the black and red wool coat the man wore. He groaned as his senses returned to him and rolled onto his knees to sit up.

Azrael swung his hands wide and closed his fists. The

world around the two slowed to a halt as Azrael brought time to heel. He spared the Fractured from this break in time. He watched as the man got to his feet and stood up. Azrael, forming his scythe from the mists and rain, held it out to the side as a crack of lightning flashed behind him and cast his shadow on the Fractured.

"What in the bloody h-" the man said, turning around with a wince on his face to see Azrael. He took a step back, looking up at the eight-foot-tall harbinger, all sense of pain leaving his body. When the man's eyes slid to Azrael's scythe, his expression changed. Replacing the awe and wonder he had a moment ago, anger filled the man's face, and he pointed a finger directly toward the face of Death.

"Well, well, well," the Fractured yelled. "If it ain't me old mate from the past. The bloody Angel of Death, big bad Azrael, making an appearance for little old me?" The Fractured spat at the wet ground, the spit instantly washing away in the downpour. "Fuck off, mate. Ain't nothing you can do to stop me now."

Azrael brandished his scythe, and in that movement, the Fractured raised his hands and shot a stream of soul glass at the angel. Azrael dodged the volley and twisted from it to swing his scythe parallel to the street to cut the Fractured from the side. The Fractured responded, sending out a blast to deflect the blade and another at Azrael's face. Azrael was momentarily surprised at the deflection, a heretofore unknown effect that the Fractured could do to his weapon. He regained himself to wave away the soul shards and ready his scythe again. He used his hand to pull on the Fractured's soul, dragging him on his heels and sliding him across the pavement into the path of his weapon that he swung from overhead, coming down at an angle to the ensnared man. But the Fractured aimed a blast at the ground, and instead of shooting out free shards, he propelled himself away using his soul like an appendage, retracting it back within himself when he landed a few feet away.

"Poltergeistism," Azrael said in small wonderment as he looked at the microscopic abrasions the Fractured had caused to the physical matter of the cement.

"What, mate? Didn't quite catch that." The Fractured flung a rush of soul stuff down again and shot himself into the air above Azrael's head. As the angel tracked his movement, the Fractured raised his arms and exuded a long, undulating tentacle from each that he lashed down at the angel's shoulders. Azrael raised his weapon and blocked both with the length of it before pointing a hand at the Fractured and flicking his finger, sending the Fractured flying. The Fractured had not let go of the scythe, and when shot back, he wrenched it out of Azrael's hands and retracted it to himself, even as he landed on his back on the hard concrete several dozen feet away.

The Fractured wasted no time. Using his soul to propel

himself to his feet, he raised Death's massive weapon in his own hands and charged at Azrael. He bounded a handful of feet before Azrael pointed his hand and locked the Fractured in place. He then raised his hand further, and the Fractured could only watch in frustration as his soul and the body that housed it complied and levitated in the air. Azrael reached with his free hand and pulled, his scythe responding to its master's call, ripping from the Fractured's hands and flying back into his own.

"Enough with this," Azrael said, "if you are so bent on plaguing me with your defiance, I'll remind you what mastery of souls truly is. You are mine now. You will pose no further threat to creation."

"Piss off with that shite!" The Fractured said, struggling against Azrael's control. "Don't make me the bloody poster boy for your fascism! You never gave a toss about me before, and now that I'm in your way, you want to crush me out?"

Azrael paused, looking over the Fractured. He spread his hand, and the Fractured screamed as his soul expanded against his will, pushing out beyond the confines of his body and billowing like a bloated corpse. Azrael reached out and pulled a thread of shards toward himself, looking at each individual piece of soul glass.

"It is too late," Azrael said, "you have become too powerful. Your soul acts like that in reverse to the Agglomeration." He let the thread go and watched it fall back into place as if attracted to the center of the Fractured's soul. Azrael shook his head, looking the Fractured in the eye. "And, you have reached poltergeistism. Containment is no longer tenable. There is no other outcome to consider."

Azrael pushed the Fractured back through the air to give a little distance. He took in a deep breath as he looked down at the scythe in his hands. He hesitated, rolling the weapon's shaft back and forth, puzzling out if he was making the best call. He steeled himself and looked back at the Fractured.

"Do you even recognize me," the Fractured barked, "or am I just another one of your fuckups? Does the bloody Archangel of Death ever make mistakes?" He thrashed against his restraints, pinpointing the areas of pressure and snaking his tendrils around the points of contact, curling around whatever was holding his neck, back, and chest in place. "And even if you did screw up, would you have the bollocks to own up to it?"

The Fractured then retracted his tentacles, ripping through the force like saw blades on ice, freeing him from Azrael's telekinetic grasp. He fell to his feet and blazed his soul, raising it out of his body in a whirlwind of glass and spectral storm.

"Why didn't you take me?!" he yelled, charging at Azrael.

Azrael looked at his hand that had held the Fractured back. It burned from having his tether severed. He watched the enraged soul-thing as it reared up at him, its essence whipped into a fury and wildly flaring out tendrils in all directions like an eldritch horror. He looked at the ground, the hard concrete that split and crumbled under the Fractured's advance, watching as the powerful soul pushed on and broke physical matter as he flung himself into the air again. And then he watched as the Fractured reached out with his tendrils, wrapping them around the drain spouts of the buildings to either side of them, around the posts of parking meters between them, and around the cars behind them. He saw the Fractured pull tension on all of these tendrils, using them to rip himself toward Azrael with superhuman speed, tearing off the spouts, ripping up the posts, and overturning the cars.

"Stop."

With but a word, the Fractured stopped. Frozen in time, Azrael decided to no longer let him exist outside of it with him. With a wave of his hand, he erased the tendrils and then, like rewinding time, set the broken bits of the world back in place. He sighed as he gripped his scythe again and then reached out to touch the Fractured on his forehead, releasing only his head from the stasis.

"Wh—what have you done?" The Fractured said, his eyes darting around, being the only things that could move.

"I am truly sorry," Azrael began, "that you have tied your entire existence upon a choice I made five centuries ago. You must know that would I have seen you for what you were when you took your first body and fractured your first soul, I would have reaped you then rather than now, on the precipice of our demise."

"What?!" The Fractured exclaimed. "You're pinning this on me?! This is *your* fault, mate. I didn't ask for this. I *became* this."

"I am allowing you to witness your end out of respect for what you were. Not who you are. You were a precious thing, one of a very rare few made to usher in the entirety of the human race. You have children in this world, innumerable in measure. Copies of you and your brothers and sisters from which all humans arose."

"Cut the shit, Seraph," the Fractured said as Azrael readied his weapon once again.

"In your quest to topple the system that you so abhor, you have become the catalyst for its total destruction. You are its twilight, and so would you be of all the world and the worlds beyond." Azrael raised his scythe, lighting it ablaze again in a light that was not light. "You. You are Ruin."

"Go ahead, you sanctimonious prick," The Fractured seethed. "I beg for nothing."

Azrael lifted his scythe over his head and reeled back.

"Azrael, stop."

Samael's hand reached out and touched Azrael's shoulder. After a moment, Azrael relaxed and let his weapon drop. He peered at his friend and saw him looking back with a deep pain in his eyes.

"Don't do this," Samael continued, "don't make my mistake."

"I must, my friend. It is the only way." He looked at the Fractured and then back to Samael. "The system is broken. If I don't do this, nothing will stop him. There is no check in place to hold him, nowhere for him to go that won't end at the Agglomeration. The rules protect him twice over, and," he turned to face the Fractured fully again, "I am prepared to accept my punishment if it means saving us all."

Azrael pulled away from Samael to square up with the Fractured again.

"There's another way," Samael said, his wistful smile appearing on his lips, "I told you there was, and I found it."

"What?" Azrael turned back, searching his friend's eyes. "How?"

"Me," came the response from over their heads.

An angel dropped to street level from the rooftop he had perched on. Samael smiled as before them stood an angel with the vestments of a Virtue on his silver tactical armor. An angel of light brown skin, black, shoulder-length hair, and a short goatee lining his pointed chin. He rested his hands on his weapons, two dirks that hung on either hip as he nodded to Azrael and then looked to the Fractured.

"Cael!" yelled the Fractured. "You piece of shit! You wanted a villain; well, there he bleeding is!"

"I'm afraid he's right," Cael said with a shrug and a smirk as he looked at the Fractured.

Azrael growled, leveling his gaze upon Cael.

"I remember. It was you who fractured this soul. It is at your feet we can lay all the death and fracturing that has happened since," Azrael's eyes began to emit their necromantic energies as his presence darkened, "and what can you do here that I cannot?"

Surprised at Azrael's reaction, Cael's smirk disappeared, and he raised his hands up defensively before Azrael.

"Atone! I-I can atone like you said."

"He's agreed to shoulder the burden, Azrael," Samael said, gently laying a hand down on Cael's shoulder. "He wants to make up for his sin by committing another in your stead. He has chosen to save you from the fate that awaits you if you don't let him take this on."

Azrael looked between them, wearing the shock on his face. But then he shook his head, denying the thought of it.

"No. A Virtue cannot be allowed to commit the cardinal sin," he looked to Samael, "the system is taxed enough as it is. We cannot afford to surrender a commander of a legion to the punishment, *two* punishments, that would have to be suffered to end this threat." Azrael shook his head again. "I will do this. They can select another for my role like they did for you."

"You must let him," Samael said. "It is that very station of his that might allow him to escape judgment. It's his job, after all, to protect the humans, and it is his legion, specifically, that polices the realm against rogue celestials. There is no one better suited to do this, and we think there is a valid argument in all that we can use with Raziel."

"This is why I respect you, Azrael," Cael said, turning away from them and facing the Fractured. He walked over to Rook and reached out a finger, touching his cheek gently, even as the Fractured tried to bite it in between hurling obscenities.

Azrael thought hard. He looked at Samael, whose face pleaded with him to agree, and at Cael, who taunted the suspended Fractured.

"Very well," he said, lowering his head and stepping aside. "Do it and be done with it. Leave nothing; it must be a total soul destruction."

"Oh, no," Cael said, looking back to Azrael with his smirk returned, "I'll do it, but it's got to be my way."

"What?" Azrael looked up at him.

"That's the deal," Cael said, looking back at the Fractured. "We end this where we first met. You remember that day, don't you Fractured? The day I showed you what you really were? Where was that, broken one? Do you remember?"

The Fractured spit in Cael's face, and he sneered as he wiped it off.

"All Saints Church."

Chapter Ten

1950...

Rook slid his horned-rim glasses off and placed them on the sturdy library study desk before him. He rubbed his eyes, trying to refresh them. He could only see a blurry outline of a vaguely-book-shaped mass and a white rectangle in front of him and didn't know if it was fatigue or the lack of corrective lenses that was causing his difficulty. With a sigh, he grabbed the glasses and slid them back on. Seeing that the image before him was clearer but still blurry, he removed the glasses again, deciding he was tired.

The library was nearly empty. Save for the staff librarian, two students from the nearby university, and a man using the lack of eyes as cover for his day drinking, the only other people Rook could see were beyond the window on the sidewalk outside. At least, he wished this to be true. Paying any more attention than was necessary to the dozen shadows that surrounded him, ghosts reminding him of the lives he ended to extend his own, was a weight he desperately wished to ignore. As long as he didn't make eye contact or give them cause to react, the ghosts tended to merely remain near him, slowly forgetting their former lives and succumbing to some numbness that would eventually overtake them. It was already too much to bear their lives ending, Rook felt. He didn't want to think of what happened to the souls that refused to move on. Of their eventual fate because of him.

He loosened his buttoned shirt collar and flapped his trench coat, trying to let in some cooler air. It rustled the newspaper and book he had before him, and he looked at the image printed over the first page of the international section. Even without his glasses, he could still make out the larger elements of the Korean War spread, detailing the United States' entry into the conflict. Rook had already read this article, and the commentary the editor had conspicuously written between the lines. Their disapproval of how the U.S. handled its affairs was unmistakable, and how he felt British involvement would surely shore up the war effort came through in the writing.

Rook turned the pages again, blinking hard and squinting over the print. He passed over other articles that he had read despite his disinterest. There was an editorial on the new threat of communism that was washing over the world. It highlighted terms like "Red Scare" and "Red Menace" as shadowy threats, bullying conservatives into action against the perceived liberal, anti-religious, and atheist agendas that would surely tear down society. The sweeping praise of Winston Churchill and his stalwart defense against the threat finished the piece in a grand gesture that reminded Rook of the treatises of Luther from centuries past. There was a column detailing the conviction of a spy from London thought to have sold British secrets to the Soviet Union, snuggled up to and filling out the communist fearmongering that overtook most of the paper. The recent Belgian government collapse took a section of the fourth page, a story that Rook got a chill reading, feeling the similarities between it and the spark that started the First World War. But none of this was deemed worthy of further digging for Rook right now.

Rook continued until he returned to the article he had come to the library to read. A small blurb, barely an article, told about communist Poland enacting a law to take possession of properties owned by Roman Catholic churches. This is what Rook truly marveled over. Despite how invisible such a story would have been to a news outlet just half a decade earlier, Rook could now read news from around the world that covered even the smallest changes in the status quo that refreshed daily. The papers pushed every story, no matter how trivial, to compete with the unedited, nearly live video reels that one could see on the new television technology. In fact, the banner posted over the newspaper stand in the library boasted just that: *Up-to-the-Minute News: As fast as television, affordably in your hands*, it read.

He pressed the article flat to keep the paper from folding and slipped his glasses back on, shaking off the fatigue despite the dull pain he felt in his neck. He read over the entry again, picking out the details that had caught his attention before. Tracing his finger along the lines of text, he read the few locations and names of surrendered properties listed. Though the article was vague, providing just enough to be considered news and focusing on the ease with which the religious organization caved, it did mention a church that was effectively given a free pass to remain Roman Catholic, given the dilapidated state of the site. No pictures and not much detail, but there was a name: *Monomakh*. The article read out like a muted facsimile of the Lutheran raids of his time, trading popular uprising for political sovereignty and the shifting of assets seemingly on the whim of the government. But Rook saw the hint of something more in the text he had searched for.

Reaching for the book, Rook checked its title before opening it up. *Ważne starożytne teksty polskie*, it read, or "Important Ancient Polish Texts." Long done with artifacts such as crucifix fragments, bones of saints, or the Holy Prepuce, Rook had recently turned his attention to more tangible and reliable evidence of the divine: first-hand, written accounts. Confirming against the information found more than halfway through the book, it seemed Monomakh had, reportedly, an almanac, first written in German and then translated into Polish, in its possession that was supposedly written by a fallen angel, one sent to pay penance on Earth, teaching the locals the secrets to farming. More importantly, it had markings in it that looked like no known human language. Markings, the book assured, that had been painstakingly copied from the original German version into the Polish one housed at Monomakh.

Rook checked the newspaper again. The name matched. So did the location. As he read further in the blurb, Rook's heart skipped a beat when he got to the article's last lines. *Despite the state of it, Monomakh will continue to operate as a Roman Catholic church but without a priest or congregation of its own. Instead, it will only be allowed to practice the rituals and ceremonies outlined in its Holy Liturgical Almanac to continue to feed its parish and surrounding areas, which is noted to always be in abundance no matter the time of year.*

Rook smiled and stood up. The scratching of his chair caused the librarian to look at him, but Rook only smiled back and then gathered his materials. Rolling up the newspaper and placing it under his arm, he picked up the book when he felt a twinge in his left arm. The book fell from his hand and landed with a thud on the table, sending a shock of sound through the quiet room and provoking another stare from the librarian. Rook smiled again, trying to hide his concern, and felt his left arm with his other hand. It was numb, somewhat cold. At first, Rook didn't know what to make of it, but when he reached out for the book again, realization burst on his face as the memories flew back into his mind of similar reports he heard a few times in war. He searched his mind, through each of the conflicts he had been in, to recall what the diagnosis was. He shook his head, dismissing what he knew it to be. Shell shock? Anxiety? Gross Stress Reaction? No, he was beyond that. That couldn't be it.

Rook successfully scooped up the book the second time and held it tightly as he returned it to its section among the rear shelves of the library. The brisk movement to reset the book winded him, and he felt his heart flutter against his chest out of his control to slow it. After he pushed the book into place, he paused, leaning against the shelf, and forced himself to breathe deeply. Sweat rolled down his forehead and along the back of his neck. His breathing became labored. The room began to spin.

"Ey, you okay?" asked the drunk man, poking his head out from his hiding place between the back aisles.

Rook looked at the man, trying to see him through the double and triple copies of his face spontaneously appearing in his vision. He turned toward him and thought up the words he was going to say, of some platitude that he was alright and to thank him for his concern. But Rook's body gave out, and with a sudden sensation of suffocating, he collapsed onto the floor. His sight quickly faded, and though he saw the room above him darken as the drunk tossed his flask in a rush to tend to him, Rook couldn't hear him anymore. Nor could he seem to catch his breath. Worse still, Rook could no longer feel his heart that moments earlier had been beating like a hummingbird.

Rook died. An occurrence Rook had weathered before in no small amount, but nothing so sudden when off the battlefield. As he rose above his body, looking down at it in mild shock, he only then pieced it together that this poor shell had a heart attack. He looked it over —this newly dead body— and was at a loss to explain it. He was healthy, lightly athletic, and young; had he missed a detail or flaw that was ultimately fatal? Rook shook off the thought; the young man didn't give up his life to be ranked like cattle. He deserved better. But all Rook could do now was to offer him the prayer of Eternal Rest, as he did for every soul and again for every lost body before he had to go. Rook already felt the pressing of time against him, and he had to search for a new body right now, but the prayer would be said first.

Quickly finished, Rook took his leave of the library. He didn't want to cause a further scene and decided it was best to find someone alone and away from the commotion here. He hated this part, the hunting and selecting, so he tried to push it from his mind and take to it as though it was a habit or need. If he put it to the very back of his mind, he could tell himself he was divining out the next host. That the hand of God guided him to the proper body. He only had moments left to find someone, so he put himself in the sky and closed his eyes, letting his intuition or divine guidance give him a sign.

Rook heard the ding of a shopkeeper's bell. A solid tinkling of noise passed through Rook and drew his attention to a pub just down the road. The sound was tantalizing to him, ringing clearer than any of the other noises on the London streets, and so it made perfect sense to follow it. The English pub invited Rook, he could hear a bluesy song on the jukebox and see the smoke hazily wafting from the recently opened door, and he heeded his divine call to pass inside.

The interior of the establishment matched Rook's expectations. A dingy carpet remained from the decades of use it must have seen, no doubt held together by the smoke and dried liquor stains that saturated it. The lights were dimmed, both to give atmosphere and hide the blemishes. But it held a decent amount of people for its after-noon reopening, and Rook could see them enjoying some local food concoctions alongside the traditional drinks.

But Rook didn't spend his time admiring the eatery, though he made a note to come back sometime later. He set to work watching the people and settling on a choice of target. Being no stranger to such places, he knew that his best luck would be had near the bar, where he hoped to find someone alone or a few people drunk enough not to kick up a scene. And, as his luck would have it, several individuals were bellied up to the bar, perched on their stools with drinks in hand or nearby. But, in this particular bar, none of them were truly alone. Surely some of them were here by themselves, Rook thought, but none were set up far enough away from another for his comfort. He couldn't tell if any of them were without company.

Something grabbed Rook by his chest, tugging on his core. It pulled him down from his flight, setting his feet on a floor that he knew he might soon be falling through if he didn't hurry. He resisted, not letting it pull him back away from the bar, and lurched forward toward the patrons by putting his metaphysical foot down and straining. His time had run out, and the underworld beckoned. He only had moments before he was sure the pull would be too much.

A man coughed roughly and slid off his stool. Taking the rest of his beer down in a single swig, he lumbered by Rook and plodded his way toward the toilet at the back of the pub. Rook followed. Though he didn't like the choice that was being made for him, he saw no alternative, and he could not wait for one. The man wasn't overly tall, nor were there any prominent features that merited concern, but that cough sounded deep and painful, and Rook wondered if it was going to be a problem. But he caught that line of thinking and reminded himself that he couldn't objectify the man, that if Providence were selecting this one for him, he would be grateful for it.

Rook entered the private room through its closed door. On the other side, the man had stepped up to a urinal and prepared to relieve himself. Pushing through the walls and checking the stalls for anyone else, Rook was satisfied they were alone and hovered in close to the man. He braced himself, in as much as a ghost could, staying focused on the man to resist the pull of death as he waited for him to finish. Rook refused to take someone so exposed, so undignified. He would push his will to its limit to let the man have his last relief in this mortal life, and he gritted his teeth and tore against the pull to ensure it. As he watched and waited, he muttered his prayer of Eternal Rest for the man and his soon-to-be-released soul, and he desperately hoped the man would make the choice to move on.

The man finished. He zipped up his trousers and reached for the flusher but did not get to touch it. Rook slammed into the man, sending his soul through the urinal and into the wall beyond it. The empty shell collapsed, slumping down onto the tile floor, and Rook dove after it. Sliding into the man's flesh, Rook felt the pull of death subsiding as he delved deeper, feeling it release him entirely once most of him was inside the body. From there, he slipped into the void at the body's center, as though he was fitting on a new suit, and relaxed himself into the spectral juncture that connected him to the body. It resisted him, a sensation not unlike pairing two like poles of a magnet together, but Rook overcame it and made his connection.

He started with his heart. That had to come first. But once that was done, he needed to breathe, and with that, the fiery pain that followed next. Rook screamed. His first breath was always a scream.

He screamed to fill his new lungs with air but also to bear through the pain. His chest, his shoulders, his arms and legs, head and eyes, all burned with an intense sting akin to fire. He gritted his teeth and forced himself to ground the pain, to take it into himself and to accept it as penance so he could take on the gift that was a new body. The pain dug in deep, the cool tile of the dirty floor soothing his forehead, but he managed it and worked through it. The scream died in his chest, wasting away to a whine and a wheeze, and Rook could finally replace it with deep, erratic breaths.

Rook pulled himself off the floor. He felt weak. He shook his new head and blinked his new eyes, rubbing them as he rose to a shaky standing. He felt his heartbeat throbbing through his head, which felt thick and oppressive. Each thud he swore he could hear, that anyone near him could hear. And he felt a fog in his brain that didn't burn away. Rook expected an adrenaline spike by now, a body's response to such a traumatic event, but he didn't feel anything like it. Just a pain behind his eyes and something stuck in his chest.

He reached out and flushed the urinal. The door opened behind him. He could hear a man talking, but he didn't quite catch what was said.

"John? Are you alright?"

Rook blinked, and the words finally made sense when they were repeated.

"John, are you alright? Did you have another episode?"

Rook nodded his head and took the man's offer to assist him out of the room and back into the pub. To Rook's surprise, he wasn't rushed away or was treated in any way. Instead, the man took him back to his stool and slapped the bar top.

"Oi, another round," the man yelled, waving the barkeep down. He then looked at Rook and smiled, squeezing his hand on Rook's shoulder. "This one's on me!"

Rook scooted onto his stool and accepted the drink with a sheepish smile. He brought it to his lips and took a sip. As he pulled the pint glass away, he caught something emerging from the toilet room door, darkening the air around it as it formed fully on the other side. Rook slid his eyes away from it, the shattered thing that slowly hovered closer and joined the other dozen spirits that were in his tow. Rook took another sip, a larger gulp this time, and set the glass down on the bar top. He stared at it, watching the suds slide down its edge.

"You chose poorly," Rook said softly, his eyes closing as he gripped the glass. When he opened them again, he saw the dark, broken tendrils of John's ghost passing through his vision as it languidly tried to rejoin its body. Rook shook his head and took another drink.

Rook stumbled out of the bar. The ring of the last call bell was still sounding in his ear, as was the laughter and singing that John's friends forced the poor man through as they continued to buy him beers and celebrate him through the rest of the night. Rook had no idea what the occasion was or why the interactions felt bitter-sweet. He only understood that they loved this man and were glad he was there with them. To Rook's relief, they didn't seem to notice or mind his reserved reactions. He knew nothing about this man and didn't know how to act, but no one there called him out for it.

Out on the street in the cool night air, Rook felt somewhat refreshed. It had taken longer than usual to get accustomed to this body, never quite feeling comfortable in it. But the fresh air seemed to revitalize him, the coolness, a welcome change. Rook took in a deep breath and let it fill him for a moment before he let it out. The something that was stuck in his chest got caught in the contraction of his lungs, and Rook coughed uncontrollably. He doubled over, attempting to hack out the obstruction, but it never came.

Instead, the coughing fit eventually subsided, and it left Rook dizzy and tired.

Rook's concern couldn't be put off any longer. He felt through the pockets of his trousers and coat and found a wallet, pulling it out and opening it to find John's identification card. It was old, likely the original WWII-issued card everyone got during the war. It showed signs of wear but was in good enough shape. It only had one address on it, indicating that John had never moved residences in the decade since it was issued. The address was nearby. Walking distance. And he had keys. He dug his hands into his coat pockets and walked along the sidewalk toward John's home.

Behind him, all thirteen ghosts moved with him. For the ones that had been with Rook a while, they seemed more tethered or tied to him than anything else. Where Rook was, they needed to be, and so they moved to stay within a certain range of him. If Rook didn't move for a moment, as he did when stopped at a crosswalk and waited to cross the street, the old ghosts would hover, their black fragments knitting and unknitting loosely as if shifting in an ethereal wind. Once Rook moved again, they followed, nothing more. The spirits newer than that still remained active, choosing to flitter away or come in closer as they saw fit. Still, they didn't show much beyond the thoughts of animals, reacting to the stimuli of the physical world but doing nothing to it, and even sometimes leaving Rook entirely to pursue something new. No such luck with these, though. Rook remained their loci, and they scrambled to stay within sight and threatened a flurry of activity if Rook happened to look through one, even to look across the road.

The newest ones posed the largest issue for Rook. They remembered him. They resented him. As he walked down the street, these were the spirits that would dash across his sight just as a car drove by. They would rush him out of the corner of his eye and try to startle him. The newest, they could still speak, whispering loathsome things into his ear and droning on endlessly lamenting their deaths at his hands. And they could scream. Screaming in Rook's ear when he least expected it. To Rook's satisfaction, John's ghost didn't do any of this. Despite the dozen others in his company showing off their examples, John merely hovered close, snaking his long, wispy tendrils into Rook whenever Rook stood still long enough.

Rook saw John's apartment building. A five-story building with a flat top and austere concrete walls that stood stark and cold among its fellow buildings along the street. It was a pre-war building, apparently making it through the conflict intact, and didn't benefit from the rebuilding effort of the last five years. Its face was worn and stained from decades of rain and fog, the hedges and small bushes outside were in dire need of tending, and the front gate looked more ornamental than protective. Rook crossed the street and opened the gate, finding it unlocked and squeaky-hinged, and entered the building.

There was no lobby to speak of. The door opened to a hallway that proceeded for the length of the apartments on either side before spilling into a cross that ran the length of the ground floor. Following the path to its fork, Rook could look right or left and see the rows of apartment doors on both sides of the carpeted path. In front of him was the only stairway that led to the upper floors. Now understanding the building layout, Rook was relieved that he would only have to climb one flight of stairs to reach the proper floor and proceeded to ascend the stairway.

One floor was almost too much. Rook's body felt fatigued and worn by the climb. Reaching the landing of the second floor, Rook had to grab the railing and take a moment to regain his strength. It was unlike the winded feeling he had earlier tonight in the library; this was a whole new kind of drain. It scared Rook, and he pulled on the railing to peel himself off the wall and walk into the hallway. Fishing out John's ID card, Rook followed its suggestion and found the apartment door he sought. A quick key turn, and the door opened. Rook took a breath and prepared himself for what he might find inside.

As the door swung open, Rook could see the living room unfold before him. The first thing Rook noticed was immediately on the other side of the door, a plaid, hessian armchair, turned at an angle to face the corner of the room toward the door, and a brown square tray table set up to its right, both on a large, square dingy carpet all set up on the dark brown, varnished wood floor. As the door opened further, Rook could see the square living room terminated into a smaller, rectangular kitchen split apart by a hallway that ended with a door on either side. When Rook entered the apartment and closed the door behind him, he could smell the lingering soot of cigarette smoke and guessed that the film he felt covering the walls and floors was made from years-long nicotine buildup. A small television sat on a table across from the armchair, a round wooden table and four matching chairs finished the kitchen, and pictures hung along the walls and hallway depicting collections of faces Rook had never seen.

It didn't appear to Rook that John was a wealthy man. Nothing in this part of the apartment was new. The chair had its arm sections worn down enough to fray the burlap into sharp bristles. The television was small, necessitating its placement closer to the chair. And the rug was matted and worn. And the apartment was cluttered.

With the larger details out of the way, Rook could now notice the stacks of boxes in the corners of the kitchen, several buckling under the weight of the ones above them and appearing to hold several things wrapped in newspaper. He also noticed pictures or artwork in frames stacked against the walls; their faces turned away. It all gave Rook the impression that John had prepared to move out at some point but then decided against it. Or he moved in and never fully unpacked. Either way, the clutter had the same layer of old cigarettes on it and so had been here for a while.

Rook saw a folded paper lying open and face down on the armchair. It sat mostly on the arm but overflowed onto the end table, where a torn envelope sat near it. Rook picked up the paper, revealing an ashtray on the table. It had been used, and used a lot over the years, as the build-up of old ash and grime proved, but it was otherwise cleaned and emptied. There were no cigarette packs or loose tobacco on the tray, the only other thing on it being an empty drink coaster and a hand-written note about TV programming and related channels. Rook turned the paper over and read the contents.

It was a typed letter. Addressed from a local physician to a John Moore. As Rook read it, his heart sank.

Dear Mr. John Moore,

This letter acknowledges the receipt of your request to have your medical information sent to you due to your declining ability to appear in our office. This letter also seeks to inform you of your latest results and our recommendations for your continued care.

Your X-ray scans show the carcinoma masses in

your lungs have expanded, and there is extensive damage to surrounding tissues. The carcinomas may have become malignant and could appear in other tissues in your body, but more scans would be needed to confirm.

In regard to your hesitancy to undergo chemotherapy, we suggest a treatment of megavoltage radiation therapy to target the cancer and destroy the cells, giving your body a chance to heal on its own. However, we must, for fairness and completeness, conclude that this therapy will only improve your quality of life in the near term and will not alter your prognosis. This treatment may extend your life expectancy, but at this stage of your disease, it will not cure it. Given your prior choices to defer the matter of treatment with our office, we are prepared to offer letters of residency for any hospice or long-term care facilities you may consider.

Included is a prescription. It is for morphine. John, if you do nothing else, please take this for the pain.

Yours,
Dr. Johan Doll

Rook dropped the letter. He stared at it in disbelief as it glided down into the seat of the armchair. Where it landed, a light blue, glossy paper caught Rook's eyes, stuck in the crease between the seat cushion and armrest of the chair. Pulling it out, Rook could see a flowing script heading the pamphlet prominently displaying *All Saint's Church* as its origin. Below it was a rudimentary graphic depicting a pair of hands with a Catholic cross laid in them with an aura surrounding them. Then, in bold letters underneath, it read: *God Heals: Faith Healing and You.*

Rook's eyes shot open wide.

"No! No, no, no! Tell me you didn't, John!"

Rook flipped the pamphlet open and looked across its spread, his mouth slowly opening as he read it. He read the healing declarations it urged its believers to master.

I release miracles of healing in my body in the name of Jesus, Heavenly Father.

I come before You today with a heart burdened by illness and seeking Your healing touch.

We believe all teaching and healing is an expression of the love and mercy of the Lord Jesus

Christ.

Below that, it listed numerous quotes from the Bible as if to prove the existence of the power.

"But I will restore you to health and heal your wounds, declares the Lord."

"He gives strength to the weary and increases the power of the weak."

"He heals the brokenhearted and binds up their wounds."

"Lord my God, I called to You for help, and You healed me."

All without citation. Finally, below that, it gave a list of days of the week and times that a support group would gather.

"Oh, John, no! It isn't real!" Rook said as he dropped the pamphlet. He looked around as if for an answer and then directly at John's ghost. "Did you even think about it? Did someone convince you it'd work?"

As if in answer, Rook's head burst with a splitting headache, and he grabbed it, wincing in pain. His vision grayed out, seeing nothing but bright spots on a slate field of view. And within his chest, he felt the stuck thing pressing against the tissue of his lungs, causing him to break out into a coughing fit again.

Rook stumbled, pushing the armchair forward as he used it to leverage himself into motion toward the rooms down the hallway. He had two choices to make and decided the water closet would be on the same side as the kitchen. He fell through the door and planted his hands securely on the rim of the sink as he coughed into it, the pain causing him to hunch over it. Rook spit up blood, coughing it out and splattering it across the white basin. Rook's sight returned to see the spew, watching the drips and then the color of his blood as it gathered around the drain. Rook felt his skin flush, cold and clammy, as he focused on the drain to steady his swirling vision.

Rook looked up and saw John's face staring back at him in the mirror. He saw the sunken pits of his eyes and the paleness of his skin. The corners of his eyes were irritated and red. He reached up and grabbed the edge of the mirror, ripping open the medicine cabinet behind it, and reached in to grab whatever medication John had secured. But there was none. Rook stood up straight and backed away slowly as the horror of what he saw sunk in. There was no medication in the cabinet at all, not a single prescription bottle, no cough medicine, not even a tin of aspirin. All alone, the only thing in the medicine cabinet was a black mass, in glaring contrast to the white of its surroundings. It was a book. It was The Holy Bible.

"John, you fool," Rook whispered. "How could you throw your life away?"

Rook stepped forward and picked up the Bible. He opened it, rifling through its pages in the distant hope that it was more than it seemed. But it was not. It was just a common reprinting of the Bible. He let it fall to the floor.

Rook turned on his heel and made for the living room. On his way out, he finally noticed that articles and newspaper clippings on faith healing were scattered around the kitchen and on the table. Several more pamphlets from other churches were mixed in, even a few brochures on faith healing facilities. Rook's hands wiped across the top of the table, sending all that false hope careening to the floor. He leaned against the table, needing the support, as he felt his heart pounding in his chest.

"You couldn't know this, John," Rook started, "you haven't seen the things I've seen. You probably haven't been where I've been. So maybe you didn't know."

Rook gripped his fingers against the edge of the table.

"But you had to know. You had to understand that you

were throwing your life away. Right?"

Rook looked up, gazing directly at John's ghost.

"Why would God choose you? I've served him for hundreds of years, I've healed the sick, I've administered to the pained. I've helped countless souls into His hands. He has never once rewarded me with his presence, John. I've only seen the Archangel, never heard his voice. How could you think, seeing less, knowing less, that He'd heal you?"

Rook lowered his head, staring at the table, his grip tightening until it hurt. Then, he relaxed and let it go.

"Faith," Rook said, almost with a laugh. "Faith, that's how."

Nodding to himself, Rook stood up again.

"I get it," Rook said, looking skyward. "I understand. You're right."

Rook walked away from the table and took a few steps toward the apartment door. He stopped and looked at John again.

"This church of yours looks promising. I think we're meant to go there together. So, then let's go."

John slowly reached out with his smokey-black appendages and passed them through Rook, another tepid attempt at reaching out to embrace his old body. Rook nodded again and, passing through John, walked to the door, leaving the apartment.

Rook slipped through the large, ancient, ornate double doors of the All Saint's Church, a gothic, Victorian cathedral. The massive stone structure was larger inside than it had appeared from the street. An enormous, open space flooded Rook's eyes as he entered, his vision adjusting to the dimness in contrast to the sunlight outside. Rook held his breath, taken aback by the lavishness and intricacies of the frescos and stonework, and he paused in reverence.

Every surface visible was carved from polished or lacquered granite, alabaster, or marble. Nothing but gold and wood tones filled the space between the stone. Gilded statuettes of Jesus were the focal points for sprawling gold fillagree and molding covering every wall. Owing to the Victorian aesthetic of maximalism, not a single spot larger than one's hand was empty or undecorated along the walls, pillars, or floor, flaunting colors clearly chosen to pop against the fossil greys; autumn reds, warm Sienna, and cool Irish greens.

Rook passed under a giant, pointed archway supported by pillars, shined to a mirror gloss, and held up a ceiling that felt impossibly high above him. As he passed through the foyer and looked around to get his bearings, he felt amazingly small and tiny compared to the scale of this place. But he, somehow, also felt too tight, claustrophobic. As if, despite the open and negative space, something weighed upon his very soul here. As though the building itself demanded of one to confess their sins, lest the weight of the might of God crush them.

Shaking his head to focus again, Rook noticed a lack of pews. A staple of any church, Catholic or otherwise that Rook had frequented over the years. This church, instead, opted for rows of interlocked wooden chairs. Square and boxy, each furnished with a kneeling cushion for comfort against the unbearably flat floor, reminded him more of formal seating than worship spaces for the masses. The dozen rows of these chairs, with more than a half dozen seats on either side of the aisle, dismissed the notion, as did the disparate groups of people sitting in them. A family of four sat in one section, the mother dutifully praying as the father wrangled the kids. A group of tourists sat in similar awe as Rook near the front, their body language communicating their fear of touching any surface or displacing anything that would get them removed from the premises. Singles and couples sat scattered throughout the nave, most in silent contemplation or prayer. Only a man in the back row seemed truly at home here, sitting with a leg across his knee and hands along the backs of the chairs to either side, appearing almost relaxed as he surveyed the people before him.

Rook stuffed his hands deeper into his pockets and brought his shoulders to his ears. He looked down at the floor, feeling shame bubbling up being here, whispering to himself that he was sorry for staying away for so long. He looked to the spirits that hung with him and then forward at the depictions of Christ at the front of the nave in the chancel, a series of visages in fresco rather than carved wood. Shown was the deity in his stages of ascension, first his birth, the second dying on the cross, and the third on a throne of clouds. In place of an effigy of Christ on the cross was a gilded crucifix on the altar, centered in the middle of sixteen candles, most taller than the cross they bolstered. Rook was caught off guard, pleasantly surprised that the tropes of Christianity were being eschewed here. But, the grandiose displays of opulence that were ever-present in the church weren't overlooked, and Rook saw the point that Luther had made.

Rook's heart clenched in his chest. He didn't know if it was one of his body's symptoms or a pain all his own. His ghosts didn't help the feeling, their forms hovering closer and closer to him, filling his space, closing in on him as if they sensed his weakness. He felt oppressed and burdened. He felt their judging. And John wouldn't stop reaching for him, through him. Rook heaved a breath and waved them off, walking down the aisle and heading for the front row of seats. He slid in a few seats deep and sat down, pushing the cushion aside and landing with a thud against the wood backing before he placed his head in his hands.

Why, Rook thought, looking up at the paintings of Christ. *Why are you silent?*

No reply came, not that he expected one. But he wanted one. The need for one burned in his chest right alongside the cancer mass, equally painful and equally undeniable. Rook took the cushion and placed it on the floor before him. Sliding off his chair, he kneeled on the cushion, clasped his hands, and stared at the altar cross.

I celebrated my four hundredth and seventy-seventh birthday the other day. I have entered into Your grace among the long-lived children of Adam. But they walked with You, Lord, and I do not. I have been left bereft of You.

Rook lowered his head and closed his eyes.

I have done all I can with this gift You've given me. In times of conflict, I was a chaplain and a doctor, Lord, I enlisted or conscripted myself into service to spread Your word and love. Through the Wars of Reformation, I upheld You. Through the strife of the aftermath and every small battle held in Your name, I joined them to defend You. Even through the horrors of the World Wars, I stitched muscle, set bones, sutured skin, and alleviated disease at the front line. I gave every fallen soldier in my way a path to You. I sent them into Your hands, O' Lord, each and every one.

Rook clenched his eyes tighter, the knuckles of his hands turning white as he gripped them together.

I took only what I needed to survive. I never abandoned a

host before it was time. Surely You have seen that. I give thanks to Your blessing and to them for their sacrifices. I assure them they are helping me achieve the greatness You've set aside for me. Even if they don't go, they are in Your grace. All in Your Grace.

Rook's eyes shot open. Tears filled them. He did all he could not to let his emotions burst.

But am I lying? Why didn't You help me? Surely I am worthy of it, but You don't see it fit to tell me? You didn't take me when I blasphemed before You with the Lutherans. But You also didn't bless me with the ability to heal the sick and wounded that were beyond my skill. You didn't help me when I died over and over, never letting me see the light of Heaven. Am I being punished? Is this body You have given me a punishment? Should I die with it and join You in true death? Is that the point of it? Am I being tested to have faith in You though I see no light and to take this death willingly and commit myself into Your Kingdom a full spirit?

Rook shook his head, wiping his tears.

No. That is blasphemy, too. To willingly die and not take a new vessel? That is suicide. I would not join You in your Kingdom, I would find my fate in Hell. That is not the answer. You would not condemn me to Hell. I... I...

Rook shook his head again and stood up. He stared at the cross, unmoving, until the black whisps of John's ghost passed through his vision and broke him from his fervor. He wiped his eyes and forehead, looking at the dampness in his hand. And with one more look back at the cross, seeing nothing in return, Rook turned and walked away from his seat, leaving the cushion on the floor.

"I have heard a lot of prayers over the years here," a man said from the seat just behind where Rook had been sitting, "but nothing so interesting as yours."

Rook stopped short of entering the aisle. The man he had seen earlier, in the back of the church, the one who sat casually in the last row, had moved to the seat behind Rook. Looking at him now, Rook took in the man's features. He had light brown skin and shoulder-length black hair that matched a thin goatee edged on his angular jawline. He wore a gray suit and matching slacks with black shoes, but his blazer was unbuttoned, as were the top buttons of his shirt. He had the look of someone who dressed to dress, not to fit in, and had an air of roguishness about him that was complimented in his smile Rook didn't appreciate. The man's presence unnerved Rook, and he thought the comment was tinged with lunacy. Still, Rook offered a polite smile and a nod as he walked into the center aisle. He hurried past the man's row and continued toward the back of the church.

A candlestick whizzed by Rook's head. Rook dodged; too late to avoid contact had the aim been a bit better. He spun to see from where it came, but Rook saw no one. He looked around the nave, seeing the others in the church turning their attention to the loud clang that rang through the quiet hall, but none appeared as though they had tossed the object. From behind, Rook could hear the scraping of something hard along marble or stone and turned toward it. He saw another candlestick from the fifteen that remained on the altar drag along the altar's surface, getting caught on the cloth under it. Rook strained to see what was moving it, seeing a dark figure labor with it. Just as he recognized what he was seeing, he saw the glowing red voids of anger burning from where one should have eyes as John's ghost flung another candlestick at Rook.

Rook dodged again, this one surely finding purchase had he not moved in time. He backed up, watching the other churchgoers scream as they pointed at the movement, unable to see what caused it. Several drew signs of the cross on their chests, and others scrambled over themselves to get away. All but the man who spoke to Rook earlier were frightened.

"John, no, don't do this!" Rook yelled, hands out, trying to calm the raging spirit. But John wouldn't listen. A second and third candlestick flew at Rook, the last one finding its mark. Heavy metal collided with Rook's collarbone, sending a sharp shock of pain down his arm, knocking him to the floor. He tumbled over onto his back to see the hateful ghost blur through the lines of chairs and slam into him, passing through him and through the floor beneath him.

Rook skidded his shoes and got to his feet. He backed away, looking all around for John. Suddenly, the spirit shot up from beneath the tile, sending the thick stone bricks into the air and shattering the granite flooring. John reached the ceiling, tearing off pieces of the alabaster skeleton that held up the roof, and flung the chunks at Rook. Rook had to run, dodging the ballistics and hiding behind a pillar.

"John! Please!" Rook gasped as he leaned against the pillar, his body already pushed to its limit. "Don't give in to anger! Let go and go with God!"

The pillar began to shake. Over Rook's head, dust and fragments of stone began to rain down. He backed away from it, watching cracks spider through the pillar, the section of the ceiling it held buckling under the shift in tension. Then, when Rook saw the top of the pillar dislodge, he threw himself to the floor as the massive stone structure collapsed behind him, peppering him with sharp shards of stone that sliced into his back.

Rook rolled over, his blood streaking across the floor as he pushed himself back with shaking arms and legs. Over him, John's specter descended from above and slammed into Rook, this time sending a shock of white-hot pain through his arm as John dug into it with black claws of glittering, broken smoke. Rook struggled to free himself, but John had his arm pinned, and the flesh of it was flayed before his eyes.

Rook screamed and flailed his other hand toward John but found nothing to strike. His hand passed through the shade repeatedly, everything about the wretched thing being incorporeal except what John willed to be otherwise. His claws solidified into shards of glass just before they sliced into Rook's arm and then dissipated into a haze again when he pulled them away. With that, John had him pinned, the swirling mass of darkness made solid in his arm and glued him to the floor beneath. Rook couldn't break free.

"Please, John," Rook wheezed, blood sputtering on his lips. "Stop."

And John did. He paused his slashes and slowly rose above Rook. It was enough to let Rook pull his arm in, but he still couldn't move. John had fused himself to Rook's legs. And as John moved over Rook, he fused more and more of Rook's body with his ghost form. John, still, was trying to reclaim his body, working his mass over Rook and solidifying himself within him. Rook felt the crushing pressure moving up his body. And he could feel the edges of his soul being pushed and strained. It felt like a profound sadness as his soul reacted to the attack, as though being dislodged was breaking his spirit, literally. Rook felt it sending waves of pain through his body, and a terror arose inside him he hadn't felt in more than four hundred years.

John bore down. His hips fused with Rook's. And then his intestines. And then his stomach. Rook felt his heart slowing down. Slowing. Slowing...

With a scream, Rook willed his soul out of his body and drove it against John. The jettison of his ethereal form rocked John, sending the ghost through the church nave and shattering him even further. Shards of John, broken free and glinting in the light, fell like embers as they left him, burning away in a pale, green glow until they were nothing. Rook watched this in horrific fascination, but John cleared the space between them in a flash. Rook shot himself forward and clashed with John again, turning his shoulder into the impact and breaking John in two. As one of the pieces fell away, consumed in the green soul fire, the other hovered. Its remaining shards knitted and re-knitted, spreading out to fill the gaps, siphoning John's essence to spread over his form to return it to a humanoid shape. This left John with less substance. Less of his spirit remained. Less of what was John.

John fully succumbed to madness. There was no longer any sense to his flailing. His glass-like claws and jagged edges swung wildly, slashing through the air and through the other ghosts bound with Rook. In his convulsions, John broke chunks off some of the other ghosts, causing their shattered forms to break further. In response to their damage, they began to shudder and quake as well, Rook watching in abject horror as their eyes, too, began to glow red.

Rook felt nothing but panic. He slammed into John again, sending him to the floor and breaking him even more. He slammed into him again. And again. When one of the other spirits dove for Rook in their newfound rage and power, Rook turned his aggression on them, shattering them further and burning their shards away just as he had done to John. And as another enraged, Rook turned on them, too.

"I'm sorry!" Rook cried out, unrelenting in his assault on the ghosts. Rook slammed into each spirit here, wild or not, pummeling them over and over and over again. Each shattering sent Rook further into despair, feeling the breaking underneath him twice over for the innocent ghosts he beat to pieces. When the last fragments of the last soul burned in green fire, Rook sunk back into John's body. And once inside, he could do nothing else but cry.

"Bravo, bravo!" The man finally stood up from his seat, clapping slowly as he walked toward Rook.

Rook snapped himself out of his sorrow and got to his feet. He held his wounded arm tightly against his chest and eyed the man who was walking up to him with a confidence that raised alarms in Rook's head.

"What an interesting fight," the man said, stopping before Rook and gesturing to the destruction of the church. "I've seen wraiths go feral before, but I've never seen a living soul beat others into submission. Truly impressive!"

"Please," Rook said, turning away from the man and pulling his arm tighter against himself, blood dripping onto the glossy floor, "leave me to my madness. Don't join me in it."

"You think I'm mad?" The man laughed. "I saw the wraiths. Thirteen of them."

Rook turned and looked at the man incredulously.

"It must have been something else," the man continued, "to have so many wraiths locked to you. Don't think I've seen that before, either."

Rook's eyes widened, and he cocked his head, mouth opening to ask the man how he saw. But he shook it off.

"Please, I've got to go," Rook said, turning away again.

"I get it," the man said, stepping in front of Rook so quickly that he had no choice but to stop suddenly. "Between the wraiths and your prayers, you're in a bad place right now. And, no, I'm not like you or your friends Cristof or Nadir. I'm called Cael."

When Rook looked at Cael with the question of *how could he know?* on his mind, Cael responded by tapping his own temple and then giving a knowing nod. Rook blinked.

"You can read my mind?"

"Oh, I can do more than that," Cael said. He sighed and looked over the church nave. "I like to come here between missions and listen to the prayers. It fills me to hear the people asking for help. But it's always God or Jesus they ask, never the rest of us." The man chuckled.

"Wait," Rook said, "y- you're an angel?"

"You tell me," Cael said. Raising his arms into the air, two glorious pure, white wings burst from his back. The feathered appendages stretched across the expanse of the nave, and the gust of wind they caused blew out many of the candles in the church.

"My God," Rook gasped, dropping to his knees and turning his eyes downward despite the blood from his arm dumping on the floor. "Heavenly Father, thank You for showing Your messenger to me! I am forever in Your light! Take me, I am ready!"

Cael laughed.

"I'm not taking you anywhere."

"What?" Rook opened his eyes and looked up at the angel. "Aren't you an answer to my prayers? Didn't God send you to take me home?"

"God? What God? Your God?" Cael's wings relaxed and hung at his sides as he put his hands on his hips.

"Y... yes?" Rook got back on his feet, struggling to do so without using his arms.

"My God, humans are arrogant," Cael said with a smirk. "Sorry, that's just an expression —my God— there isn't one to call to. Not like that. Never was."

"O-okay, but you're here to take me to Heaven, right? I'm finally being rewarded for my years of faith and stewardship. O-or confession! You're here to hear my confession so you can absolve me and let me in."

Cael laughed again and turned away.

"No. No one goes to Heaven." Cael looked back at Rook to gauge his reaction and smiled when he saw Rook's mind racing.

"No one?"

"No human goes to Heaven," Cael said, turning back to Rook. "And even if they did, it wouldn't be you."

Rook's eyes widened.

"I'm to go to Hell? Are the sins I've committed unforgivable?"

"What?" Cael laughed again. "No, no. Humans don't go to Heaven or Hell. That's for us." He reached out and placed a hand on Rook's shoulder before pulling it back and looking at the blood on his hand. "No, you're going to go where all humans go. The Agglomeration." He flung his hand toward the ground, trying to get some of the blood off.

"I-I don't understand. The scripture said-"

"The scripture is wrong. No one has it right. You humans take one little bit of evidence or interaction with us and create whole religions around it." He turned slightly to point at the fresco of Christ on the wall over his shoulder. "Take this guy, for instance. A millennia ago, Lucifer told some guy named Peter that he couldn't get into Heaven any more than that carpenter across the valley, and so Peter dreamed up a whole reason for it and, bam, now look at it. The greatest misunderstanding ever told."

Rook's jaw dropped, and he slapped a hand over his mouth as he looked up at the images of Christ.

"And, yes," Cael said, turning fully toward Rook again, "you got Lucifer wrong, too."

"Th-that can't be…"

Cael's expression changed. His face softened, and a look of sympathy crossed it.

"It's nothing to worry about," he said, "you do have a place to go, a purpose to fulfill once you're done." He balled up a fist and gently hit Rook's shoulder with it. "You get to make future humans better."

"How?"

Voices floated through the air, reaching Rook and Cael. They both heard people approaching as they neared the nave of the church. Rook turned toward it, looking at the hallway where he heard the sounds. Cael raised a finger, and all the doors and windows slammed shut. Runes of blue energy flamed into existence around the doorways and then settled into a dull glow. Rook could hear the people trying to open the doors, unable to get in.

"I like this conversation," Cael said, "but it's just between us."

Rook looked at Cael again.

"How?" he restated.

"How?" Cael raised a brow.

"This afterlife you're talking about. If we don't go to Heaven or Hell, then where do we go? Is there bliss or pain? How do we make future people better? Do we teach them?"

"Oh, that," Cael said. "The Agglomeration. Think of it as a swirling ball of people. Your souls all go there to join the ball. There's no afterlife or eternal reward or anything. I don't think it's painful, but then again, I'm not sure if you feel anything." Cael shrugged. "And it takes a while, but your soul eventually dissolves away, and your experiences increase the collective experience of that ball. When a new human is born, they come from that ball better primed for your world."

"Purgatory? Are you saying that no matter the life we live —that even though there are gods, angels, and demons— we're only headed for confinement? That we're stuck somewhere waiting to fade away? You're describing purgatory!"

Cael raised a brow, thinking about the parallel.

"I suppose it is."

"How could a loving God allow that?!" Rook yelled. "How can that be my reward for being a good and faithful person? To be lumped together with killers and rapists? Tossed into the same sleepless dream that Hitler gets? When these hands have brought the dying back from the brink of their deaths, or were clenched into fists to defend those who couldn't? I refuse to believe it!"

"Good and faithful?" Cael's face darkened. "You are not."

"What?" Rook's indignation evaporated.

"You didn't join those wars to save others. You joined them because 'truths have a penchant for being unearthed when the ground is shaken and burned,' which is a wise thing your friend Nadir said, but it is as selfish as fighting for personal gain or glory is.”

“No, th-that’s not true.” Rook shook his head. Fresh blood dripped from his arm onto the floor again, the pain of the wound finally starting to set in.

“You put yourself into harm’s way, knowing full well you could just take another body,” Cael continued, a frown forming on his face as he stepped toward Rook, seemingly taking in new information from Rook’s mind. “You even took the bodies of those you were trying to save.”

“I-I had to,” Rook said, stepping backward.

“No,” Cael said, tilting his head and letting out a small, derided laugh. “My job is to hunt down rogue celestials. To put to the blade the Divine and Unholy who risk the protection of mankind. I can tell when someone is hiding the truth from themselves. And you, you’re willfully delusional. In your lifetime, you have harmed and killed more people than even the best of killers outside of war. Were you anything but human, you’d be dead at the end of this chat.”

Cael drew a dirk from somewhere under his blazer. The short weapon’s blade extended to a stiletto, the metal igniting into a blue fire.

Rook’s eyes shot to the weapon. He tripped over himself to back away from it, falling to the floor with a thud and sending blood splattering in all directions.

“Do you know what that makes you, human? That makes you evil.”

"No!" Rook exclaimed. He raised up both hands before him, the flayed flesh on one breaking open again, causing rivulets of blood to run down his arm. "Please! I need forgiveness. I need your mercy! I need answers!"

"I don't have any more answers for you," Cael said, his wings pressing against his back and disappearing. "I have seen that you are no one. You're nothing."

"Please! I can't continue suffering like this. It can't go on like this."

"If you want your suffering to end, you should just let go and die. Your opportunity is coming up shortly."

"N- N-," Rook attempted to speak but began to cough violently. Each racking cough sent blood into his throat and onto the floor. It was a darker color than the blood from his arm, congealed masses of disease and clot. He looked up at the angel, his eyes blurred from the tears that had welled up.

"There it is. You can let it just take you."

"W-why?" Rook managed to get out. "Why do th-this? Why w-won't you help me?"

"You're not worth helping. You end up where you end up, even if it takes you a few hundred years longer to do it than most." He gestured up and then down to illustrate his point. "The Divine belongs in Heaven, the Unholy in Hell, and you, my worthless human? You deserve your fate. Purgatory, you called it?" Cael leaned in toward Rook, sneering as he looked him over. "No, it's worse for you. You're locked in this endless cycle for eternity."

"No!" Rook shook his head. "It's not fair!"

Rook's soul rose from his body, letting the husk fall onto the floor, and lifted to his full height before Cael. He steeled himself in his anger and screamed, throwing himself against Cael. But Rook was stopped cold. The angel's body was just as solid to Rook's soul as it was to his flesh. He bounced off, ricocheting from the unexpected block, and tumbled to the side.

Cael laughed at the attack. A full and hearty laugh as he watched Rook regain his bearings and line up before him again.

In a blind rage, he dug into himself again, pulling as much will as he could to the surface, and rushed at Cael. If he couldn't damage him, he'd have his body instead, Rook thought. He plummeted into Cael's form, connecting with his surface and smashing into the impenetrable wall. Rook was stopped again, bouncing off Cael and spinning in a daze.

Cael reached down and picked up Rook's body. With an effortless motion, he tossed it at Rook's soul, and as the body passed through his spirit, his soul attached to it out of reflex, finding its anchor again and latching on. When the body came to rest on the floor, it housed Rook's soul once again, and Rook felt the pain wash through him.

Cael jumped across the distance and picked up Rook by his neck, choking him and causing him to gasp for air.

"Is it vengeance you seek?" Cael said, dangling Rook's limp body around as he turned and faced the effigy of Christ. "You mourn for your broken faith? Maybe I'll give you a gift. Maybe, I'll give you a taste of the evil you've been spreading every time you take a body." He pulled Rook in close to his face. "Maybe you will finally break when you know what it's like to be Fractured."

Raising Rook up over his head, Cael flattened out his other hand and placed it against Rook's chest. Then, in a quick motion, Cael pushed. A gush of blue energy poured out from Rook's back in a billowing eruption. Like a raging river, the energy flowed through Rook, catching his soul in the current. Rook felt as if his soul was in a tug of war. He tried to hold on, but the compounding pressure from the wave and overbearing sense of loss and despair took him. He couldn't remain anchored to the flesh. Rook's soul snapped free from the body, tumbling out of the shell and into the air. Cael stopped and waited.

Rook felt something inside him break. Starting from where he was previously connected to the body, he felt an odd sensation travel up his soul. Numbing, deadening.

Impossibly, he saw the smokey ephemeral form of himself crack and break. Somehow, spirit stuff that had never been hard or rigid shattered like brittle glass. The shards had edges, shorn, jagged facets, that clinked and gathered around each other as the breaking continued up his form. Worse than this,

Rook felt his mind changing. His rage and obsession with Cael amplified, consuming him with an all-powerful hate. At the same time, he felt his warmth die. The concern he had for himself, the souls he destroyed earlier, and the countless he touched over the years, they felt a million miles away from him now. The details remained as though he had woken up from a dream, but his emotions attached to them faded. Rook looked himself over, feeling the transformation within him, watching himself grow long, razor-like claws on each hand. His vision, once nothing but grays and blues when outside a body, began to tint red. He turned toward Cael, and with an undying, feral hatred fueling him, he shot toward the angel.

Cael threw John's body at Rook's soul again. Rook passed through it, but when he emerged on the other side, Cael appeared before him and shoved Rook back into the body. Helpless against the angelic force, the body closed in around Rook's soul, robbing him of the burning anger that powered him and locking him into the flesh. Cael slammed the body into the ground, and Rook's eyes opened to see the world in full color again.

Cael laughed. But Rook couldn't read the expression. He saw Cael's face, the upturned mouth, and the squint in his eyes, but he could no longer fathom what the gestures meant. Cael was laughing at him. Was it mocking? Genuine? Why would he be laughing? An intense fear flowed through Rook as he realized he didn't have these answers anymore. That he did once, but now they were gone. It felt alien to him, these gestures. And so did the body. Like an overriding need or a phobia taking its first root, Rook felt like he needed to be rid of the body. He felt his skin crawling, feeling an itch too deep to be in the flesh. He didn't know what it was, only that he needed to leave.

Rook moved to get up, and without Cael there to stop him, he sat up. When he did, the doors to the church burst open, and the dozen people who had been trying to get in finally spilled into the foyer and nave. They pointed at Rook and started to run over to him, but he didn't care to stay. Rook abandoned the body, discarding it like trash and leaving the corpse for the church personnel to deal with. He phased through the wall and went outside.

Rook looked up and down Margaret Street. It was thick with pedestrian traffic. Rook could tell the tourists from the locals, and he could see those who seemed to travel alone or in small groups. Even the alleyways were full of people pushing their way past each other to get into the streets. But Rook also knew something else, that it is often when the crowds are thickest that the biggest details are missed. And in this case, no one would notice someone having a bit of trouble when there were just so many other people in the way. He scanned the crowd, looking for the inevitable loner to waltz their way through the dense field of flesh. It didn't take long, and once he had the target in his sights, Rook only waited for the man to take his turn into the alleyway before he descended upon him.

Rook screamed. Every first breath in a new body was a scream. But the streets of London didn't hear it. No one more than glanced at the poor bloke who pulled himself off of the concrete behind the trash bin. It was of no concern to anyone when the man stood up, brushed himself off, and doubled back on the route he had taken just moments earlier. For the first time, Rook felt something he never had before as he waded through the throngs of people on the busy street in the shadow of the palace. He felt like he had lost something of himself. He felt free.

As he walked along the streets, Rook caught a reflection of himself in a window and stopped to look at it. *What a nice coat this kid is wearing. Black leather, red lining. How avante garde*, he thought. *I think it's my kind of style.*

Chapter Eleven

A heavy downpour drenched Margaret Street and kept it in darkness. It did little to stop the late-morning crowds brave enough to fight the rain. A mix of locals and tourists filled the avenues and alleyways armed with umbrellas and raincoats in defiance of the dark clouds blocking the warming sun. They had all expected this weather in some manner, and those prepared for it were eager to be about the streets just the same. But, there was nothing they could have done to prepare for the sight that greeted them, the only thing that could turn their attention away from castles, kingdoms, and the Almighty.

The crowds parted like a seismic wave. At the fore, people stopped abruptly, standing like walls against the surging tide behind them. Those behind pushed against the barrier, unsure why the movement had slowed or stopped. As the wave moved through the mass, those who saw its source could not process what they saw. The people parted out of instinct, awe, or terror. An eight-foot-tall dark angel, with wings black as night arched on each shoulder, and his scythe pointed before him, blazing with amethyst static like a thunderstorm, marched a captive down the street. His prisoner, shackled by his necrotic energy and suspended a foot above the ground, growled as the people separated before him. Sent through the crowd on this dead man's walk, escorted by an emaciated Dave Vanian in a double-breasted black suit, Rook glared at the church that was slowly, inevitably, growing in the distance.

The faces Rook saw in the crowd weren't looking at him. They looked at *him*. They looked at the symbol of his —of their— captivity. He saw their astonishment. He saw them making signs of blessing and mouthing words of prayer. He pitied them. He pitied them all for their ignorance. He knew they didn't know —that they couldn't know— the truths and secrets he'd uncovered, not when beings like *him* would never tell them. He pitied their fates, their inexorable ends, their stories barely told, and their memories doomed to be forgotten.

Rook scanned the crowd, looking past their flesh to the black souls underneath. He didn't buy into the dogma that they were all products of an ever-churning system and saw differences and variations in their souls. Most were pure and intact. Others had rough edges. Some were thicker, like campfire smoke, while others were thinner, like steam rising off the stove. For all that was the same about them, there was so much that was different. They weren't copies. They were unique. Never to exist quite like this again, even if they would live another life in time. Rook hated this fact down to his very being. This robbed him of all notions of destiny or free will. The philosophical fight was reduced to a laughable parody. Did you exist for a purpose? Do you make your own choices in life? Are you here, right now, witnessing your proof of the divine because it was predetermined? Or because chaos and variability convened our paths together?

The truth, the great secret, was that it didn't matter. Not when everything you are is locked inside a gilded cage. Rook wouldn't have it. The Angel of Death wasn't escorting him to his destination to die. He would deliver him to their reckoning.

Azrael came to a stop outside the gates of All Saint's Church and lowered Rook to his feet. With a gesture from one of his skeletal hands, Azrael parted the crowd between them and the open doors of the church. As the corridor of people formed, something caught Rook's attention. A flicker of color stood out amongst the dark ocean of souls in the corner of his vision, and he slid his eyes to look at it directly. A singular person stood out. A woman with exquisitely crafted features and haunting beauty stared at Rook. She smiled, purposeful and deterministic, as she locked eyes with him. But beneath the veneer, Rook saw a mingling of orange and red emanating from her. Rook smirked, and in response, the woman nodded and looked to the church doors. Rook turned his eyes back to the path before him.

Azrael brandished his scythe forward, and Rook was compelled to lurch in the commanded direction. But Rook didn't resist the force and instead pulled on the angel's tether as he dug his feet in, trudging toward the church. Once he crossed the threshold, Azrael's magic faded, and Rook was released. Looking over his shoulder at the shroud of death, Rook flexed his hands and readjusted his Spector, flipping the collar up and flaring out the sides of the coat. He watched as Azrael brought his scythe to his side and leveled his eyeless gaze at him in return.

The doors slammed shut. The sudden closure of the portal sounded like thunder and rattled the church. Rook turned and watched as he saw unseen runes that lined every inch of every door and window, set along every sill and frame, blaze into fiery blue existence. The door was sealed, every gap filled with solid, nearly liquid, blue energy. All exterior windows were filled with a thick frost, blue crystalized energy covering their surfaces and blocking all light. Rook saw himself locked into this arena, the blue energy lining the bones of the church.

He surveyed the people locked inside here with him. They were those who had been unaware of the spectacle outside and only turned to look once the door was closed and their silence disturbed. But now they saw Rook, and all around the reaches of the church, they saw the blue lines of their confinement burning brightly. Mutters of confusion came first, followed by sounds of questioning and wonder. Rook stepped aside as a man rushed the door behind him and pushed on it, his concern piquing into fear as he slammed his shoulder into the unmoving barrier and felt no give. He tried twice more, and when his results were seen by the others, a wave of screams followed, and a dozen others ran for the other doors only to find them equally barred. They looked at Rook, too, backing away from the only calm one among them, their fear of him apparent on their faces.

Rook saw them, too. His eyes passed over the people, seeing the black human souls within, as he slowly took in the crowd. He saw them as they separated, families pulling their children closer, friends or familiar faces flocking together as they left the prayer seats and went for the doors. He met the eyes that stared him down, but he didn't linger on them. He scanned through them, looking at their souls, seeing the auras that gleamed vibrant in their darkness. Until he saw one that wasn't. A boy, young, most likely in his late teens, held tightly by his mother, who had taken them back into a corner of the church. This one had a different color to his aura. Rook looked and looked hard at the green hue that smoldered within the child.

"It's poetic, isn't it?" A voice carried over the crowd, drawing everyone's attention to the man who stood alone before the altar and crucifix. "You and I, here again. Full circle."

"I don't think you know what 'full circle' means," growled Rook as he turned toward him.

Rook saw before him a man cloaked by the blue aura of the Divine, but he didn't need to see it to know it was Cael. The angel's armor shimmered in the light of the votive candles on the bye-altar, the facets and fillagree of the silver breastplate and armguards reflecting their light back into the church. His crossed arms didn't hide the lightweight armor of his station, nor did they hide the two bladeless dirk hilts fastened to his sides. The angel smiled at Rook, a grin stretching in response to his words.

"I'll admit, sometimes your human colloquialisms escape me, changing as often as they do," Cael's smile grew even larger, "so let's speak plainly, then. Hello, Fractured. Welcome to the end. You're fucked."

Rook looked at the people to either side of him, watching them cower in the shadows at the corners of the church.

"Ain't this a sight? Our pal Cael here's got himself an audience," Rook said, looking back at the angel, "more prayers you want to hear and do nothing about? Maybe have a wank while you're at it?"

"Oh, no, they're here for you," Cael said, gesturing at them with a sneer. "For your body-hopping pleasure. And for your new little trick, too. In case you get hungry."

Rook cocked his head and took a few steps closer,

reaching out to run a finger along the corner of a row of prayer seats.

"How bloody diabolical, fitting of an angel, luring innocent sods to their doom here," Rook said slowly. "So much for your golden rules, eh? What's another dead meat bag if it means taking down the Fractured? Must feel mighty good, being able to wash away your sins with a one-way ticket straight to absolution."

Cael laughed.

"You see these wards?" Cael asked, pointing a finger up at the glowing runes. "These are my special runes. Crafted myself from excerpts of various treaties from the Tome of Divine Law. While they stay lit, nothing can get through. Nothing cosmic like you, nothing celestial like me. Nothing short of a Throne could break through unless I want them to." Cael returned his gaze to Rook, his smile easing though his eyes remained bright. "No one will know what happens here until I emerge to tell of it."

"There it fucking is," Rook said, "behind all the bullshit and preaching, that's what you are. A bloody killer, just like me."

"No!" Cael yelled, projecting a force that caused all the church's seats to slide away from him as if pushed by the sound of his voice.

"I am nothing like you," he continued, speaking through gritted teeth. "You are nothing. A mistake. A broken piece of cosmic energy that needs to be erased. Nothing more. You won't even leave behind an emptiness when I destroy you, and the universe will be a better place for it."

"You really so sure?" Rook smirked as he walked toward Cael. "You're the one to blame for all this. Do you think offing me is going to erase that little bit of history? You fractured me. You did that. And everything I've done since is just a result of that."

"You were killing people and fracturing souls long before I did that, Fractured," Cael said, lowering his arms to his sides and resting them on the hilts of his dirks.

"Maybe so. But you can't even call me by anything else, can you? That's all you see. Me: fractured." Rook stood before Cael, the height of his body slightly shorter than the angel, causing Rook to tilt his head to look him in the eye. "I would've gladly died for you if you had lied just a little. All the murders before? They were nothing compared to what I've left in my wake since you revealed what you all really are. Hundreds? Thousands? That's on you, buddy."

Rook shrugged.

"But I reckon that don't mean shit to someone like you," he continued, "someone who just sat idle and watched as humans butchered each other by the millions. Don't act like it's all about morals now. You're just pissed 'cause your precious fucking soul machine is in danger." Rook sneered, inches from Cael's face. "I fucked with your bottom line, and like some greedy corporate cunt, they sent their best bloody wanker to cover it up."

Cael roared and backhanded Rook across the chest. Rook flew through the air like a rag doll, his body no match for the physical force flung against him. Having no time to get his bearings, Rook instead flared out his soul and enveloped his body within it. When he blew through the seats and the bye-altar at the far end of the nave, Rook's soul took the impact instead, burning some of the shards of the souls he'd collected to shield him from damage. Rook came to rest on his knee, his wraith receding back into himself as he turned his eyes onto Cael.

"How dare you?!" Cael yelled, walking quickly toward Rook and tossing debris out of the way. "You shameless parasite! You mock your very reason for existence. *Our* reason to exist!" Cael reached down and snagged Rook by the neck, easily raising him high over his head with one arm. "This system was built for you, but all our lives are tied to it! You fucked up by unbalancing it. Your death will save us all!"

Cael turned and yanked Rook over his shoulder, throwing him through the nave. Rook braced himself as he broke through a pillar, smashed through more seats, and came to rest in the center of a crater of cement that was once the main church altar. Rook's wraith retreated again, its shielding keeping his body intact, though this time not perfectly. Rook stood from the rubble and adjusted his coat again, finding his arm bruised and tender.

"I only exist because *you* fucked up," Rook said, rolling his shoulder as he let his wraith extend from his body. "*Your* system is fucked. *You* ignored me. And now *you* can't fix me." A whirlwind of glass began to swirl around him, and the floor rumbled in response to his growing power. "Your grand system, feeding on human souls like oil in a fucking machine, should never have broken so easily." Loose debris plummeted from the ceiling, causing heavy tiles to fall like hail around the church. "But you know what, mate? Humans should never have been so callously created in the first place. We're not your experiment anymore. You've become mine."

Rook shot up a tendril from the floor under Cael and wrapped it around him, dragging him down to his knees. A second tendril extended from Rook's side and scooped up a large section of the destroyed pillar, swinging it into the angel and shattering it to dust upon impact. The blow sent Cael hurtling through the broken seats and sliding along the polished stone floor until Cael came to rest a distance away and rolled onto his feet.

Despite taking the hit directly, Cael showed no signs of damage as he stood. He unhooked his weapons from his belt and held them at the ready. As Rook approached, Cael evoked the weapons and sent crackling blue energy, like that of living lightning, to form the blades of the large daggers. Armed, Cael dashed forward toward Rook.

A wall of glass shards erupted from the floor between them and slid toward Cael, but Cael skidded to a stop and slashed out with his dirks. The soul wall split apart from the arcing of his weapons, opening a section for him to pass through as the wall continued on. Rook winced, feeling the damage traced back to his soul, and turned his shoulder toward Cael to unleash a deluge of shards at the angel. Like a laser beam, Rook aimed directly at Cael and swept it across his path.

Dodging the blast, Cael rolled under the stream but felt it slice into his shoulder as it was brought down upon him. The soul energy tore his skin, gouging out a chunk of celestial flesh that dissipated into the same thick blue smoke that Cael's blood did as it poured from his body, expanding out to fill the open air like oil in water. But as Cael continued forward, so did the blood, congealing together and back into his wound, instantly healing the damage.

Cael reached Rook and swung his dirk upward from below. Rook attempted to deflect, bringing his hands down on the angel's arm and wrist, twisting them to dislodge the blade. But Cael's strength and speed were immense, and the angel bore through Rook's attempt as though Rook hadn't even tried. His blade continued the arc, and Rook could only manage to bring his body out of its path by pushing away from Cael's arm. When Cael reached the apex of his swing, he turned to stab at Rook with his other dirk, just missing as

Rook fell away.

Rook tumbled toward the ground. Cael rushed up on him again and shot the tips of both of his dirks forward, directly into Rook's center mass. Rook had no hope of dodging and could only encase himself in his wraith again as the blades pierced through. He took the attack, stopping the tips from touching his flesh by the sheer amount of soul energy he put into the defense, and fell to the floor, having burned through another reserve of energy.

Cael raised his foot and tensed, ready to bring it down on Rook's head. A lasso of shards snaked up Cael's leg and then retracted, slicing and sending heavy blue smoke from his wounds again. Rook propelled himself up with a push of his wraith and swung a tendril toward Cael's arm, wrapping around it and working the shards up his shoulder and neck. Cael grunted under the pain of the slicing edges but brought his free hand over to cut through the appendage with his holy dirk, severing the mass and shattering it like a fallen mirror upon the floor. Cael's damage was severe, but his blood floating in the air soon reversed its flow, sucked back into his body, healing his wounds.

Rook, however, felt the severing and destruction of his soul run through him like a cold, sharp pain. It caused him to back up and clutch his torso, where it felt the part of his soul was sliced from, the pain too great to ignore. Cael took advantage of the pause and appeared before Rook, bashing him and sending him flying through the air again, smashing through tables and chairs on his journey through the foyer. Rook managed to absorb the damage but felt the cost of his impaired soul. As he got to his feet, he felt the gashes and scrapes he had gathered along his body. And he looked to see his Spector had been torn, the shoulder seam ripped.

Cael stood tall and laughed.

"Are you holding back, Fractured?" Cael said, showing that his body had healed from all the damage he had sustained to this point.

"I am so bloody sick of you calling me that," Rook said, taking off his coat and folding it up. "So many other colorful things you cunts have called me, but you keep going back to that."

"Is this your last wish?" Cael laughed. "Alright, what would you like me to call-"

"My name is Ruin," Rook said, tossing his coat into the confessional at his side. "My name is Vengeance." He turned to face Cael. As Rook summoned the energy from deep within his wraith, the lights inside the church began to wane and flicker. "My name is No One..." He began to walk toward Cael, whose smile had faltered, fading as he watched the lights dim. "And No One is calling."

Each lightbulb, fluorescent tube, and LED light in the church burst, sending a cascade of sparks and bright flashes across the church before plummeting it into darkness. A scream swam across the people still trapped by Cael's ward. Still preventing any outside light from entering, the nave was shrouded in an inky black. The only light came from Cael's weapons, offering slight illumination, his angelic eyes reflecting a supernatural shine.

"My name is Heartbreak, my name is Lonely," Rook's voice carried in the darkness. He spoke, but his voice was augmented. No longer speaking with just his flesh, his wraith now commanded the words, too. Reverberating with a crackling and grating that ignored physical space, his voice permeated deep into everyone and everything in the church.

Despite the darkness, Cael and Rook's eyes remained locked on each other. Cael, thanks to his angelicy, could see Rook clearly, while Rook could see Cael's aura like a bright beacon of light. Cael watched closely as Rook moved closer to a group of people that had gathered in a nearby corner. The humans couldn't see him, but they could feel his presence dominating the electricity in the air, and they tried desperately to pull away from it. Cael smirked, Rook continued.

"My name is Evil," Rook said. A dim light of his own cracked across his body, arcing bolts of spectral energy as his wraith pulsated with inborn rage. "Call me Broken, call me Shameless..."

A storm of pale green lightning burst from Rook like a tempest, casting back the darkness as his body rose into the air. Bolts of ethereal lightning scorched the ground, leaving black ash in their wake. The power burned through Rook's clothes, igniting fragments into cinders as the arcs of electromagnetism charged the air while ferrous metals were flung from his presence like bullets.

"Call me whatever you want. But know, my name's a war song! And I'll bring you a new war!"

Six ghostly bolts of lightning shot through the people near Rook. The crackling power ripped their souls from their bodies as the arcs boiled their skin and charred holes through them. The bodies disintegrated into clumps of smoldering embers. Above them, their trapped souls were impaled on his jagged spikes. The lightning then reversed, and the flash bolted back into Rook, dragging the shattered souls with it. This breaking of human souls sent a painful spike through Cael's brain, compounded six times over, and he fell to his knees as he screamed in pain. Reflexively, Cael's wings exploded from his shoulders and wrapped around him, trying to protect him from the otherworldly agony.

"I'll tear your world open!"

Rook's tendrils snaked out in every direction. Wrapping around every banister and pillar left standing, wrapping around Cael himself. The tendrils that found anchors all contracted simultaneously, sending Rook forward at blinding speed. As he crossed the distance, Rook covered himself in the erratic energy and slammed a jagged, spiked fist into Cael. The blow sundered Cael's defense; a wing buckled and gave way as the edges and points of Rook's attack shredded angelic flesh and shattered bone. Rook's spectral fist blew through Cael's body, turning his arm, side, and leg into bloody blue chunks that splattered across the walls of the church behind him like it was a children's finger-painting canvas. Nearly half of Cael's body was eviscerated, the other half toppling to the ground as Rook landed behind it. Rook turned, the energy of his wraith electrifying and shocking the bits of blood mist in the air as he faced Cael's remains and stared at his husk with burning, ghostly green eyes.

Then it faded. The six souls Rook consumed were used up. His reserves dry again. Rook dropped to his knees, out of breath, heart racing. He clutched his chest as this body began to fail as well, the exertion having burned up his connection to the Animus. As Rook looked at the fallen body of Cael, he slumped forward, unable to keep himself aloft or alive any longer.

As the body died, Rook rose from it slowly, falling to his spectral knees on the floor. The gray and blue hues of his ghostly vision pushed away all the shadows, allowing him to see the church and the damage it had sustained. Though he could see the auras of everyone here despite the darkness before, now he could see the faces of the people who were still alive, as well as the burnt bodies of those who weren't. He saw their fear, exacerbated by the lack of light, as they tried to understand what had happened. Though the light from Cael's dirks remained, it wasn't enough for them to see much, so they clutched each other and hugged the walls for safety.

Rook rose from his knees. He felt the ache and exhaustion even without a body as he stood. He looked at himself, at the shards of himself that made his soul. He had never seen so few. Even when he was first fractured, he had a full soul's worth of shards, maybe even a bit more after dealing with the feral wraiths. But now, he was barren, his wraith barely held together by the traces of his essence that bound the remaining shards together. He felt decimated and knew he had to consume again to stay whole.

As he looked over the survivors, he selected one and began his approach. But as he moved, he saw the dim light shift in the church. Dismissing it as a trick of his senses, Rook continued until he saw the light shift again. Turning, Rook saw, to his horror, Cael on his knees. In one hand, he had picked up one of his dirks, its movement causing the light to shift. The light illuminated the eerie sight of Cael's blood and entrails evaporating from the floor and walls to waft through the air back to the angel. Cael was reforming right before his eyes. Rook turned back to the survivors and moved to grab one.

"Uh uh uh," Cael said as a dirk buzzed past Rook and stuck into the floor before him.

Rook looked back, gauging if he had the time to take a

body before Cael could reform enough to kill him.

"How the hell is that possible?" Rook asked the angel. "I've put your kind down with less; how the fuck are you still here?"

Cael stood, his body now fully reformed, his wounds closing fast. He reached out for his other dirk, and it heeded its master's will, lifting from its resting place and flying into his hand. Cael looked at Rook and cracked his neck before pointing the tip of the weapon at him.

"You've killed a few Acolytes, so what?" Cael said as he started to walk over, gesturing at his broken armor to mend itself with whisps of white-blue energy. "I'm no Acolyte," he laughed, "and I am no Seraph, either. Devas bow to me. I am a Virtue. I command legions."

"And yet the Seraph Azrael has you shitting in your boots?" Rook scoffed.

Cael lunged, but Rook was unbound and kept his distance easily. Cael laughed and lunged again, forcing Rook to fly away from the humans in this corner and out into the open church.

"What happened to all that vim and vinegar?" Cael asked, inspecting the electric tip of his dirk. "'My name is Vengeance,'" he mocked, "pretty good speech, but not as much impact when you don't complete the kill. Just a little tip from me to you," Cael said, using his dirk to illustrate the point before shrugging. "Not that you'll need it after today."

Rook hovered in place, watching the angel. His form giving off a dim, ghostly light.

"But, you're right," Cael continued, "we don't call you anything but Fractured for a reason. I suppose it's harmless to tell you now."

Rook remained silent.

"Rook, Rook, Rook, Rook…" Cael repeated, tilting his head with each utterance, showing his disdain. "It's all the realms can talk about. Rook the Fractured. Rook the Destroyer. Rook the Anti-Agglomeration." Cael looked at Rook, his voice filling with venom as he continued. "Rook the Separatist. Rook the Liberator. Rook the Original Soul." Cael spit on the floor.

Rook watched and waited.

"We're all in this mess because you're an Original Soul! Do you think you're special because of that?!" Cael yelled, swinging wide with a blade. "I can kill you just the same!" Cael stopped and looked at the floating wraith, his cracked, gray form a mockery of the black human souls he had sworn to protect. "Who will miss you, anyway? There'll be ninety-nine of you left."

Cael brought his dirks to his sides, their blades extending into stilettos as he unfurled his wings. He shot toward Rook, up into the air and through the open space. But Rook was ready. In an instant, Rook had crossed the distance Cael moved and then some, continuing past him.

Unimpeded by a body, Rook's speed eclipsed even Cael's. Before the angel could register that Rook was no longer there, the wraith had descended upon a human and struck their soul. The fracture blasted Cael from behind, knocking his head forward and causing him to tumble once in the air. When he turned to look, he could no longer see Rook but saw a human on the floor in the midst of a seizure.

Rook tried to gain control as fast as he could. He forced his soul through the body's extremities and struggled to get his eyes open. He felt the coming rush of pain and adrenaline, the body beginning to respond to him when he suddenly felt nothing. The body was dead. Rook pulled himself from the corpse to find Cael kneeling next to it, his dirk buried to the hilt in their forehead. Cael turned his head to Rook as he emerged from its chest, a look of wild exhilaration in his eyes.

Rook fled the body and blinked across the room again, his speed crossing the entire distance of the church almost instantly. Again, Cael could not track the quick, short-range teleportation and again had to withstand a spike of pain in his head when Rook attempted another residency, but he shook it off and swung his eyes around the room until he saw another person struggling to keep consciousness through Rook's hostile takeover. This one was leaning against the wall, and the seizing was minimal, but Cael determined this was the one. With a flap of his wings, Cael was on the body. He poised his dirk above the breast of this host, where he knew the human soul was housed. His hand shook as he considered driving it deep into the heart of this body and into Rook himself, ending this fight once and for all, but he couldn't give up this euphoria yet. He'd never have this moment again. Locked in a fight with the Fractured, all of these deaths blamed on him, Cael could finally cull these worthless sheep and even be praised for it. He realigned the dirk to the body's brain and drove his weapon in deep and slow. Again, Rook abandoned the body and took to the air.

"Keep going, Rook!" Cael yelled. "Only a few dozen left to go!"

Rook reached out and, with his arm forming a long spectral whip, lashed at the person next to the angel, sending another painful spike through Cael. Cael yelled and covered his eyes, and Rook took that opportunity to descend into the floor. He couldn't go far, though, as Cael's ward blocked him even there. Still, it was enough, and when Cael regained his sight and stood looking for the next sign of Rook's possession, nothing caught his attention.

"Come out, come out, wherever you are!" Cael called as he stalked the room. All he could hear in reply were the whimpers of the remaining people hiding along the edges of the church.

Rook watched Cael's aura from within the stone of the floor. Diminished through the dense material, Rook's sense of the angel was dulled, but it was enough to track him.

Further, Rook could still see all the human's auras, but they were hazy and undefined. He couldn't pinpoint a soul like this; their auras were so diffused they overlapped. All except the odd green one. Rook noted he could still see it and that it shone slightly brighter than the rest. Almost as bright as Cael's blue.

Rook moved through the stone of the floor and positioned himself under the green aura. He couldn't breach the walls, so this was as far as he could go. He rose slowly, unearthing himself and rising next to the teenager. He was being held tightly by his mother, both shivering with fear and fighting the tears in their eyes. They were no different than any of the other humans in the church, and Rook could see nothing else about the child that would explain his green aura. But Rook thought about it; he had seen Lucifer in the crowd before he entered the church, and he gave Rook an indication to push forward. He despised the thought of being Lucifer's pawn, but that didn't preclude him from accepting one of his gifts. Perhaps this was something Lucifer prepared for him.

Fuck it, Rook thought, *what have I got to lose?*

Rook turned his attention back to Cael and waited for him to roam to the furthest gathering of people. When the angel turned his back to pick up a human by their hair, Rook sent a tendril across the expanse of the church to strike them. Again, the proximity caused Cael to recoil, the closest one yet, and Cael regretted it, waiting for the pain and the white haze to fade from his eyes.

Rook faced the child and reared up a tendril. He whipped it around the boy and pulled, but the soul didn't dislodge. More over, the boy didn't react as Rook expected. Instead of immediately coughing or sending him into convulsions, the boy merely flinched and looked around. And the attempt didn't seem to shock Cael at all. Rook tried again, wrapping his tentacle around the boy and pulling. But again, nothing. It was as though his soul was too solidly anchored.

Rook looked back, Cael was regaining his senses and was shaking off his blindness. He turned to face the boy again. Sending out tentacles to wrap around the broken pillars and debris in the immediate area, expanding himself out to twice his size, Rook fell upon the boy's soul. He used his tendrils to pull himself down and wrap his entire wraith around the soul. Rook engulfed it like a deep-sea predator, swallowing the child and his soul, anchoring himself in place until he could consume it. The boy fought back, his body not succumbing to the delirium or shock such an attack would otherwise cause, and Rook found his soul to be as hard as stone. But Rook wouldn't relent, and when he had folded over the entirety of the soul down to its Animus juncture, he used his remaining strength to pull down.

The boy screamed and tried to move away, but the invisible force choking him kept him in place. He couldn't tell what was happening, and his screams were echoed by his mother, who quickly fell into hysterics hearing her child calling out in anguish. Cael, too, was called by the screaming and flew up to see Rook's wraith consuming the boy's soul. He dove for the octopus-like aberration, bringing the point of his dirks to bear and homing them in on his target.

Rook felt the soul finally snap. The Anima broke free of the Animus, and the break sent an explosion of vibrant, emerald green through the church. The blast buffeted Cael, bursting his eyes and rupturing his ears before getting caught up in his wings, flinging him back against the far wall of the church. Cael thudded against the immovable warded barrier, cracking his skull. He slid from the impact, trailing blue blood along the surface.

Rook consumed the soul. The shattered, jade fragments joined his own, and Rook felt a rush of energy and power. As though each shard of green was worth a dozen full souls or more, Rook felt himself become gorged on endless cosmic energy. All his shards —his original, the remnants of those he consumed, and the shards of the child— blended together seamlessly as the boy's power filled in the gaps of his soul with molten, emerald filament.

The body, too, behaved like none had before. Perhaps it was the boy's soul so completely infusing with Rook's, or perhaps the body sensed the presence of a powerful soul, but it offered no resistance to him. Like slipping into his favorite

Spector coat, sliding into place within this body felt right. Felt natural. It welcomed him, and within seconds, Rook could feel himself blended with the body. He expected the familiar sting of his takeover to well up inside and overwhelm him with pain, but it never came.

Rook took his first breath, but it was not a scream. It was a gasp of cool, invigorating, clean air.

Rook opened his eyes and looked at the church. The lightless void seemed less complete. He could see the people huddled in each corner, even across the foyer and nave. But it wasn't just their auras he could see, like before. Now, he could see their faces as clearly as on a moonlit night. As he looked, Rook scoffed, realizing that the boy hadn't even fallen over. Holding his hands before him and seeing his aura now a body of gray glass chunks solidly fused together with green crystal veins, Rook marveled.

The sound of scraping caught Rook's ear. His eyes shot across the church to where Cael had pulled himself from the wall. He was healing quickly, bracing against the wall. Rook watched as the last of Cael's wounds knitted closed; the gash in his head all but disappeared. Cael glared at Rook, calling his weapons back to him.

"That's a new one," Cael said, shaking out the last of his daze and standing tall again. "Didn't think that could get any worse. That's on me. Never again."

"I've got plenty more tricks up my sleeve, cunt. Let's go."

Cael pushed off the wall and charged at Rook from the other side of the church. Bracing, Rook expected to see Cael in his face within the blink of an eye, but that didn't happen. Though still fast, Rook could track his movements, and dodged just before Cael could make contact. As he rolled out of the way, Rook exploded spikes of his soul through the skin of his fist and slammed it down on Cael's back, the green-lined and gray-filled spectral spikes impaling him in the side, sending the angel into the ground.

Cael rolled from the impact but was on his feet again in a deft movement, springing into attack with no wasted effort. Despite the gouged holes within him, he slashed at Rook, sending one dirk in after the other in a flurry of strikes. The attack was quick, and Rook couldn't cover his arms fast enough before the azure blades sliced into his flesh. Though the flame sizzled and seared through Rook's new flesh, the pain was less than he was expecting, allowing Rook to maintain his focus on the fight. And when his soul covered his arms, he swung with them, connecting his Anima with the blades and knocking them from Cael's grasp. With a hand free, Cael twisted and brought his wing forward, sending a rush of wind to pummel Rook, pushing him back, his feet sliding along the polished stone floor.

Rook was amazed. He used his soul as he had before, but burned through none of its power. He felt just as strong as he did moments ago. He looked at Cael, who himself had some misgivings of Rook's newfound power and no longer kept up his facade. Gone was the brightness in his eyes, and all but a memory were his arrogant and boastful laughs. Rook saw now in Cael a look of pure determination, one of calculation and grit.

"What's the matter? Did I break your knob?"

Cael hunched down and summoned his celestial power.

"Laial tol zna!"

Cael's words resonated with purpose, their syllables causing their desired effect as fast as the sound traveled through space. As soon as Rook heard them, he translated them to mean *stop all movement*, but Rook already felt a familiar sensation robbing his perception of time and sapping his movement. Rook watched as the command spread, crystallizing everything into stasis. All things, from the debris in the air to the beating of everyone's hearts, ceased, freezing this moment in time. Rook watched as Cael called his blades again, seeing them zip through the air at double speed. Cael moved hyper-fast, deactivating them and reattaching them to his belt. Rook tried to puzzle it out; Cael's command didn't exclude him. Why was he not totally frozen? Before Rook figured it out, Cael moved across the floor and squared up. Cael approached in a blur and swung a fist at Rook's face.

At the last second, which came incredibly quickly, Rook pulled his head out of the way. Though his movements were slow and sluggish compared to Cael's, the Virtue's ultimate power was proven less-than-effective as Rook managed to avoid the blow. His shock quickly turned into rage as Cael followed up with a second punch that connected with Rook's side and sent him through one of the remaining pillars, through a side-altar, into the stone floor, and then through it for some distance, tearing a path of rubble across the thick slabs and foundation beneath. Rook had no time to bring his wraith out to protect himself, and so his body took all the impact as it scraped across the stone, streaking blood along until he came to rest in a new crater across the church.

Rook opened his eyes and pushed himself off the ground. He felt the remains of the stone falling from his back as he pulled himself out of the crater. As he stood up and looked at Cael, he saw the angel's face twist into a visage of terror. He looked over himself and saw that despite the utter destruction to his clothes and several large superficial gashes on his arms and legs, he was otherwise unharmed.

"Huh," Rook said, looking at the torn-up stone, granite, and wood he just traveled half the length of the church through. "Well, ain't that something?" He looked at the stones that had just been on him, seeing them still floating in the air where they should have fallen. And when he looked around the room, Rook noticed that everything else was still frozen. He looked at Cael and smiled.

Cael's face dropped into a mix of horror and disgust. He reignited his blades in his hands again and pointed one at

Rook.

"Nephilim!" Cael yelled, panic coloring his voice as he spat out the word before his face contorted into a manic expression of levity. "Ha! Hahaha," Cael laughed. "You're nephilim now?!"

"Is that right?" Rook said, looking himself over again.

"Come, nephilim," Cael said, a blue shine overtaking his eyes, "let me show you the horror that awaits those of your kind!"

Rook leveled his eyes on Cael and let the darkness sink into his face.

"You have not known horror until I have shown it to you."

Cael charged, and though he was faster than Rook with time stopped, Rook had caught up considerably to the lag. Rook ran forward as well, but before him, his wraith flew faster. Somehow, he felt his soul and body would act as one, and death wouldn't come so easily as it had to all the others. His heart remained strong and steady, his body remained in motion, and in front of it, Rook rose like a feral beast brandishing long, razor-tipped spectral claws and gnashing, scissoring teeth that dove for and sunk into Cael's shoulder.

As Rook bit down, he raked Cael's arm and chest with his claws, opening long gouges of flesh to expose his divine blood again. As Cael struggled with the wraith, stabbing at it and cutting off chunks that instantly rejoined like globs of ferrofluid, he could not prepare for the second attack. Rook's body, somehow still operational without him in it, stepped up and threw a kidney punch that jettisoned the angel into the ceiling, where he scraped along it before gravity took over and plummeted him onto the floor.

Cael moaned in pain, his face and torso shredded to ribbons, but he pushed himself off the floor. Rook was on top of him before he could regain his speed. He pressed a foot into Cael's back and grabbed onto his wings. And then, pulling with all his might, Rook tore one of Cael's wings from his back.

Cael screamed as he doubled over, writhing in pain, reaching for a wing stub that wasn't there and finding only a gaping hole. Rook grabbed him again and tossed Cael onto his side. He picked up one of Cael's dirks and stabbed it deep in the stomach, dragging it along from front to back over his hip.

With Cael's concentration broken, time resumed, and a cacophony of terrified screams filled the room as the people saw the horrendous and visceral scene lit by Cael's weapons. They watched in horror as the teenager who had clutched his mother just moments before reached for and twisted the angel's remaining wing, grinding him into the ground until the boy's foot could press upon the angel's neck. And then the unthinkable happened; this boy pulled, and through the squelching sound of the angel's flesh tearing and the popping and cracking sounds of his bones breaking, the boy tore off the other wing and tossed it to the side.

Cael cried out, arching his back and screaming to the sky. Rook caught him from under his throat with his arm and, with his knee in his back, pulled backward to the point of straining. Holding the angel like this, he leaned in and placed his mouth against Cael's ear.

"Now it's full circle..." And then Rook pulled until he heard Cael's back snap and watched him fold unnaturally upon himself.

Rook dropped the squirming mass of broken angel onto the floor. He breathed hard, wiped his brow, and looked out over the people. He walked around Cael until he could face them all and looked at each of them in turn. In every face, he saw nothing but abject horror. Not one saw him as fighting for them or could fathom the significance of this moment. But it didn't matter. The message had to be sent, and he had to be the one to send it. He looked down at Cael, who pitifully reached out and tugged on Rook's pant leg. He pulled himself away from the grip and placed his foot on the angel's folded back. He took in a deep, fulfilling breath. And then he stomped.

Rook's foot crushed the angel's bone. Rook stomped again, and his foot tore flesh. Rook stomped again and again and again, and in his mind's eye, Rook saw the poor wraiths he had to beat down in this same church seventy years ago.

He stomped again, just as he slammed into them back then. He stomped again, just as he had to do to the feral ones. He stomped again, just like he did to the innocent ones. He stomped again, but it wasn't out of fear or preservation. He stomped again because he wouldn't allow himself to suffer any longer. And he stomped again because he was Rook Maison.

Rook looked down at Cael. There wasn't much left of him. The angel's blood no longer hung in the air like incense smoke. Now, it had begun to drift to the floor like snow. It pooled around the body and in the cavernous hole at its center. And it coated Rook's leg.

He then looked at the people, who stared at the mangled angel with profound sadness or deep despair. Some reached out, stretching their hands from the safety of their hiding spots, to mourn their Heaven's fallen and cry for him. Rook watched, repressing the frustration he felt seeing these people not understanding or simply disbelieving he had destroyed a monster, not their angel. He wanted to spew out obscenities, chastising them for their rigid beliefs and unwillingness to accept the greater truth. And he wanted to despise them for what he knew so well, firsthand experience of their zealous faith and blind followership. But he didn't.

Turning, he walked away from Cael. He bent over and picked up the bladeless dirks, turning them over in his hands and shifting the only source of light in the church. They were deceptively light and felt as though they were made of tin or even plastic. He couldn't tell if it was the nephilim strength that made them feel flimsy or insubstantial to him or if that was one of their celestial properties, but Rook liked the feel of them anyway. He held each one out and tried to turn them off, but they didn't respond. Even if he knew how to do it, he figured only Cael could manipulate them. Still, they would make great souvenirs, and he placed both in one hand.

A woman ran forward and stumbled over the viscera on the floor to reach Rook. She took him in her arms and hugged him tight, tears dripping from her soaked eyes as she held him.

"Michael!" The woman cried in his ear. "Michael, are you okay?"

When she felt no embrace back, she pulled away and looked at her son. Though she recognized his face, she didn't recognize his eyes as the cool, expressionless Rook stared back at her.

"Michael?" she whispered.

Rook slowly shook his head.

"I'm afraid not, love," he said. "And maybe you saw this coming, I think." He gestured toward the bloody angel.

The woman fell back and sat down in shock and disbelief. She blinked at Rook and then looked at the destroyed angel herself. She no longer moved. After a moment, Rook left her there, turning away.

But before Rook could leave, he heard a sickly wet sound.

He looked around at the people, but none of them were making any noises that sounded like that. As he scanned the church, Rook turned his eyes over Cael's body and saw the faintest flicker of blue still within it. It was slowly gathering what it could of the blood and flesh of the corpse, attempting to heal yet again. He stepped closer and cocked his head at the little sprite of energy.

"The wards work against even you, eh? Didn't think about that, did you?"

Rook reached out and slid a spectral tentacle around the angelic essence. He pulled it from the body and held it aloft before him. Though it cast the faintest of light that the others could see, only Rook saw it for what it was. He smiled as he held it, a grin spreading across his face.

"Fuck it."

He shoved the essence toward himself and let his wraith gnash down on it like he did to so many souls before. He took into himself this equivalence of an angel's soul and devoured it. When it was gone, the wet noise stopped. And Rook felt a tingling inside him.

Rook dropped to the floor as a torrent of energy surged through him. He convulsed as the celestial essence spread through his wraith and fused with his own and the nephilim's souls. Like an overriding imbuement of power, he couldn't contain the surging outpouring of energy, and it rushed forth, spilling from him. A cascade of light erupted from Rook, shining like a star that illuminated the church with the light of a bright summer's day.

As quickly as it started, it was over. Rook blinked, looking at the dark church ceiling above him as the last of the light faded. He sat up and laughed, feeling his wounds healing. He pulled back the tattered shirt sleeves to see the scars from Cael's blades smoothing over, leaving nothing behind of their once cauterized disfigurement.

Rook stood up and brushed himself off. His hand touched one of the dirk hilts, and he felt a warm sensation from it. Taking it into his hand, he held it forward and willed it to shut off. It obeyed. He then willed it to ignite again, and a blade of blazing, blue fire, mixed with static, blue electricity, formed from nothing.

"Too right," he said, turning off the hilts and fastening them to his belt.

A creaking began to well up from the depths of the church. The sound of the pouring rain began to fill the silence. The runes that covered every angle and edge of the church began to fade, and the outside light started to flood through the windows. One of the side doors broke from the pressure of the people leaning and pushing against it, bursting open and spilling them into the hallway. Another door flew open as people on the other side finally broke through. But most ran for the main entrance and clamored to pull it open.

And when they did, they froze because another angel stood in their way.

Chapter Twelve

Azrael stood beyond the threshold. His massive form heaved slowly, his barely restrained anger apparent as he gripped his weapon with both hands and stared through the entryway, waiting for any sign of Cael's successful completion of his task. He didn't even see the people before him, the mass that had stopped cold and fell to their knees at the sight of his dark presence. His wings cloaked them all in a darker shadow than storm clouds or rain ever could, but they were beneath his notice so long as their souls remained black and human.

Rook saw the massive blue aura blazing vibrantly through the church wall. He sighed and walked to the confessional, reaching inside to grab his Spector. As he slipped it on, the coat fell onto his new shoulders, draping from him in sublime perfection. Rook felt the silk lining slide across his skin as if feeling it for the first time. The wool of the outer shell felt thick and sturdy but warm and soft to the touch. He smiled as he smoothed out the coat and popped up the collar. The damage it sustained during the battle could be repaired, and he would see to that, but right now, his new favorite body and patched-up soul were of the same mind about his favored coat. He turned and faced the door and the Cataclysm beyond it. He was ready.

Rook walked towards the door, and as he did, he reached out with his tentacles and swept the people aside. He didn't reach into their bodies or grab their souls. He didn't need to. His will was enough to solidify his spectral arms to part the people from his path gently. He moved all those still inside the church, setting them off to either edge of the foyer.

"Go on, now, no sense in getting hurt caught up in all this," he said as he set them down, watching them reel from being moved by unseen hands. When all that remained were those kneeling at the doorframe, Rook took a breath and prepared himself. He reached out, grabbed them all, and yanked them from the door. And then he stepped through.

Rook emerged into the torrential London rain. The streetlights reflected in the raindrops as they fell, casting refractions onto the crowd outside and the dark angel who stood before them. As he stepped forward, meeting his eyes with Azrael, he caught lightning streaking across the sky from the corner of his eye, forking through the clouds behind the angel's wings. He watched Azrael's eyeless face, as flat and devoid of emotion as it was, betraying his anger as he took in the sight of Rook before him. His nose crinkled, and his eyebrows lowered. Azrael's grip tightened, and his already pale knuckles whitened further. He squinted at Rook and slowly cocked his head as he read everything there was to know about the boy who exited the church, the boy who looked back at him and smiled.

"Impossible..." Azrael said as his breath left him, his eyes widening. "No... I will not have this."

"Azrael," Samael cautioned, eyeing Rook but reaching out to touch his friend on the arm. "Don't..."

"He has become nephilim!" Azrael roared. He pointed the shaft of his scythe at Rook, the weapon surging to life with currents of amethyst and azure energy. "The Fractured has destroyed the Virtue!"

Azrael's wings exploded in a flurry of black feathers, his massive wingspan pulling him into the air as his eyeless voids blazed with purple fire. The force of his ascension sent the crowd crumpling to the cement, the beat of his wings crushing them further with each oppressive, downward thrust. As if at Azrael's command, the forces of nature were sent into chaos. Lightning slammed into the streets, and thunder crashed through the buildings, shattering glass and sending it down like rain into the crowd. The people's cries rose, their terrified screams shrieking through the quarter as they covered their ears and heads, scrambling over each other and trampling their fellow kind as they desperately tried to get away. The ground rumbled in response, quaking under the mounting pressure of Azrael's wrath. The streets cracked, the sidewalks buckled, and the streetlights sparked and exploded as they fell. Azrael evoked his title and set a cataclysm upon the streets of London.

Rook's soul shimmered into power. Tentacles burst from him in every direction, wrapping themselves around All Saint's Church behind him and snaking along its walls and the ground beneath him. Spectral tendrils pushed and pulled on every surface, lifting him into the air. The outpouring of his soul shone bright with gray light, every shard of glass in his wraith edged with a thick line of green like kintsugi, and his substance throughout was speckled and dotted with swirls of blue stars and galaxies. A storm grew within Rook as the shards broke free and whirled around through his phantasmal extremities. As the lightning struck around him, so too did pale green electromagnetic discharges, coursing through Rook's body, arcing along his haunted soul, sending bolts of lightning chaining through the raindrops and frying them with pops of steam. His whirlwind became a flurry of razor blades, slicing through and severing brick, stone, and metal along the street. Rook's stare never left the Archangel of Death as he matched him in his display of power. All the world would tremble on the precipice of their battle.

"Come on, you raging fuckstick!" yelled Rook. "You ain't getting any prettier!"

Azrael dove for Rook. Rook vaulted for Azrael. Samael yelled for them to stop.

Rook and Azrael hurtled toward each other, their bodies tearing through the wind and rain, ripping them asunder. The people were thrown through the streets.

And then it all slowed. As Rook and Azrael raced toward their collision, the distance between them grew to infinite, even as it drew closer to an end. The world around them restrained, coming to a halt, as they, too, felt their bodies fall into stillness. As if under protest by time itself, both Rook and Azrael slid to a stop a finger's width apart as they, and the entire world, froze.

"I want an explanation."

A white light blinded Rook and the angels. From between the celestial spheres, a slit was cut in the fabric of reality, and pure light poured through. A massive thick tome emerged first from the gap, leaving the brightness of its origin and becoming drenched in the shadows of our world. A book containing pages beyond count, pages made of individual panes of light bound within a cover of blackness, reflecting impossible purple hues which had no source. The book was infinite made manifest, and it was held in the pale hand of the being who followed it.

Diminutive in stature compared to the Cataclysms, a man emerged from the portal of light bearing golden, shoulder-length hair and a light complexion. Dressed in a stone gray three-piece suit tailored to fit his slim build, he stepped onto the street with black, wingtip, brogue oxford shoes. As he emerged fully from the other side, the slit in reality fused shut, sending a shimmering spark of silver up the line as the fabric mended. The man faced the combatants locked in their opening volley and let his tome leave his hand where it chose to hover at his side as he clasped his hands together before himself.

"Oi," Rook spat out, finding himself able to speak and look despite having no other control over his body or soul. "Who the fuck are you?"

"I am Raziel," the man said. His voice was pleasantly toned, even, and cordial, though his eyes were hard and stern as they looked at Rook. "I am the Arbiter of Celestial Law. I speak for the Thrones. And I will address you momentarily."

"Raziel," Samael pleaded, "let me explain."

"Samael," Raziel said as he turned toward the Angel of Despair. "No, no explanation is needed from you." Raziel turned his attention back to the Angel of Death and the Fractured. "I want to hear from you, Azrael."

Azrael's eyes returned to nothing. He let the fire of his anger extinguish, signaling to Raziel that the fight was over and he was listening, even if he had no choice but to. The rest of Azrael's body was locked in place, including his scythe, which remained gleaming.

"The Fractured is wanted on over a thousand violations of Celestial Law," Raziel continued, "most of which would not have occurred had you followed through with the duties of your station and reaped the soul at his first violation."

"Sir, he would have had no reason to look for a human possessed by an Original Soul. It was unprecide-," Samael spoke up, stepping closer to Raziel. But Raziel brought a finger up to silence him.

"Samael," Raziel said, glancing at him, "you are guilty of no violations. You learned your lesson well. But don't make the mistake of thinking that you can absolve him of his." Raziel looked back to Azrael. "You need to explain your actions, Azrael. Perhaps the nuance of the situation can save you."

"A thousand?" Rook laughed as he sneered at Raziel. "That's gotta be a record or something, yeah? What do I get for that?" He glared at Raziel, letting his sneer drop. "Free pint at the pub?"

"Fine," sighed Raziel as he turned to Rook, "let's address you first."

Placing his hand, palm up before himself, Raziel waited for the tome to fly up and hover over it. The book popped open as he looked at it, pages fluttering of its own accord until settling on a page. Though the face of the pages was visible for all to see, Rook couldn't make out anything on them. They were just light. But Raziel appeared to read from them just the same.

"Original Soul, creation of Min, named in this path as Rook Maison," Raziel said, looking to Rook before turning his eyes back on the page before him, "you are hereby bound by law. For your one-thousand, six hundred and seventy-two known violations of the written Celestial Laws, you are to be imprisoned." Raziel's eyes returned to Rook's, and he pointed a finger of his other hand at the suspended man. "You are bound to this nephilim shell, never to exist beyond it for the rest of its natural life. You are rendered powerless, never to access the nephilim or celestial resources within you so long as you remain a soul, and your properties afforded to you by your nature as an Original Soul are now repressed."

Rook was released from stasis as Raziel spoke and dropped to his feet on the pavement below him. With each of Raziel's declarations, Rook watched and struggled as the words imposed real, metaphysical constraints. Golden and blue energy appeared before Rook and then snapped into place around his neck, wrists, and ankles. He watched as the tendrils of his soul all around him, still locked in time, sizzled and were erased by the same golden and blue hues. Rook fell to his knees as Raziel read the last of his decree. An overpowering and oppressive gold glow appeared above him and wrapped his body like a cellophane sheet. When Raziel finished, Rook was free, the last of the light fading into his skin.

"What in the bloody-," Rook said, looking at his hands and where the light had sunk into his skin. "How fucking dare you, mate? Who the fuck do you think you are?!"

Rook tensed and tried to unleash his wraith, but he felt nothing quicken inside of him. He tried to well up the power within him, to empower himself even within this body, but it didn't happen. And when Rook decided to rush up to Raziel to sock him one across the face, he found himself shackled to the ground, glowing chains of gold and blue limiting his range of movement to only a few steps. The only power Rook seemed to retain was seeing the blue auras in front of him.

With Rook sufficiently bound, Raziel also let Azrael free from his moment in time to join Samael. None of the power or anger behind Azrael remained; his frozen magic dissipated as he gently set foot on the street. Raziel turned his back on Rook and faced Azrael fully, dropping his hand and letting the tome return to its position at his side. He once again set his eyes on Azrael and clasped his hands before him, waiting.

Azrael and Samael looked at each other before stepping up before Raziel. Now next to each other, the difference between the three angels was apparent. Azrael and Samael, being Cataclysms, towered over the less-than-six feet of Raziel's height, but it was clear who was in charge here, at least to Rook. He saw the mighty Angel of Death suppress his anger to address Raziel with the respect they felt he deserved. It was revolting to Rook, and he spat on the ground to express it.

"I..." Azrael began, his voice returned to its low, grave baritone. "Acknowledge the transgressions of my station and of the Celestial Law that you stand here to bring." Azrael paused. He looked at Raziel for a long moment but then glanced at Samael before continuing. When they met eyes to voids, Samael nodded, and Azrael continued speaking to Raziel.

"But I do not agree with them."

"Your acceptance is not a condition of adherence, Azrael," Raziel said, "your violations do not factor in your intent, which I am allowing you to interject. The law is clear; by endangering the safety and health of human lives and souls, you stand against the law."

"I argue that my inaction, or even appropriate action, would have not prevented a larger loss of life than what I have done."

Raziel lowered his eyebrows, turning his nose downward ever so slightly as he heard Azrael's words. Rook raised a brow, listening in.

"Go on."

"Had the Fractured been allowed to roam free without my decision to intervene, it would have been a dereliction of my duties," Azrael started. "Had I done nothing, the Fractured would remain at large, breaking souls and consuming them. The Agglomeration would be set for sure destruction should any circumstance occur in which the Fractured returned to it. Had I returned with this information to a Throne such as Gaia, I would have been tasked as I was to continue my hunt for the Fractured, resulting in no net change from the outcome tonight. And, had we taken the issue up with you, would it be incorrect to say that the matter would be judged by you and all future measures would be under your jurisdiction?"

"What are you insinuating?"

"That I pursued the only course left available to me. The only one where failure could be contained."

Raziel paused, taking Azrael's words into consideration. He looked down, nodding to himself as he worked it out. After a moment, his eyes flicked back to Azrael, and he nodded his agreement.

"Be that as it may, Azrael, had you reaped the Fractured when he violated his first law and possessed another human, the entirety of this series of events would have been prevented."

"You are right," Azrael said, "but you forget to acknowledge my right as Cataclysm of Death to reap at my sole discretion. Setting aside that the Original Soul possessing another human was an unprecedented feat predictable only by Min, or Thoth, and that I would not have known the act had taken place without inspecting every human at every death, you would have to be asking me to be present and reap every soul that expires for me to be deemed culpable. And unless you are suggesting that I, as adept as I am in my role as Cataclysm of Death, am capable of being at over one thousand and forty-three deaths simultaneously each hour, with the spare time to inspect the living in the vicinity of each occurrence, then I cannot see how the blame can be leveled at me." Azrael lowered his head as he gazed down at Raziel. "I performed my role and continue to do so excellently."

Raziel frowned, looking up at Azrael. He brought his finger to his temple and pressed, blinking rapidly, a sure sign he was fighting the onset of a headache. Rook smiled, despite his misgivings, listening to his enemy standing up for himself.

"This does not excuse the involvement of a Virtue in your affairs, a decision that ultimately led to his total destruction."

"A choice made by the Virtue," Azrael stated, "under my protest."

Raziel brought his hand to the bridge of his nose and pressed, closing his eyes. Silence fell across them all as they watched him gather his thoughts.

"Ha, fuck you!" Rook yelled with a laugh. "It ain't all black and white, is it?" He continued to laugh until it fell darker in his throat. "You cunts are all the same, but at least this one has some integrity."

"Enough," Raziel said, holding back his true reaction. "It is settled." He held his hand out again, letting the tome fly over and position itself above it. It flipped open and fluttered through the pages until stopping halfway through. Raziel took in a breath and spoke his decree. "Azrael, I find you cleared of all violations set against written law.

Though it should be noted that this administration finds your methods to have been crude and poorly executed, there is no enforceable violation at this time." And with that said, the book slammed shut.

Samael let out the breath he had held. He smiled wistfully at Azrael and Raziel and gestured at them both.

"I'm glad that this is resolved!" Samael said, clapping his hands together once. "All adjourned, then?"

"Not quite," Raziel said, turning toward Rook. "Azrael, please escort the Original Soul and deliver him to Malakut."

"Malakut?" Samael said, looking back and forth between the two.

"Yes," Raziel said, turning back to Samael. "The Original Soul must be imprisoned where he can't harm anyone else. Malakut is cut off from the flow of the Agglomeration, so there is no danger of him returning to it while there. And it is infinite, inhabited by the Cataclysms of mankind; if he ever sees another face there again, it'll be yours."

Samael's face dropped, but Azrael nodded and stepped forward. He raised a hand, and a glowing blue chain phased into being between him and Rook, the length of it landing in his hand while the other side attached to Rook's neck. Azrael pulled, and Rook lurched forward under the weight of the chain.

"Hey, what the bloody fuck?!" Rook said, pulling against his restraint. "You let this wanker get away with putting the whole city asleep and starting a bloody war with nothing but some strong words, and I'm stuck rotting in some sodding dungeon for eternity? Why?!"

"Because you have committed a grievous number of sins," Raziel said, stepping up to Rook. "You have violated every law we have in place to protect the Grand Experiment and have threatened its existence like no other ever has. You've condemned yourself."

"Let's go," Raziel said as he looked at Azrael and gestured with his thumb.

"So I get punished because I didn't play right within your rules? Locked up for not playing your bloody game?" Azrael put tension on the chain, and Rook fell a step forward. "Oi, don't I have a say in this shitshow?"

"No, but I do."

"Beast!" Azrael said, looking at the woman who interjected. She walked through the frozen background of destruction, stepping lightly as she approached the group and came before the Arbiter.

"Tobit," she said, looking up at Azrael, "Though, for once, that name does not suit you."

"Why are you here, Lucifer?" Raziel asked, the first tinge of annoyance finding its way through his tightly curated persona.

"Because the condemned deserves his case to be heard," Lucifer said, saying the words with a melody as she smiled at

Rook. "And if no one else will speak on his behalf, let it be me."

"Fine," Raziel said, his eyes narrowing at the Lightbringer. "What would you say in defense of this soul?"

"Let him go." Lucifer trained her eyes onto Raziel's, her smile hanging softly.

"What?" Azrael interjected, mirrored by Samael's step backward and Raziel's every attempt not to glare.

"It is as I say it," Lucifer continued. "Let him go."

"Your word is not law, Lucifer," Raziel started, "no matter what you are. Unless you have an argume-"

"He is bound," Lucifer said, cutting Raziel off. "He is powerless. Harmless. Let him live out the rest of his life here on Earth." She turned to Rook and looked at him. "All he ever wanted was to exist like someone normal. He deserves that much from us." She turned her eyes back on Raziel. "This all happened because we chose to keep his nature a secret from him. We did not shepherd our children when they sought the truth, Raziel, and that is on us."

Raziel quietly rejected Lucifer's words, straining to keep a polite veneer. It interrupted his ability to think, and he found himself stalled with what to say.

"And just because I do not care for your tone, Raziel, I will remind you. It was Min's wish to let his Original Souls go through the rebirthing process ad infinitum. The One Hundred shall pass through the Agglomeration whole and intact each time for a purpose that you do not dare to question. You will not get in the way of that. Let him go."

The shock was apparent on Raziel's face. Samael, too, made no effort to hide his astonishment at the argument. It was only Azrael whose face did not bend or change upon hearing the Beast's words. And it was he who spoke next.

"Lucifer's right," Azrael said, tossing down the chain.

"W-wh," Raziel muttered, the logic so inconceivable in his head. He hated it, and he shook his head to be free of it. "No. Entire Eorthian days have to be erased from the minds of the humans because of that thing. We have to protect the Agglomeration from him, we have to-"

"And we will do just that, will we not?" Lucifer asked, her smile returning. "We will find a use for this incredibly rare and unique soul, just as we are meant to."

They all fell silent, each in turn looking to Rook, who looked at the blue chain that hung from his neck.

"If I promise to be nice, I can go outside and play?" He said with a growl, leveling his eyes at Raziel.

Raziel shook his head and gestured for his book, but it refused to come. Lucifer smiled.

"It seems the tome agrees with me," Lucifer said.

"Fine," Raziel said slowly, looking out at the frozen crowds along Margaret Street. "So be it."

Raziel's tome flew away from him, and in the openness of the nothing around it, it split apart the veil between worlds and spilled the light from the other side once again. Raziel followed the book as it held the portal open but stopped before going through it. He turned and looked at Lucifer and then the others.

"Two days. Poveglia. Midnight."

And then he stepped through and was gone.

The shackles burst from around Rook's neck and then his wrists and ankles. The shattering gold and blue energy sundered like ice and flitted away into the air.

When Rook looked back at the others, Azrael and Samael were gone, and only Lucifer stood with him.

"Sounds like we have someplace to be in two days, eh?" Rook asked, smoothing out his coat.

"Not you," Lucifer said. "And do not pay it any mind."

"Alright," Rook said, shrugging, "on my best, then?"

Lucifer smiled.

"Have fun. Just not too much."

The world lurched forward, rushing to come alive and catch up to the flow of time. The torrential rains resumed, and Rook was doused anew. The raucous noise of a city unburdened filled the space and he looked around to see the street as it was earlier that day. No signs of the destruction his war had caused remained, Raziel apparently making good on his task to erase the conflict from history. Rook looked back for Lucifer, but they were gone, replaced by the ever-surging flow of people that passed him by. As Rook looked around, he heard a voice calling over the crowd, and he turned toward the All Saints Church to see that it was calling for him.

"Michael!" yelled a woman, waving over the crowd at Rook as she left the church. "Alright, Michael, let's go!"

Rook watched as people filed out of the church, morning Mass over, ready to continue their lives. He caught his reflection in the window of a nearby building and saw himself for the first time. His brown hair was pressed against his head from the rain, and he had the handsome features of a young man. But what caught his attention most were his eyes. One was green, the other brown. He smiled and adjusted his Spector, leaning in to walk toward the church.

Epilogue

A hot Mediterranean wind blew through the untended, wild trees of a small island in the Venetian lagoon. A storied island sat alone in the view of Venice and Lido, Italy, a forgotten monument to ancient diseases and crude medicine, still served as a tomb to over a hundred thousand souls who lost their lives as refugees, plague victims, and at the hands of mad scientists. Poveglia was haunted as much by those who died on its shores as by those who visited its forbidden land in life. It was a doomed place. Invisible to all except those searching for the macabre, the most haunted place on Earth held presences that no ghost hunter or death tourist would ever uncover. A secret no human had ever known. Among the echo and locked wraiths that roamed the dilapidated *Reparto Psichiatria*, even angels and demons may walk deeper into its hidden spaces.

A rotunda, submerged far into the soil of the island, long since impassible by human means, stood against the crushing earth above it, housing the grandest library of works ever known. Though libraries of lore, like that of great Alexandria, would dwarf the content here by sheer count, they could never compare in content. Surrounding the curved walls of the large round room were bookcases, cabinets, credenzas, and breakfront bureaus overfilled with texts written by celestial hands. Books penned by angels covering every subject in their purview sat tumbled and piled among the other tomes of their kind.

Interspersed were the writings of demons and devils on the topics they governed, offering their own truths and alternate viewpoints whenever their matters overlapped. Not far from the walls, in a circle around the central space, large pillars served as separation markers by topic and age. Each had mounted, ever-vigilant sconces that housed mystical candles, forever casting their light with flames caught and frozen in the brightest moment of their lives. Their light flooded the old stone cupola, illuminating a grand, Victorian, mahogany writing desk burdened under the mass of a dozen volumes of celestial legal precedents. Behind it, opened and offering its curios and smaller publications, a Wootan-style cabinet stood overflowing. Between them stood the angel Raziel, the last of the Seraphs of the Throne of Order, the last living representative of the long-dead God of Law and Destiny.

His companion, the sentient and ever-present tome of knowledge that was older than even he, found its home here, nestled in the Wootan cabinet. The endless abyss that was its cover sat closed and leaned against the oddities in the cabinet, sleeping until it would be needed again. It was the representation of all knowledge in the universe, a tome of the highest Throne, and the master of this place in the stead of the only book that would be higher if it wasn't missing. Thoth's library was open only to those it deemed worthy, such as the beings who now occupied its room. Chief among them, Raziel served as its mouthpiece and Arbiter of all Celestial Law, no one more suited in all the realms to contemplate and pour over the endless nuances of details that were both fixed and always changing at once. No one more fit to speak for the Thrones than the one chosen to enact and enforce celestial decrees. But also present on this night were the Cataclysms Azrael and Samael and the one known as Lucifer, granted temporary passage to be reviewed by the Arbiter. They sat in cathedras forged from libre as they cast their eyes at Raziel and upon the artifact placed prominently over the Wootan behind him. The symbol of his order and the relic of his master Jupiter, the bident known as Siderium, hung mounted as a reminder to Raziel and all who saw it of the price Order paid for free will to flourish.

Raziel pushed aside the papers and books in front of him, sliding them to the edge of the desk. He leaned forward, hands flat on the polished wood surface, and stared at each of his three guests in turn. When he spoke, he did so through gritted teeth.

"Complacency is at fault here," he began. "Each of you

has a measure of culpability as defined by precedence and measured by law that should strip you of your rank and hold you bound to the lowest order."

Raziel looked at Azrael.

"Azrael, with your wild endangerment of human lives during your vigilante quest to bring down the fractured Original Soul and your negligence in securing or remediating damage caused by your actions or the actions of the Fractured, you were a danger to both the entire realm and the Great Experiment."

Lucifer smiled at Azrael, who sat tall and stoic in his seat as Raziel went on.

"But it was your continued disinterest in pursuing the anomalies you encountered when cleaning up after the Fractured that caused the most damage. At no point during his string of possessions and murders did it seem to cross your mind to look just a little deeper. Perhaps it is my mistake to believe that such odd and aberrant circumstances would pique your interest, and maybe I am misguided in thinking that anyone would perform above their duty when inconvenient, but it is this failure on your part that can be held up as an example to all others as to how complacency can, and will, eventually lead to chaos and collateral collapse."

Azrael frowned, his eyeless gaze unblinking as he watched Raziel speak. When Raziel saw no reaction, he sighed and then looked at Samael.

"Samael. You have broken no laws and trespassed on no legal grounds I can find. Perhaps that stands as proof positive that the judgment handed down to you for your past transgressions had the desired effect, and I first want to commend you on your adherence to the law on the matter."

As Raziel spoke, he feigned appreciation to Samael lightly, offering a plastic smile with his words before letting the gesture fall flat.

"But you, too, have fault here," Raziel went on. "I am told that it was you who identified what caused the damage to the influx of wraiths coming into the Agglomeration. That it was you who correctly deduced the mechanism of that damage. That you knew of the only ways in which that damage could be caused. And that you had first-hand knowledge of the powers and capabilities of the Original Souls that could result in the damage we were seeing. And yet, none of this was brought to the Thrones."

"If I may," Samael spoke up but was stopped by Raziel raising his hand.

"Gaia confirmed that once she had issued you your task, she had heard nothing back about it."

"Yes, but you know tha-"

"Yes," Raziel sighed, "I'm aware. But it is no excuse that you did not try. Even if you had not gained another audience with Gaia or none of the other Thrones would see fit to grant you the five minutes it would have taken to hear your report, that does not stand as a reason not to make the effort. All requests to them, through proper channels, would have come before me, and that, at the very least, would have offered you all tools and resources that would have prevented the fallout we had to repair."

Samael nodded, putting his hands back in his lap.

"At least," Raziel said, placing his hand on his forehead and closing his eyes, "I could have gotten ahead of the renewed distrust between the Divine and the Unholy."

"Azrael did a fine job of preventing any lasting damage from that," Lucifer said with a smirk.

"Which brings me to you, Lucifer," Raziel said, opening his eyes and standing up straight to cross his arms and point his nose down at the man. "I cannot even begin to fathom the willful disregard you may have interjected into this. No one has a finger so tightly on the pulse of the human condition than you, so I find it utterly laughable that you would not have known what was unfolding here. Either you decided to let this play out as some amusement, or you decided that this was so beneath you not to warrant your attention."

"I would argue it was anything but."

"And would you like to expand on that?"

Lucifer smiled. The casual, yet proper, lounging position in his chair made of book scraps belied his intent with the statement.

"I have been aware of Rook for some time. Since about

1530?" Lucifer said, turning his smile to his companions on his side of the desk as they both turned to look at him. "Oh, be away with that look. I did nothing as such to put him on his path. I merely told him that God would approve of what he was doing."

Lucifer placed his elbow on the arm of the chair and leaned his head into his hand, his finger touching the edge of his smile.

"Not an incorrect statement, mind you. I very much did."

Raziel's face finally fell into a scowl, the implication of Lucifer's words tracing spiderwebs of interconnections and logical conclusions in his head. His eyes darted back and forth as he followed the thought paths before settling them back on Lucifer. He lowered a hand to the tabletop and leaned against it in Lucifer's direction.

"Was this another one of your plans? Was this the fruition of another one of your coups against the Thrones working to an end right before our eyes?"

Lucifer's smile faded, though nothing else about him moved.

"Careful," he said. The word caused Raziel to straighten out and stare at him.

He read Lucifer as much as he could, then looked over the other two before he turned away and gestured toward the cabinet. The infinite tome slid from its place and came to a stop on the writing desk, opening itself to flutter through the pages until it came to a rest. Raziel turned back and looked down at the open pages before speaking again.

"A Virtue is dead. His essence destroyed. The fractured Original Soul now empowers a forbidden creature's body. Killing him, by law, would be the right thing to do, but his joining the Agglomeration would spell doom for us all," Raziel said, his voice lower, his composure returning. "Containment of an Original Soul could only be commanded by a Throne. Otherwise, its confinement is impermanent, and so not an option that is available at this time. Nor is destroying it. Binding it," Raziel's eyes snapped to the three, "is the only viable option, it would seem."

"And so you have," Lucifer said. "The nephilim body, as it is, cannot stand up to a Cataclysm should your hand be forced. Not an easy fight, but without access to the skills his soul could afford him, he would hardly be the one to bet on winning." Lucifer glanced at Azrael and smiled. "But nephilim resilience does reduce the likelihood of the poor soul expiring naturally before you can find a more lasting solution to this problem."

"We are to neglect one of the highest laws to protect the wishes of the Thrones," Azrael growled, his face turning toward the floor.

"Should be familiar territory for you, Tobit," Lucifer chuckled.

"Which is why," Raziel said loudly, regaining all eyes on

him as his patience had clearly thinned, "I have come up with a solution for the situation at hand. It solves all these problems in one, leaving plenty of time for us to solve the final one."

All his guests looked at Raziel, eyebrows raising.

Raziel turned the book, letting all three look upon its pages of light to read the words only celestial eyes could see.

"Cael's role, as was mandated, was to be the assassin of celestials who endangered humankind. He shared that duty with his legion. And while no other Virtue should have to carry the burden of that distasteful job, his legion is capable of carrying it out in his stead, even as their ranks are disseminated into the other legions."

The three looked from the book to Raziel.

"While Cael's role was to punish those who caused the Fractured, and to prevent those who would use the naturally born Fractured for their own ends, we will employ the Original Soul in a different manner. He shall clean up the fractures entirely."

"How?" Azrael asked.

Raziel smiled and turned the book back toward himself. The pages flipped on their own until they settled again. Raziel read the words aloud.

"The Original Soul, Rook Maison, is hereby remanded into our service. The term of service is no less than the time it will take until we can process his fractured soul and those that are within him without damage. The duties of his service include the location and absorption of all fractured wraiths, the abolishment of any and all mechanisms of fracturing wraiths, and the punishment of all who fracture wraiths. To serve this duty, the Original Soul, Rook Maison, shall be ferried to the known location of Fractured activity by a celestial harbinger and have his bonds temporarily lifted to fulfill his duty. His jurisdiction will cover all spheres. At the conclusion of his duty, he will be returned to his previous location and be rebound. Such will be his penance."

"What?" Samael gasped. "You're making him your attack dog?"

"No," Raziel smiled, a dark expression overriding the platitude, "he will be our sink trap."

"If all fractured wraiths go into him..." Azrael began.

"And none go into the Agglomeration..." Lucifer continued.

"Then, between him and the Noden, we could finally undo the damage that was first created by the Necroacennan event," Raziel said, a gleam in his eye that unnerved both Samael and Azrael. "Even the natural-born Fractured wouldn't return to pollute the soul mass. The remainder would finally be solved!"

Lucifer smirked and leaned back in his chair, but Azrael sat forward.

"Have you thought this through? Sending the Fractured

to absorb all other fractured wraiths would compound his power exponentially. He'd become... Become..." Azrael fumbled for the words.

"The Anti-Agglomeration," Raziel said. "Finally, all the corruption, all of the scarring that the Agglomeration has endured can be safely stored away. The Noden, another of which we will soon bring online, can heal the wounds without constantly fighting the damage new fractured wraiths bring. In a few scant centuries, the Throne's intended vision of a pure soul engine could finally be restored."

The book slammed shut.

"I don't think this is a good idea," Samael said.

"It is already done. The decree is set. All that is left is to inform the indentured. And I believe I'll let that responsibility fall upon you," Raziel said, curling a dark smile toward Lucifer.

Lucifer looked up as if this conversation had lost interest some time ago and glanced at the others before he smiled and shrugged.

"If you insist."

"Of course not, Lucifer, no such command would leave my lips and fall upon your ears. But I suggest it. You seem to know our dear friend better than any of the rest of us."

Lucifer stood and smiled politely, offering a slight bow to Raziel and a nod to Azrael and Samael.

"Then I suppose I shall be about it. I tire of the bibliosmia in here. It is rather oppressive." Lucifer walked from his seat and into the space between the pillars. He turned back and flashed a smile at Raziel, "Get some fresh air, Raziel. I fear the musk is getting to you."

Lucifer stepped forward and walked through the veil between worlds, leaving the Cataclysms and the Arbiter behind. Raziel looked at his remaining guests.

"Dismissed," he said, turning away. The book on the table lifted into the air and found its home in the cabinet, nestling between the loose pages on its shelf. It leaned against a glass-enclosed skull in a jar and rested, its black form in stark contrast to the empty space left next to it for a companion book that had long been absent.

Azrael and Samael stood, looking at each other uneasily. Samael shrugged and opened his mouth as if to speak when Azrael shook his head. The two communicated wordlessly their intent and nodded in agreement before turning away and stepping out from the center of the room. Looking back just once, they, too, faded from view, leaving the Earth realm.

With the others gone, Raziel let out a long breath and closed his eyes. He nodded once, then twice, and then shook his head. And then, after another short pause, he opened his eyes and looked upon the Siderium.

"It is as you said it would be."

Raziel paused again, seemingly listening to the relic's unheard words.

"I know, sire. I am just tired of the constant deviations and contrition. Tired of our most important duty being made into a mockery."

Raziel nodded and closed his eyes.

"Yes. It is only a matter of time. Your order will be restored."

The Siderium pulsed with a violet glow and then subsided.

"I will see to it."

The light of the candles, frozen and unmoving, was doused. In the darkness, Raziel's eyes shined as he gazed at the holy relic. The dim blue energy that sat behind them flickered as the subtlest hint of violet dust scattered the light.

Rook leaned back in his wide, plush, first-class seat. As the plane came out of a gentle bank to level with the horizon, a light on the console above him went dark, and a chime played over the cabin speakers to indicate that they had reached cruising altitude. The pilot's voice, crushed from the bad noise compression, cut through the din of the engines to let everyone know it was now safe to walk about the aircraft. Rook reached over, across the empty seat to his left, to slide up the porthole cover. He watched as the clouds passed by and saw the land that had been his home for centuries give way to endless water.

It wasn't long before the attendants had brought up the refreshment cart to the front of first class, and Rook turned his attention away from the sky to watch the tight-fitting contraption get pushed between the seats on its way to him. He chuckled to himself, judging the attire the poor attendants were forced to wear. The woman at the rear of the cart pulled it with her as she asked each side of the aisle what they would like to drink, deftly crafting and serving the orders she was given. The man on the other side of the cart did the same, matching her skill with ease, filling the orders for the other row. The woman smiled at him when the cart got to Rook's row.

"Traveling alone?" she asked, pulling the cart to align with the row.

"Ah, yeah, seems so," Rook said, smiling back.

The woman let out a small gasp, looking into Rook's eyes, her own darting between both of his.

"Oh! Your eyes are different colors," she said, "one green and one brown! What do you call that? Hetero-uh..."

"Heterochromia," the male flight attendant jumped in, smiling at his coworker and nodding at Rook.

"Well, you must be quite the hit with the ladies," she giggled before correcting herself and glancing at her partner, "or the guys." He returned her look with a sideways glance as he fulfilled another order.

"Yeah," Rook said, his smile lingering.

"What will you have, handsome?"

"I'll take one of those little bottles of whisky you got," he said, flipping up a credit card between his fingers. "Best of the lot."

"Aren't you a little young for that?" the woman asked.

"I'm old enough to take you to the loo and knock boots above the clouds, love," Rook said, snaking a smile across his lips. When the attendant responded to his advance with shock, he looked at the other attendant.

"Or you." Rook laughed and then looked at the woman. "Or you both."

"Sir," the man said with a roll of his eyes, "I'll only warn you once about that kind of behavior here."

Rook's expression dropped, replaced by confusion.

"Oh, I thought..." he gestured at the woman who was now trying to get the cart past his seat. "I thought it was genuine."

The male attendant handed Rook a soda and a plastic cup, staring at him with a disapproving glare. Then he pushed the cart beyond Rook's seat and out of view.

Rook looked at the soda can and thought for a moment but dismissed it as he leaned out over the arm of his chair to look at the cart. Seeing the bottles of alcohol clinking together in their storage at the bottom, he reached out with his hand and tried to will his soul to do the same. But nothing happened, and Rook gave up settling back into his seat.

"I believe you would call that a 'swing and a miss,'" Lucifer said, occupying the previously empty seat next to Rook.

"Oi!" Rook exclaimed, startled by his sudden row companion. "Where the shit did you come from?"

Lucifer only smiled and placed a plastic cup of golden-brown liquid on the tray in front of Rook. Rook took it and sniffed it, and when he smelled the familiar smoke and bite, he nodded and held it up to a toast before sipping it. He tossed Lucifer the can of soda in thanks.

"Romantic folly aside, it seems you are on your way to new ventures," Lucifer said, looking out the window.

"I thought it was genuine," Rook grumbled, taking another sip. "Feeling what others feel ain't my cup of tea. Been a long time. Bloody confusing." He leaned back and looked out along the aisle in front of him.

"Oi," he said, turning back toward Lucifer. "How old is this body anyway? Like, sixteen or seventeen?"

"Ha," Lucifer said, turning his head back to look him over. "Twelve."

"You're shitting me!" Rook set his cup down and dug in his Spector until he could pull out a passport. He flipped it open, seeing this boy's face staring back at him in print, and looked at the birthdate. "Fuck!"

"I would not worry," Lucifer said, "you are a nephilim

now. You will age at a rate unusual to human experience. In two or three more years, you will look to be in your twenties. You will reach the thirties a year or two after that." Lucifer popped open the soda and took a sip, wincing at the taste and looking at the can as if it assaulted him. "But there you will remain perpetually for most of your fifteen hundred years of natural life."

"Coming for you, Methuselah," Rook said before taking another sip and looking down the aisle again.

A silence settled between them for a few seconds before Rook looked at Lucifer again.

"What are you doing here, anyway? Thanks for the drink, but you don't seem like the kind for idle chit-chat."

"I came to ask you why you are leaving England, I suppose," Lucifer said, still looking out of the window.

"Eh, nothing left for me there—nothing but the lies and bullshit of the Old World. I stuck around because I thought I'd find some answers, but all I got was bullshit, wall-to-wall. Might as well check out the New World and see what it's got to offer." Rook took another swig. "Plus, those cunts over there have some bloody funny accents."

Lucifer nodded, bringing the can back to his lips before remembering how it offended him. He looked at it, and the sugar-liquid-filled container burst into mists that fell about his hand.

"Now, tell me the real reason why you're here," Rook said,

eying the Devil.

Lucifer looked back and watched Rook before answering.

"A judgment has been made about you," he said, watching Rook's face flatten. "Raziel has made a decree and asked me to inform you of it."

"Go on, then," Rook said, setting his drink down.

"You are to be our newest sin eater."

"Sounds pious."

"You have made this flaw in the system something they can no longer ignore, and they will use you to fix it. You will be taken to wherever they find a fractured wraith. You are to absorb it, removing it from the ebb and flow of the Agglomeration and excising the taint from the streams of life. It is their hope that, over time, you will amass all the Fractured within you, and the Agglomeration will introduce only whole souls back into the population."

"They are literally going to take me to broken souls and feed me," Rook scoffed. "How did you manage to swing that?"

"I did not. It was an idea all of Raziel's own."

"Ha," Rook said, grabbing his drink. "Unhinged."

"Agreed."

"So, how am I to do it, no powers and all?" Rook said, wiggling his fingers.

"You will be unbound, allowed full use of your abilities until the completion of the task. It is expected that you also dispatch those that would be causing wraiths to fracture, as well, so it would be a necessary risk to unleash you. And with both Divine and Unholy being sure future targets in their own realms, Raziel sees your growing power to be an asset to that, as well."

"Mm," Rook uttered as he sipped again.

"What do you think?" Lucifer asked, looking at Rook.

"Does it matter? Using me to fix the shite that made me? Using their bloody decrees and incantations to control me?" Rook sneered as he spoke. "Fuck this shite. At least these twats," Rook gestured with his cup at the other passengers, "don't have a clue about the strings attached to them. Me? I know it all too well, and you pricks don't even bother hiding it from me anymore." Rook drank the last of his drink in a single swallow. "I want to bloody torch the whole lot of it."

Lucifer smiled.

"What if I offered you an alternative path?"

Rook narrowed his eyes and looked at Lucifer. Lucifer, in turn, reached out and touched Rook's bare hand. An orange-red shock sparked across the back of it, splitting and dividing along his hair, diving under his skin to light up his tendons, bones, and then something more solid underneath. Rook felt a sharp, cold sensation race along his body, flooding his senses and permeating his body. At once, he felt as though a weight was lifted from him, that a Jovian pressure was released. And Rook saw his soul quicken under his skin.

"Are you a fan of the long con, Rook?" Lucifer said, his smile widening as he leaned back in his seat, crossing a leg over his knee. "Of course, you are, being such an old soul yourself. What if I unbind you now, never to be bound again, and we play nicely within the system for a little while?"

Rook raised his soul from his hand and watched it turn and extend as he tested, shaping it into several forms. He looked at Lucifer.

"Let's say I am. And I do. Then what?"

Lucifer produced a business card and held it up between his black-tipped fingers.

"Then I will tell you about another nephilim. Not everyone knows about him yet. His name is Dominic, and I think you two should meet."

Rook's wraith reached out and took the card, placing it in his hand. He looked over the white cardstock and read the black embossed letters.

FORD BRADSHAW & CO.
RARE ANTIQUITIES
DOMINIC NOVIKOV
826 WATER ST, PORT TOWNSEND, WA 98368

Rook will return

in

FRAGMENTS

Soundtrack of a Fractured Soul

Songs I was listening to during the creation of this novel.

- *|Matte Blvck| The entire album. Seriously. Listen to everything they've done.*

- My Name Is Ruin *|Gary Numan| If there was ever a song that was Rook, this is it.*

- Love Hurt Bleed *|Gary Numan|*

- Intruder *|Gary Numan|*

- Vivien *|†††(Crosses)|*

- Invisible Hand *|†††(Crosses)|*

- Bloodsport *|HEALTH| Soundtrack to Azrael's hunt.*

- Church Outfit *|Poppy|*

- Fill the Crown *|Poppy|*

- Do You Call My Name *|Ra|*

- Save Yourself *|Stabbing Westward|*

- In The End *|Black Veil Brides|*